Praise for

GHOST HUNTER

"Bewitching . . . Castle's new futuristic romance brilliantly blends exceptionally entertaining characters, witty prose, and a thrilling paranormal-tinged plot in a sublime novel of romantic suspense."
—*Booklist*

"Cooper stole my heart. Elly was properly feisty. Their chemistry sparkles. Highly recommended . . . It's J.A.K. at the top of her game."
—*The Best Reviews*

"Jayne Castle has long been one of my favorite authors. With each story that she writes, her special touch enhances each page. Paranormal fans will rejoice at what she has put together in *Ghost Hunter*. This book is one that offers a wealth of intrigue, mystery, and all-out sexual chemistry. Those are trademark elements of a great author. Very highly recommended."
—*MyShelf.com*

"We welcome back Jayne Castle (Jayne Ann Krentz) to the genre of paranormal romance in which she is one of the leading writers. If you love paranormal romances, *Ghost Hunter* is just the ticket for you this month."
—*Romance Reviews Today*

"Sexual fireworks laced with humor equals fizz. Fizz is a trademark of author Jayne Castle aka Jayne Ann Krentz, and *Ghost Hunter* is volatile. Go for it!"
—*Reviewer's Choice Reviews*

"As usual in a Castle/Krentz romance, you get plenty of steam, gripping emotion, and characters who come alive as you're reading . . . This one's earned four of Cupid's five arrows."
—*BellaOnline*

continued . . .

"[A] deft combination of romance and suspense . . . *Ghost Hunter* is a page-turning winner. I finished it in one day and was sorry to see it end. I hope Ms. Castle plans to write more books in this fascinating world."

—*A Romance Review*

"Returning to the planet Harmony, Castle adds intriguing new characters, including a fashion-conscious dust bunny, to her already captivating world. Characters with passion, dialogue with zip, and fast-moving action all add up to vintage Castle fun!"

—*Romantic Times* (4½ stars)

Praise for the novels of *New York Times* bestselling author Jayne Castle . . .

"Castle is well-known for her playful love stories, and this futuristic tale of romantic suspense runs delightfully true to form . . . An appealing, effervescent romance mildly spiced with paranormal fun, this novel won't disappoint."

—*Publishers Weekly*

"A fun read, as are all [of] Castle/Krentz's books."

—*The Southern Pines (NC) Pilot*

"_____der Jayne Castle, Jayne Ann Krentz takes her ____ combination of witty, upbeat action, lively sen-____d appealing characters to [a] unique, synergistic world."

—*Library Journal*

"Jayne Castle, one of the pioneers of the futuristic subgenre, continues to set the standard against which all other such books are judged."

—*Affaire de Coeur*

"As always, the characterizations and plot blend perfectly for a thrilling, funny, and fully satisfying read."

—*Romantic Times* (4½ stars)

SILVER MASTER

JAYNE CASTLE

JOVE BOOKS, NEW YORK

THE BERKLEY PUBLISHING GROUP
Published by the Penguin Group
Penguin Group (USA) Inc.
375 Hudson Street, New York, New York 10014, USA
Penguin Group (Canada), 90 Eglinton Avenue East, Suite 700, Toronto, Ontario M4P 2Y3, Canada
(a division of Pearson Penguin Canada Inc.)
Penguin Books Ltd., 80 Strand, London WC2R 0RL, England
Penguin Group Ireland, 25 St. Stephen's Green, Dublin 2, Ireland (a division of Penguin Books Ltd.)
Penguin Group (Australia), 250 Camberwell Road, Camberwell, Victoria 3124, Australia
(a division of Pearson Australia Group Pty. Ltd.)
Penguin Books India Pvt. Ltd., 11 Community Centre, Panchsheel Park, New Delhi—110 017, India
Penguin Group (NZ), 67 Apollo Drive, Rosedale, North Shore 0745, Auckland, New Zealand
(a division of Pearson New Zealand Ltd.)
Penguin Books (South Africa) (Pty.) Ltd., 24 Sturdee Avenue, Rosebank, Johannesburg 2196,
South Africa

Penguin Books Ltd., Registered Offices: 80 Strand, London WC2R 0RL, England

This is a work of fiction. Names, characters, places, and incidents either are the product of the author's imagination or are used fictitiously, and any resemblance to actual persons, living or dead, business establishments, events, or locales is entirely coincidental. The publisher does not have any control over and does not assume any responsibility for author or third-party websites or their content.

SILVER MASTER

A Jove Book / published by arrangement with the author

PRINTING HISTORY
Jove mass-market edition / September 2007

ISBN: 978-0-515-14355-3

JOVE®
Jove Books are published by The Berkley Publishing Group,
a division of Penguin Group (USA) Inc.,
375 Hudson Street, New York, New York 10014.
JOVE is a registered trademark of Penguin Group (USA) Inc.
The "J" design is a trademark belonging to Penguin Group (USA) Inc.

PRINTED IN THE UNITED STATES OF AMERICA

10 9 8 7 6 5 4 3 2 1

Another one for those who
love dust bunnies.

A Note from Jayne

Welcome back to my other world, Harmony.

Two hundred years ago a vast energy Curtain opened in the vicinity of Earth, making interstellar travel practical for the first time. In typical human fashion, thousands of eager colonists packed up their stuff and lost no time heading out to create new homes and new societies on the unexplored worlds. Harmony was one of those worlds.

The colonists brought with them all the comforts of home—sophisticated technology, centuries of art and literature, and the latest fashions. Trade through the Curtain flourished and made it possible to stay in touch with families back on Earth. It also allowed the colonists to keep their computers and high-tech gadgets working. Things went swell for a while.

And then one day, without warning, the Curtain closed, disappearing as mysteriously as it had opened. Cut off from Earth, no longer able to obtain the tools and supplies needed to keep their high-tech lifestyle going, the colonists were abruptly thrown back to a far more primitive existence. Forget the latest Earth fashions; just staying alive suddenly became a major problem.

But on Harmony folks did one of the things humans do best: they survived. It wasn't easy, but two hundred years after the closing of the Curtain, the descendants of the First Generation colonists have fought their way back from the brink to a level of civilization roughly equivalent to the early twenty-first century on Earth.

Here on Harmony, however, things are a little different, especially after dark. You've got those dangerously sexy ghost hunters, the creepy ruins of a long-vanished alien civilization, and a most unusual kind of pet. In addition, an increasingly wide variety of psychic powers are showing up in the population.

Nevertheless, when it comes to love, some things never change. . . .

If, like me, you sometimes relish your romantic suspense with a paranormal twist, Harmony is the place for you.

Love,
Jayne

Prologue

〜

HARMONY
Two Hundred Years after the Closing of the Curtain . . .

SHE HAD NEVER LIKED THE PARKING GARAGE, ESPECIALLY at night. It was dark and gloomy, and the disturbing echoes of the heels of her classic pumps on the concrete made her uneasy. Sometimes she heard other people's footsteps as well.

But tonight the garage was eerily silent. The instant the elevator doors opened she went briskly toward the space where her car was parked. She kept a tight grip on her purse and stayed as far away as possible from the dark canyons between the few remaining vehicles.

Not that there had been any recent incidents reported, she reminded herself. Several months ago a rash of car prowls had caused management to tighten building security for a while. The guards had caught the thieves in short order. Unfortunately, the new security staff had been let go in an economy move a few weeks later.

Tonight her own footfalls were the only ones she heard.

She walked faster, all of her senses, normal as well as paranormal, fully alert.

Her car was in sight now. She had her key ready in her hand.

She sensed him when she went past the deep shadow cast by a support pillar. He was less than three paces away, waiting for her. The floodwaters of his twisted, unwholesome psychic energy lapped at her, a rising tide of rage that was just barely under control.

Panic struck. She bolted toward the vehicle. Only a few more feet. If she could just get inside, get the door locked . . .

But he was moving fast now, bounding forward like a great beast charging its prey. There was no need to look over her shoulder. She knew who he was. His heavy boots thudded on the concrete, running her down.

She fled toward the car, but she knew she was not going to make it. He was too close, right on top of her.

His arm snaked out and caught her by the throat, jerking her to a halt. He pulled her back hard against his big frame. She tried to scream, but he tightened his grip, choking her. She struggled wildly, kicking back with one foot.

The heel of her shoe connected with his shin. She kicked back again, frantic.

"Bitch."

He staggered a little, but he did not go down. He shook her, making her head spin. Then he slammed her hard, facedown, against the fender of her car.

He ripped off her jacket, revealing the sleeveless camisole beneath.

"Stupid bitch," he said, his voice hoarse and ragged. "Did you really think I'd let you get away with saying no to me? No one says no to me. *No one.*"

She realized then that the struggle was arousing him sexually. Her stomach churned. She tried to scream, but her voice was frozen in her throat.

Out of the corner of her eye she saw him raise one hand. She realized he was holding a small object. The next thing she knew, he was pressing the syringe against her bare arm, just below her shoulder. She felt a sharp, stinging pain.

A fresh wave of icy terror slammed through her, but she could not even lift a finger to defend herself.

He held her pinned against the fender while the drug took effect. It didn't take long. Within seconds an other-worldly sense of lethargy stole over her, sapping all of her physical energy. Her body folded in on itself, leaving her utterly limp, boneless.

But the drug did not knock her out, not entirely. She remained dazed but semi-awake, trapped in a terrifying dream-like state. She was aware of what was happening around her, but she was powerless to act.

He picked her up, threw her over his shoulder, and carried her across the garage to where a large black car was parked. She heard the sound of the trunk being opened.

Then she was inside the trunk, and the lid was coming down, leaving her frozen in the darkest night she had ever known.

She had thought that her level of shock and horror could not climb any higher. She was wrong.

Chapter 1

LUNCH HAD NOT GONE WELL. THERE HAD BEEN AN UN-
fortunate scene that had resulted in a lot of disapproving
glares and rude remarks from other restaurant patrons. She
had been asked to pay her bill and leave immediately. Her
request that the remainder of her salad be put into a carry-
out bag had been met with icy refusal.

Celinda was still fuming and still hungry when she
opened the door of the office of Promises, Inc. Mostly she
was angry at herself because she had been so embarrassed
she had felt it necessary to leave a tip.

Laura Gresley was at her post at the reception desk.
Her customary smile—polite, professional, and polished—
seemed slightly off. There was a forced quality about it.

"Oh, good, you're back, Celinda," she said, clearly
relieved. "I was about to call your personal phone." She
lowered her voice. "There are some people here to see you."

"*Some* people?" Normally clients came in alone, not in
groups. "My next appointment isn't until two thirty."

"These two don't have an appointment," Laura said with
an ominous air.

"But I don't have room to squeeze in anyone who doesn't already have an appointment. I'm booked solid this afternoon; you know that."

It was the wedding season, the most popular time of the year for formal Covenant Marriages. That meant that Promises, Inc., and other matchmaking agencies were swamped. The number of weddings taking place always produced a lot of new clients. It was simple physics: weddings inspired families to put a lot of pressure on relatives of a certain age who were still single. In desperation many of the pressured turned to agencies.

Whoever the clients were, they had managed to rattle Laura. That was not easy to do. She held her position as receptionist for Promises, Inc., precisely because she was virtually unflappable. She was fiftysomething, poised, and efficient. Like everyone else on the staff with the exception of Celinda, she wore a gold ring on her left hand, signifying a Covenant Marriage.

Laura was accustomed to dealing with some of the most elite people in Cadence City, from wealthy business executives to politicians and media celebrities. If she was uneasy about the people waiting for her, Celinda thought, that meant there was a serious problem.

She glanced toward the seats in the small lobby. There was no one around. That was not a surprise, of course. There was rarely anyone in the small, expensively appointed space because Promises, Inc., went to great lengths to ensure that clients were never kept waiting in a public area. Discretion was everything when you operated the most elite matchmaking agency in the city.

Promises, Inc., worked only on referral. It did no advertising. There was nothing on the front door of the office or on the business cards that Celinda and the other consultants carried that indicated the nature of the business that was done behind the company's elegant doors.

Laura followed Celinda's glance toward the empty reception chairs. "I put them in your office."

"Why me? Why didn't you give them to one of the other consultants?"

"These two specifically asked to speak with you."

Celinda sighed. "I'm getting a bad feeling about this. You're about to drop the other shoe, aren't you?"

"Obviously you are an amazingly intuitive woman," Laura said dryly. "Neither of the two would tell me why they wanted to talk to you, but one of them carries a badge that says she is with the Cadence Police Department. Detective Alice Martinez."

"Good grief." Celinda stared at her, flabbergasted. "Probably not a potential client, then. It's highly unlikely that a woman living on a detective's salary could afford our services."

"I'm inclined to agree with you. The man with her gave his name as Davis Oakes. He did not elaborate further."

"Weird." She did not know anyone by that name. She did not know any police detectives, either, for that matter. "And weirder."

"I would have asked Ms. Takahashi to deal with them, but she's at that charity luncheon today. She won't be back until around three."

Patricia Takahashi was the owner of Promises, Inc. The fact that Laura regretted not being able to get her involved spoke volumes about just how nervous the visitors had made her.

Celinda hoisted her large black tote higher on one shoulder. "Well, I suppose I'd better go see what they want."

She started around the edge of the desk, heading for a short hallway lined with closed doors.

Laura looked at the oversized tote. "Where's Araminta?"

"Napping. She had a big lunch. Unfortunately, it was not her own."

"Oh, dear." Laura's smile was half-amused and half-sympathetic. "Another restaurant scene?"

"I'm afraid so. I've explained to her that just because the food on someone else's plate looks better than what I ordered, it does not necessarily follow that she can help herself to a stranger's meal."

"How nasty did it get?"

"Very nasty. The person whose meal Araminta swiped referred to her as a rat. I, of course, took offense on her behalf. The waiter got involved. Evidently there is a rule about bringing animals into restaurants unless they are companion animals."

"I've heard that." Laura's mouth twitched a little. "One of those boring public health regulations, I believe."

"I explained that Araminta was a companion, but by then things had become complicated."

"How complicated?"

"In the general uproar and confusion that followed the reference to a rat, Araminta took a few sample bites from some of the other diners' plates as well. A large person came out of the kitchen waving an empty garbage bag and a big pot. There was talk of catching Araminta in the pot, transferring her to the bag, and delivering her to animal control."

"Oh, my." Laura's eyes danced. "Sounds like a circus."

"Suffice it to say that we will not be going back to the Quik-Bite Deli anytime in the near future."

She went down the hall to her office and opened the door.

The waves of strong, subtle psi power slammed right through her sturdy defenses, catching her completely off guard and rezzing all of her senses. Excitement and anticipation pulsed through her. The energy was unlike anything that she had ever encountered: dark, controlled, fascinating.

The hair rose on the nape of her neck. Beneath the fabric of her neatly tailored business jacket, goose bumps prickled her upper arms. A strange, unfamiliar sensation stirred within her. She felt as if she were about to leap off a very high diving board into a fathomless pool.

Get a grip. Okay, so one of the visitors was a particularly strong psi talent. No, not *one* of the visitors; the man. This energy was indisputably male.

The ability to resonate psychically with amber and use it to focus the brain's natural paranormal energy waves had begun to appear among the colonists on Harmony shortly after they came through the Curtain to settle the new world. Something in the environment had begun to stimulate the latent ability in humans.

At first the talent had seemed to be little more than an intriguing curiosity. But when the mysterious energy Curtain that had made interstellar travel possible had closed without warning, trapping the colonists, the ability to pulse psi through amber rapidly became critical to survival.

Virtually everyone on Harmony gave off some degree of psychic energy. Most people generated low or medium levels of power, allowing them to use amber to operate a toaster or start a car engine. But there were some individuals—she was one of them—who could generate an unusually high degree of psychic energy.

Being a strong para-resonator, as powerful psychics were called, was almost always a double-edged sword. Her particular talent was the ability to read the paranormal energy rhythms and patterns given off by others. To her, human psi waves were as distinctive as faces.

Her para-rez ability was rare. She had never met anyone else who could do what she did. Then again, anyone who could read other people's psi waves as accurately as she was able to read them no doubt kept quiet about the skill for the same reason that she did. Paranormal abilities were common in the population, but powerful and unusual talents were not, and very few people were comfortable around others who possessed such powers.

She knew that most people would find her particular psychic ability especially unsettling. It wasn't mind reading, of course. There was no such talent. But her ability did allow her sharp insights into one of the most personal and private realms of an individual's personality. The truth was, if you could read a person's psi waves, you could tell a great deal about that individual's strengths and—far more disturbing to the person—his or her weaknesses. It was human nature to not want to reveal weakness, not even to a relative or a lover.

Only the members of her family and her closest, most trusted friends knew about her talent. And even they did not know her deepest, darkest secret. She had understood intuitively, ever since her eighteenth year when she had unwittingly discovered exactly what she could do with her psychic ability, that she must never confide in anyone.

There was another major downside to her ability. She had been forced to develop mental shields in order to cope with the relentless tide of psi energy that lapped at her whenever she was around other people. Had she not been able to do so, she knew she would have gone mad.

But she had learned how to control her talent, and now it was informing her in no uncertain terms that the man waiting for her wasn't just a powerful para-rez, himself; he was going to be the most intriguing, most exciting man she had ever met, the one who could rez all of her senses.

So what was Mr. Perfect doing in the company of a police detective?

Assuming a proper, professional smile, she pushed the door open the rest of the way and walked into the room.

The man and the woman inside both rose from their chairs. The woman was establishing her authority. Celinda sensed that the man felt no need to do the same. He was just demonstrating that he been brought up with good manners.

"Celinda Ingram?" The woman offered an ID encased in a leather wallet instead of her hand. "Detective Martinez. I'm with the Cadence City Police Department. This is Davis Oakes of Oakes Security."

Security. That didn't sound good.

Celinda set the tote carefully on the floor behind her desk and then took her time examining the woman's identification. She looked up and nodded once, cautiously polite.

"Detective." She switched her attention to Oakes. "Mr. Oakes."

"Miss Ingram."

His low voice rolled over her senses like a tropical ocean wave at night, darkly powerful and infinitely mysterious.

She braced herself for his touch. She had a feeling it was going to thrill all her senses.

It did. The skin-to-skin contact produced a strong resonating effect. Little tingles of excitement flickered up and down her spine. Yes, indeed, hormones on parade, just as she had anticipated.

She freed her hand as quickly as possible. This was no time to get distracted. She made herself concentrate on Alice Martinez, who had sat down again.

The detective was an attractive thirtysomething, dark-haired and dark-eyed. Her business suit was as severe as a uniform. The jacket of the suit was a tad lumpy on the left side. The bulge was a strong hint that there was a gun in a holster there.

Alice Martinez wore no visible amber, but Celinda sensed a distinctive psi pattern that indicated that she possessed some sort of fairly strong talent.

Mentally Celinda ticked off the reasons why a police detective and a man who worked in the security business might want to speak to her. It was a very short list. She suddenly went cold. The specter of fear that had become her constant companion during the past four months suddenly leaped from the shadows and wrapped icy fingers around her heart.

"Has something happened to someone in my family?" she whispered, her pulse skittering wildly.

"No." Alice Martinez gave her a quick, unexpectedly reassuring smile. "This doesn't involve any of your relatives."

"Thank heavens." The relief was so overwhelming she sagged a little against the desk. "For a minute there I was afraid . . ." She let the sentence trail off.

Davis's eyes narrowed ever so faintly at the corners. She knew he had taken note of that brief moment of panic.

"Detective Martinez and I are cooperating in an investigation," he said quietly.

She gave him a polite smile while she took stock. For years she'd known exactly what qualities she wanted in her dream man. She was a professional matchmaker, after all; she knew what to look for in a mate. The list was long and detailed: kindness, intelligence, loyalty, a strong sense of responsibility, the ability to make a commitment and stick to it, a capacity for love, the right attitudes toward money, children, and family obligations, etc., etc.

But until now she had never had a visual image of Mr. Perfect.

Her ideal man, it turned out, had hair as dark as a midnight sky and eyes of an unusual shade of silvery gray. His face was all hard edges and dangerously interesting planes and angles. He was of average height, but beneath the jacket of the dark business suit there was a lot of sleek muscle, especially in his shoulders.

It dawned on her that he had not taken his seat again. Instead, he stood quietly in that centered, controlled manner that seemed to characterize everything about him.

"As Detective Martinez told you, I'm with Oakes Security." He handed her a card.

She glanced down and read the fine print. "It says here that you're not exactly *with* Oakes Security. You're the president and CEO."

His mouth curved faintly at one corner. "Yeah, that, too. Oakes is a private consulting firm. We specialize in corporate security."

"I see." She was more mystified than ever. Nevertheless, she made an effort to appear intelligent. "Corporate security. That would be the expensive version of a private investigator?"

"The very expensive version," he agreed neutrally. "In

the same way that a matrimonial consultant is a real pricey version of what most people call a matchmaker."

Okay, no mistaking the icy sarcasm in that comment.

She smiled coolly. "Pricey is right. But we only do Covenant Marriages here at Promises, Inc. The way we look at it, the stakes are high, so our fees should be, too."

The marriage laws had been relaxed slightly in the past two centuries, but they were still extremely stringent. There was a lot of talk about loosening them up, but everyone knew that, realistically speaking, that wasn't going to happen anytime soon.

The rigid rules governing marriage had made sense two centuries ago when the colonists had found themselves marooned on Harmony. Survival had been the first and most important objective. The philosophers, social scientists, and political leaders who had framed the new Constitution had known that the key to keeping the fragile flame of civilization alive was the family unit. They had, therefore, cemented the sanctity of marriage in both law and tradition, ensuring that families remained intact regardless of the price that had to be paid.

The laws applied to everyone. Society put just as much pressure on gay people to form Covenant bonds with their partners as it did on heterosexuals.

The institution of the Covenant Marriage was a contract that, with very few exceptions, could be severed only by death. Getting out of a CM was a legal and financial nightmare that very few could afford.

But the Founders had also understood the need to provide an alternative for those who were not ready to undertake the commitment of a lifelong marriage. The Marriage of Convenience was a legally recognized arrangement that had to be renewed at regular intervals. It could be terminated by either spouse at any point unless a child was born into the marriage, in which case the contract was immediately converted into a permanent Covenant Marriage.

Families frequently encouraged their offspring to experiment with Marriages of Convenience before entering the far more stringent Covenant Marriage. Most Marriages of Convenience were, in reality, short-term affairs. Tradition afforded such arrangements an aura of respectability, however. MCs were several notches above what was often referred to as shacking up.

There were matchmaking agencies that worked with people seeking Marriages of Convenience, but Promises, Inc., was not one of them.

"Do you give refunds if the match proves to be a bad one?" Davis asked, gravely polite.

This definitely sounded personal. He was challenging her for some reason.

She went behind her desk, sat down, and folded her hands on the surface. She rezzed a bright, professional smile for him.

"Do you get paid regardless of whether or not you solve the case?" she retorted.

He raised dark brows a little, acknowledging the hit.

Alice looked faintly amused. Satisfied, even a little exhilarated by her successful parry, Celinda turned back to her.

"What is it you want from me, Detective?"

"Mr. Oakes is pursuing an investigation on behalf of his client," Alice said, businesslike now. "This morning, in the course of that inquiry, he came across a dead body. We in the Cadence PD have an interest in that sort of thing."

Celinda swallowed hard. The small sense of triumph she had just experienced evaporated in a heartbeat. Davis had discovered a dead person, and now he and the detective were sitting in her office. The situation was deteriorating rapidly.

"I see." A fresh wave of alarm swept over her. "Are you here because you think I knew the victim?"

"Good question," Alice said. "His name was Alvis Shaw. He was a longtime drug addict and small-time thief. Rez any bells?"

"Good grief, no," Celinda said, shocked. "I assure you I'm not acquainted with anyone who meets that description. What in the world brought you to my door?"

Davis's silvery eyes were as unreadable as mirrored sunglasses. "I found Shaw's body in the alley just outside a small, low-end antique shop that specializes in cheap colonial knockoffs. The name of the place was Jackson's Old World Finds."

Startled, Celinda unclasped her hands. "I was in that shop yesterday afternoon."

"I know," Davis said. "The owner of the shop showed us a receipt for an object that you purchased from him."

"I don't understand," she said. "What does that have to do with Mr. Shaw's death? The item I bought wasn't valuable. The owner couldn't even remember when or where he got it. He said it had probably come in with some things he picked up in an estate sale. He only charged me five dollars for it."

"There is a possibility that Shaw's death is connected to the object you bought," Davis said.

"*What?* That's impossible." Horrified, Celinda leaped out of her chair, seized her tote, and placed it gingerly on top of her desk. She rummaged around inside. "I'll show you, it's just a chunk of old red plastic. Probably a knob or handle from some Colonial-era machine. It's pretty, but I don't see how it could be valuable. I bought it as a toy for Araminta. She got very excited about it."

"Who's Araminta?" Alice asked.

A fluffy ball of tatty gray fur studded with two baby-blue eyes appeared from inside the tote. The small beast hooked a pair of paws over the edge of the bag and peered at Davis and Alice with great interest.

"This is Araminta," Celinda said.

"A dust bunny," Alice said in the tones of someone who is resigning herself to the inevitable. "Should have known, what with the way my luck has been running lately."

"What's wrong?" Celinda demanded, offended. "Are you allergic to dust bunnies?"

"Not yet," Alice said with a long-suffering air. "But I'm thinking of developing an allergy to them."

"Why?" Celinda picked up Araminta, lifted her out of the tote, and set her on the desk. "What can you possibly have against a sweet, innocent little bundle of fur like this?"

Araminta drifted across the desk to a glass bowl containing individually wrapped candies. She seemed to float because her six paws were concealed by her fluffy gray fur. She hopped up onto the rim of the candy jar and helped herself to one of the little bundles inside.

Alice watched her use her sharp little teeth to unwrap the candy. "Lately it seems there's been a dust bunny involved in every screwy case I get. And from what I've heard, the little suckers aren't all that sweet and innocent. They say that by the time you see the teeth, it's too late."

"Only if they're provoked," Celinda assured her.

Araminta blinked her blue eyes at Alice and then enthusiastically crunched the candy.

"I don't understand how she can still be hungry," Celinda said. "She just had lunch, a couple of them, in fact. She used to be a dainty eater, but lately she's developed the appetite of a sumo wrestler."

Araminta polished off the candy and tumbled across the desk. She stopped at the edge and leaned forward, balancing precariously on her hind paws. She chortled at Davis.

"Do you happen to have some snacks on you?" Celinda asked, embarrassed. "I think she smells food."

"I've got some crackers left over from the lunch I grabbed on the way here," Davis said. He reached into his pocket and withdrew a small packet. He removed the plastic wrapper and handed the crackers to Araminta.

They all watched Araminta take the offering in one paw and start munching energetically.

Celinda shook her head. "You'd think she hadn't been

fed in days, but she just swiped, ah, I mean she just *ate* two sandwiches, several olives, and a bag of fries. And that was after she helped herself to most of my salad."

"About the item you purchased from Jackson's shop yesterday," Davis said, looking at the tote.

"Oh, right." Celinda reached back into the tote and took out the small antique. She held it up so that Davis and Alice could see it. "It's obviously just a chunk of old plastic off some Colonial-era gadget. It's not like it's a really valuable alien relic or anything. It's not even made of green quartz."

It was common knowledge that, with one notable exception—a substance called dreamstone—the relics and artifacts left behind by the mysterious alien civilization that had first colonized Harmony were all made of a nearly indestructible, acid-green quartz that glowed in the dark.

The aliens were long gone by the time the human colonists arrived, but they had left behind the ruins of at least four large, startlingly ethereal cityscapes and an un-known number of smaller outposts scattered around the planet. There was a lot of Harmony left to be explored. No one knew how many more archaeological sites remained to be found.

In addition to their walled cities and assorted outlying ruins, they had also constructed a maze of underground tun-nels, most of which remained unexplored and uncharted. The catacombs, too, were fashioned of the green quartz.

Celinda tossed the small chunk of plastic into the air and caught it in her hand. "There's no way this could be worth much."

She watched Davis's and Alice's faces covertly, trying to tell if either of them realized that she was lying through her teeth.

The truth was, she was very certain that the red object was neither Old Earth nor Colonial in origin. She was al-most certain that it was an alien relic of some kind. No Old World or Colonial antiques gave off a faint trickle of psi energy the way this thing did. The red widget was most likely a rare and therefore extremely valuable find. She had fully intended to contact some of the upscale antiquities shops as soon as possible to see if she could get a good price for it. She did not want to turn it over to the police unless there was no alternative.

The artifact was about three inches long and an inch wide. It was slightly curved, making it easy to grip in one's palm. Although she sensed the energy coming from it, she had no clue to what it had been designed to do.

Alice frowned, head tilted slightly. "You're right. It looks like a cheap plastic drawer pull. Are you sure that's the only thing you bought at Jackson's yesterday?"

"Yes," Celinda said, relaxing a little because now she was telling the truth again. "I'm positive."

Alice took out a notebook. "I'd like to ask you a few questions. Just routine."

Celinda went very still. "You said you're investigating Alvis Shaw's death as a possible homicide."

"Yes." Alice flipped open her notebook.

"Then your questions are not going to be routine, are they?" She tightened her grip on the relic. "At least not from my point of view."

Alice ignored that. "Can you tell me where you were between midnight and three AM this morning?"

A sensation of impending disaster swept over Celinda. Great. Just great. She was a suspect in a murder. In the matchmaking business, that kind of thing was a guaranteed career-ender. Cold perspiration formed under her arms. Thank heavens she had not removed the jacket of her business suit. With luck, they wouldn't see that she was sweating.

"You think I killed Mr. Shaw?" she managed.

Alarmed by the sound of her too thin, too tight voice, Araminta tumbled across the desk and bounded up her arm to perch on her shoulder. Automatically, Celinda reached up to pat her, taking comfort, as she always did, from the contact.

"Like I said, this is routine." Alice rezzed a pen and prepared to take notes.

"Am I the first person you've interviewed in connection with this murder?" Celinda asked warily.

"Yes, as a matter of fact, you are," Alice said.

Damn, it was happening all over again, Celinda thought. Her short career at Promises, Inc., flashed before her eyes. She would have to leave town and find another job, just as she had four months ago. There were only four large city-states on Harmony. Two down and two to go. At this rate, she would soon be running the kind of low-end dating service that advertised in the Personals section of cheap tabloids.

"Miss Ingram?" Alice's voice was sharp.

Davis did not move. He just stood there, watching her. Celinda forced herself to shake off the dread that threatened to demoralize her. *Stay focused. Maybe you can manage this. Maybe your life is not about to go to green hell again.*

"Sorry, Detective," she said politely. "What was the question?"

"You were about to tell me where you were last night between twelve and three," Alice said.

Celinda moved one hand in a vague gesture. "Where I usually am at that time of night. In bed."

There was a short beat of silence.

"Was there anyone else in the household?" Alice asked.

Probably diplomatic cop talk for *Are you sleeping with anyone who can give you an alibi?* Celinda thought.

"No," she said. "Just Araminta."

Alice looked up from her notes. "So there's no one who can vouch for the fact that you were home alone?"

Celinda started to say no and then stopped, brightening a little. "My landlady, Mrs. Furnell. She lives right downstairs. I have to walk past her front door to get outside the building. Trust me when I tell you that she would definitely remember if I went out late at night or if I came in at an odd hour."

Alice did not look impressed, but she made a note. "Were you a frequent shopper at Jackson's?"

Celinda shook her head. "Yesterday was the first time. I was just browsing, but Araminta went straight to this widget and started playing with it. She seemed to want it, so I bought it for her."

It was the truth as far as it went. Celinda saw no need to add that she would never have gone into the shop in the first place if Araminta hadn't made a great fuss when they walked past the window.

"Thank you." Alice flipped the notebook shut and looked at Davis. "That does it for me. What about you? Is that the missing relic you were hired to find?"

Davis studied the red plastic object in Celinda's hand. "It fits the description I was given."

"What, exactly, was the description of this missing item you're looking for?" Celinda asked.

"I've got a photograph." Davis went back to his chair, reached down, and opened the slim briefcase he had brought with him. He took out a glossy print.

Celinda looked at the picture. The relic in the shot was, indeed, identical to the one in her hand. In the photo it appeared to be lying in a metal drawer, the kind that museums and banks use to store valuables.

So much for hoping that Davis didn't know the relic was valuable. *Easy come, easy go,* she thought.

Alice rose from her chair. "I'll leave you and Miss Ingram to talk about that red doohickey. Believe it or not, I've got some actual police work to do."

"Thank you, Detective," Davis said. "You've been very helpful."

"Gee, thanks, Mr. Oakes." Alice did not bother to veil the sarcasm in her voice. She slung the strap of her black leather bag over one shoulder and made for the door. "Be sure to mention my name to Mercer Wyatt the next time you see him. Tell him that we at the Cadence City PD just live to assist the Guild in every possible way."

Chapter 2

ALICE PAUSED AT THE DOOR. "GUESS I FORGOT TO MEN-
tion that Mr. Oakes's client is Mercer Wyatt, the boss of the
Cadence Guild."

Celinda stifled a heavy sigh of regret. So much for Mr.
Perfect. There was a saying in her business: Any matchmaker who tries to match herself has a fool for a client.
She should have remembered that bit of wisdom. But, oh,
the vibes had been so good. Correction: the vibes were still
terrific. What was wrong with this picture?

"Guess you did forget to mention that little fact," she
said to Alice. She drew herself up and gave Davis an ac-
cusing look. "I assumed you were probably working for
some high-end collector."

"The Cadence Guild is what you would call a corporate
collector," he said, unfazed by her glare. "It has a very fine
museum."

"Which, of course, is not open to the public." She gave
him a steely smile. "Like everything else the Guilds do, their
museums are operated in an extremely secretive manner."

Alice was starting to look amused again. "I'll leave you

and Mr. Oakes to discuss this in private." She turned back to Davis. "Don't forget our agreement. If you turn up anything in your investigation that I should know about, I expect to hear from you immediately."

Davis inclined his head. "Understood, Detective."

Alice looked skeptical, but she said nothing more. She went out into the hall, closing the door behind her.

Davis studied Celinda, eyes cool and enigmatic. "I apologize for any confusion here."

"My fault," she said crisply. "I obviously didn't ask the right questions."

Sensing her tension, Araminta muttered into her ear.

"I take it you are not a fan of the Cadence Guild?" Davis said.

"I am not a fan of any of the Guilds. I consider them antiquated, outmoded institutions. Not to mention arrogant, heavy-handed, and corrupt." She gave him another chilly smile. "Just my opinion, of course."

"Sure." He gave her an equally wintry smile. "You're not the only person who has some reservations about the way the Guilds are run."

"They certainly have had some bad public relations problems in the past," she agreed with alacrity.

"Which they are working hard to overcome."

She thinned her smile out a little more. "Got a long way to go."

The Guilds had been established during the Era of Discord when the colonies had faced the threat of tyranny from a megalomaniac named Vincent Lee Vance. Until that turning point, there had been no necessity for the four struggling city-states that had grown up around the original colonies to establish militias. Regular police departments had been all that was necessary to maintain law and order in the new world.

When Vance and his fanatical minions had begun to terrorize the city-states, they had staged their assaults via the network of underground alien catacombs that crisscrossed the planet. The strange alien psi energy that radiated throughout the maze of tunnels rendered conventional weaponry unreliable at best and, at worst, extremely hazardous to those who used it.

But the underworld labyrinth provided its own natural artillery in the form of highly volatile, potentially lethal balls of fiery, acid-green energy technically known as UDEMs. The acronym stood for unstable dissonance energy manifestation. The balls of eerie green fire were called ghosts, because they drifted erratically and unpredictably through the tunnels like so many lost specters.

Certain individuals with unusual parapsych profiles—commonly known as ghost hunters—could control and manipulate the ghosts, transforming them into weapons. The vast majority of ghost hunters were men, because the paranormal ability to handle the unique energy storms generated by the UDEMs was linked to certain male hormones.

Every schoolchild knew the story. Vincent Lee Vance recruited ghost hunters into his renegade army. The city-states responded by creating the militias known as the ghost-hunter Guilds. In the end, the colonies were able to put down the rebellion, thanks to the admittedly heroic actions of the Guilds.

After the Era of Discord, the Guilds were never disbanded. Instead, those in charge saw a golden opportunity to corner a booming new market. Exploration and excavation of the alien catacombs was rapidly becoming big business. Hundreds of academic, corporate, and privately financed companies were eager to go underground to compete in the search for valuable alien antiquities and the quest for long-lost secrets. And they all needed ghost-hunter teams to protect the crews from the wandering balls of alien energy. It took a ghost to kill a ghost, and only ghost hunters could do the job.

The Guilds contracted the services of their members to

those who wanted to hire them. Over the years the organizations, led by a series of shrewd, ambitious men, had become powerful, secretive institutions bound by mysterious traditions and Guild Law.

History was repeating itself once again with the recent discovery of the vast, underground rain forest. Within the last few months the Guilds, led by Cooper Boone, the boss of the Aurora Springs Guild, had moved swiftly to position themselves as the primary source of guides and bodyguards for researchers, para-archaeologists, treasure hunters, and others who wanted to explore the jungle.

There were those—Celinda counted herself among them—who considered the Guilds only a notch or two above criminal mobs.

"I don't suppose you're going to tell me why the Cadence Guild is interested in my relic," she said.

Davis smiled his faint smile. "One of the things that I offer my clients is a guarantee of confidentiality."

"Why did the Guild hire you?" she asked. Then she held up a hand to stop him from responding. "Wait, let me guess. Guilds usually throw their business at people connected to the organizations. There must be half a dozen private investigation and security firms in Cadence that are owned and operated by retired hunters. Is your firm one of those companies?"

He contemplated her with a considering expression. "I come from a family of hunters. But I turned out a little different."

"I see." More bad news. He came from a Guild family. Traditionally, Guild people married other Guild people. It was one of the many customs that, in her opinion, had kept the organizations from going truly mainstream.

How could she have been so wrong about him? So much for her psychic powers.

Sadly, all the lecturing in the world wasn't going to dampen her intuitive reaction to Davis Oakes. Something about him compelled her senses, riveted them. Probably a bug-to-liquid-amber kind of thing. Silly little bug gets attracted to the enticing, glowing resin, goes for a stroll, gets stuck and—*whappo*—the stuff hardens around her and she's trapped in amber forever.

"I'm afraid I'm going to have to ask you to give me that artifact." Davis reached inside his jacket and took out a checkbook. "I'll reimburse you for the cost plus an extra thousand for your trouble."

"An extra *thousand*?" She was stunned. "It's worth that much to the Guild?"

"Let's just say that my client is very eager to recover the relic. Fifteen hundred?"

The arrogance of the offer irritated her.

"What happens if I refuse to hand it over?" she asked.

He took out a pen, put the checkbook down on the desk, and began writing. "Why would you want to do that?"

"Gosh, I don't know." She unfolded her arms and spread her hands. "Maybe because I bought it legally. Even got a receipt."

"The relic was stolen. You are not the legal owner."

"Maybe I just don't like the Guild thinking it has the right to have a private investigator barge into my office and take it away from me without an adequate explanation."

He did not look up from writing the check. "This is Guild business, Miss Ingram."

"I love it," she said, not bothering to conceal her disgust.

He glanced up. "You love what?"

"You thinking that *Guild business* is an adequate explanation." She wrinkled her nose in disgust. "That is so very Guild-like."

He straightened, put the pen back in his pocket, tore out the check, and handed it to her. "Maybe this will make up for the lack of a full explanation."

She took the check from him and read it carefully. *Two thousand dollars* was clearly written out in a bold scrawl.

She could do a lot with two thousand. Pay her rent, buy some badly needed new clothes, treat herself to some fancy restaurants . . .

She tore the check in half very deliberately and then put the halves together and ripped them into fourths.

He regarded her with polite inquiry.

"Not enough?" he asked.

"There is no amount of money that I would feel comfortable accepting from the Guild." She shuddered. "In point of fact, I don't want anything from the organization."

"You're going to make this difficult?"

"Not at all." She gave him a tight little smile. "You can have the stupid artifact, because the last thing I want is to become involved in Guild business."

"You're sure you won't accept the money?"

"Positive."

"You do realize that this means that the Cadence Guild now owes you a favor," Davis said neutrally.

"*No*, absolutely not." She was appalled. "The Guild doesn't owe me a thing."

"You know what they say, the Guild always pays its debts."

"Sounds like a real nightmare scenario to me. Look, I'll make a deal with you. You can thank me for giving you the artifact by not mentioning my name to your client."

He thought about that briefly and then nodded once, his expression somber. "If that's what you want. I don't see how keeping quiet about your role in this will violate my professional obligation to my client."

"Terrific." She went to the door, opened it abruptly, and held the relic out to him on the palm of her hand. "Good afternoon, Mr. Oakes. I won't say it's been a pleasure, but it has been interesting."

He picked up his briefcase and walked toward the door, halting directly in front of her. "Are you a good matchmaker, Miss Ingram?"

"The best."

"I notice you're not wearing a wedding ring. I take it that means you haven't been able to find a match for yourself."

She knew she was turning red, but she managed to keep her composure. "Very observant of you."

He nodded. "Probably just as well. I got matched by a pro once."

"I can tell by your tone of voice that it did not work out."

"No," he said. "Luckily for both of us, we found out shortly before the wedding that the match was a bad one."

"I see," she said coolly. "I'm sorry you had such an unfortunate experience. All I can tell you is that what happened to you was an anomaly. Statistically speaking, the odds of making a good match are significantly improved when you employ a knowledgeable, reputable marriage consultant."

"Maybe." He shrugged. "Personally, I've pretty much decided to skip the whole happily-ever-after thing."

She stared at him, startled. Very few people went around announcing that they planned to skip the *happily-ever-after thing*. Even if one were personally inclined to avoid marriage, family and social pressure proved too strong for most people. Folks who didn't get serious about marriage after a certain point in life found that their careers stalled, invitations from one's peers—all of whom were married—dried up, and people began to regard the unmarried individual as exceedingly odd.

In spite of her annoyance, her consultant instincts kicked in immediately.

"Never say never," she said bracingly. "I'm sure the right person for you is out there somewhere." She couldn't believe that for a while there she had actually thought that person was her.

"Yeah, sure." He did not look convinced. "What about you?"

"Me?" Good grief, was that her voice? The word had come out sounding like a squeak.

"Are you involved with anyone at the moment?" he asked with an air of great patience.

This was getting awkward. She cleared her throat and tried to appear nonchalant. "No, not at the moment. Life has been very busy lately. New job, you know."

"Care to go out to dinner and discuss something besides marriage and relics?"

She went blank. "Huh?"

He smiled a little. She could see the sexy heat in his eyes. Psi energy tingled in the atmosphere, hers as well as his. She was shocked to realize that her insides were starting to melt.

"Got a feeling a date with you might be interesting." He paused a beat. "Or am I picking up the wrong signals here? If so, my apologies."

He was daring her to take the leap with him, challenging her.

"I usually don't date—" she began.

"Hunters. Yes, I got that impression. Let me make it clear that, while I come from a Guild family, I don't make my living as a ghost hunter."

"I was going to say that I usually don't date people I meet at work."

"I'm not a client."

She took a deep breath. In spite of his incredibly seductive psi patterns, they had nothing in common. Even if they got past that monumental hurdle, he had made it very clear that there was no long-term future for them together. Dating a man under these circumstances violated all the matchmaking rules, but she had never felt this way about any man in her entire life. She might never again meet someone who had this effect on her senses. Why shouldn't she take the opportunity to experience a romantic fling?

Once again she reached up to touch Araminta.

It would have to be a terribly discreet fling, of course. Professional marriage consultants had to be exceedingly careful about their reputations.

"Well," she said, "I suppose that might be all right."

"Are you free tonight?"

She stopped petting Araminta. She could do this.

"Yes, as a matter of fact, I am," she said. Belatedly, a thought struck her. "I can't stay out late because I'm going out of town tomorrow morning and I still have some last-minute packing to do. But tonight is definitely clear."

Great. She sounded just like Amberella in the fairy tale. After midnight the beautiful amber carriage turned back into a large squash, and a shoe went missing.

"If you'll give me your address, I'll pick you up at seven. I promise to have you home before midnight."

"My address," she repeated. A tiny chill of uncertainty swept through her. What did she really know about Davis Oakes? She had only just met him, and she was probably not thinking clearly, because standing close to him like this stirred all her senses.

He owned a security firm, she reminded herself. Okay, he had the Guild for a client, but he appeared to have a working relationship with a police detective. That would seem to indicate that he was not a serial killer. Still, she wasn't quite ready to break *all* the rules. Safety first.

She rezzed what she hoped was a polished, confident smile. "Why don't we meet at the restaurant? I'll take a cab."

Amusement gleamed in his eyes. "The careful type, huh?"

"We in the marriage consulting business tend to err on the side of caution when it comes to this sort of thing. First dates are tricky. If both parties take responsibility for getting themselves to and from the appointed venue, there's less pressure."

"That sounds like it came out of some kind of dating manual."

"It did. The title is *Ten Steps to a Covenant Marriage: Secrets of a Professional Matchmaker*."

"Since we're talking about a date, not a Covenant Marriage, we can forget the rule book," Davis said. "All right, how about Verdigris in the Old Quarter? I'll wait for you in the lounge."

"That sounds lovely."

He held out his hand. "If you don't mind, I'll take the relic now. The sooner I get it back to my client, the better."

Belatedly she realized that she was still holding the artifact.

"Right." She started to hand it to him.

Araminta suddenly went wild. She chortled shrilly in Celinda's ear and went into full predatory mode. Her second set of eyes, the amber-colored ones she used for hunting, and a lot of teeth suddenly appeared. Her lint-ball form sleeked out, revealing a tough, sinuous little body and all six paws.

She sprang straight down Celinda's outstretched arm, seized the relic, and bounded to the floor. With her prize clutched in her two front paws, she raced through the open door and disappeared.

"*Araminta*, come back here," Celinda called.

She rushed out into the corridor and saw Araminta dashing around the corner. She raced after her. When she rounded the corner, she was just in time to see the dust bunny disappear through the open door of the stairwell.

Jana Pace, the consultant who had the office next door to Celinda's, rushed out of the stairwell, shrieking.

"*A rat. I just saw a rat. I'm going to call the janitor.*"

Jana fled toward her office and a phone.

Celinda came to a halt at the top of the stairs and looked down. There was no sign of Araminta.

She heard Davis's footsteps behind her. He stopped and looked over her shoulder, gazing down into the empty stairwell.

"Had a feeling this case was going a little too smoothly," he said without expression.

"Hey, it's not my fault Araminta ran off with the relic."

His eyes narrowed. "She's your dust bunny."

"Araminta doesn't *belong* to me. She's a companion. She's very independent, and she obviously considers that artifact her toy. I'll bet she's going to hide it somewhere."

"In which case, she'll eventually retrieve it."

She'd known him less than forty minutes, but she already knew enough about Davis Oakes to realize that he wasn't about to give up easily. This was a man who, once he set an objective, kept going until he reached it. Furthermore, he was currently working for Mercer Wyatt, which meant he had the full power of the Cadence Guild behind him. What chance did one small dust bunny have?

She needed to find a way to take the heat off Araminta.

She dashed the back of her hand across her eyes and put a tremor in her voice. "Araminta has probably run away for good. I'm going to miss her so much. She was my little pal."

"In my experience, once dust bunnies form a bond with a human, they are fiercely loyal," he said, showing no signs of sympathy. "Your little pal will be back. She'll probably be waiting for you when you get home tonight."

So much for that ploy. Nevertheless, she sniffed and blinked furiously, as though trying to suppress a flood of tears. "I have your card, Mr. Oakes." She added a delicate sob to her voice. "I'll give you a call if she ever shows up again and brings back the relic."

"You do that." He went back out into the hall. "If you'll excuse me, I've got some work to do. See you at seven tonight."

That stopped her cold. She cleared her throat. "I, uh, sort of assumed that this new development meant our date was probably off."

He paused and looked back at her. "Guess again, Miss Ingram. You and I are going to be spending a lot of time in each other's company until that damn relic reappears."

She knew a threat when she heard one.

"No offense, Mr. Oakes, but under the circumstances, I don't think it would be a comfortable evening for either of us. What do you say we postpone the issue of a date until we see whether or not Araminta comes back with the artifact?"

Chapter 3

SHE MUST HAVE SENSED THE ENERGY THAT HAD PULSED between them. He couldn't have been the only one who had felt that high-rez stuff ricocheting back and forth back there in her office. Or was he?

Davis got out of the parking garage elevator and made his way through the rows of cars to where he had left the Phantom. He was still half-aroused.

Max was waiting for him when he reached the car. The dust bunny was napping on the passenger seat in his favorite position, flat on his back, all six paws up in the air. When Davis opened the door, he stretched, opened his blue eyes, rolled over, and made little chortling sounds.

"Hey, there, buddy."

They did the brief greeting ritual, which consisted of him patting Max on the top of his furry head and Max bouncing up and down a little.

"I should have taken you in there with me," Davis said. "You might have saved the day. Takes a dust bunny to catch a dust bunny, I always say. As it is, we've got a whole lot of new problems."

He set the briefcase on the floor on the passenger side. Max hopped up onto the back of the seat where he had an excellent view. Max liked riding in cars.

Instead of rezzing the engine, Davis sat for a moment, hands resting on the wheel, trying to suppress the unfamiliar sense of anticipation and hungry excitement that was flooding his veins.

"Damn near knocked me off my feet, Max. Felt about nineteen again. And it's not like she could ever get hired to read the evening news on the rez-screen. I mean, she's attractive, okay? But not in the usual way. She's, I dunno, *different*."

Max made understanding noises.

Different. That was it, he thought. She wasn't perfect. In his experience, perfect was pleasant to look at, but it was never interesting for long. Perfection never made you curious. It never raised any questions. Everything was on the surface with perfect. You knew in your gut that, in the end, perfect was going to be boring long-term.

No, Celinda Ingram was not perfect. What she was, he thought, was fascinating. Fascinating always carried some risk.

He looked through the windshield at the Slider parked nose to nose with the Phantom and summoned up a mental image of the mysterious woman in the office four floors above him.

Hair the color of rich, dark amber, caught up in a severe knot at the back of her head, a couple of wisps dangling down in front of her delicate little ears. Big, hazel green eyes, soft mouth, assertive nose and chin. There was an elegance and dignity about her. He liked that in a woman, liked to know that she thought enough of herself to carry herself like a queen.

He had also sensed a whisper of power. She had worn an amber bracelet on her left wrist. Could have been a fashion statement, he thought, but it could have been something more. Everyone could generate a little psi energy, but power-ful para-rez talents like himself often carried tuned amber in some form to help them concentrate and focus that energy.

Whatever else he had been expecting when he and Mar-tinez tracked down Celinda Ingram, it had not been the deep rush of sexual excitement that had made him long to throw her over his shoulder and take off into the rain forest.

How the hell could she be a matchmaker? He didn't trust any of them, not after the fiasco of his engagement to Janet.

But what the hell, he wasn't looking for long-term. He could overlook the matchmaking thing. He wondered why she wasn't married. And then he thanked his lucky amber that she wasn't.

"If nothing else, it's going to be a really interesting eve-ning, Max."

The thought cheered him. He hadn't had a really inter-esting evening in longer than he cared to recall. Ever since the fiasco of his close encounter with a Covenant Mar-riage, he had devoted himself to his business. Life was simpler that way. At least it had been until today.

He rezzed the Phantom's engine. Beneath the gleaming hood, flash-rock melted. He backed out of the parking slot and drove out of the garage, heading toward his office in the Old Quarter.

A short time later, Max on his shoulder, he pushed open the door of the offices of Oakes Security.

Trig McAndrews, seated behind the reception desk, looked up from his computer. His bald, shaved head gleamed in the overhead lights. So did the gold ring in his ear.

Trig was built like one of the Colonial-era buildings in the Quarter: not too tall but solid as a brick right down to the foundation. He looked as if he moonlighted as a pro wrestler. The elaborate tattoos enhanced that impression.

"Any luck, boss?" Each word sounded like it had been dragged through crushed gravel.

"Yes and no."

"I hate answers like that."

"Me, too."

Max hopped down off Davis's shoulder, landed on the desk, and greeted Trig with a small chortle.

"How's it hangin', big guy?" Trig patted Max on the top of his head and then looked up at Davis. "So, what happened?"

"The person of interest Martinez and I interviewed had the relic in her possession," Davis said. "She was apparently willing to turn it over to me. But, in what may strike you as an amazing coincidence, her dust bunny ran off with it just as I was about to take possession. Bunny and relic disappeared."

Trig's expression did not change. "A dust bunny ran off with our client's artifact?" Each word was very carefully spaced.

"Miss Ingram says the bunny thinks the relic is a toy, which means that the little sucker will bring it home soon. Dust bunnies don't like to be parted from their toys for very long."

"Gonna be a little hard to explain this chain of events to Mercer Wyatt," Trig observed.

"I don't plan to tell Wyatt what happened. Not as long as there's a chance of getting that relic back. Keep the client in the dark whenever possible is the company motto. You know that."

"What do I say if Wyatt's assistant calls again for an update?"

"The usual. Tell him that we're making progress."

Trig nodded. There was no need for him to say anything more. They both knew how important recovering the relic was to the future of Oakes Security. It was the first big case the firm had landed since Davis's world had gone to green hell six months ago. A lot of old clients had been unwilling to take a chance on him after the disaster. He was well aware that if he screwed up, it was a good bet they'd never see any more business from the Guild or any other high-profile corporation.

Trig snorted. "Sounds like you'd better keep an eye on the matchmaker. If she didn't know the relic was worth a lot to the Guild before she talked to you, she'll know it now."

"Don't worry, I'm going to put her under close surveillance tonight."

"Stakeout?"

"Dinner date."

Trig's heavy black brows bounced up and down a few times. "You're dating someone who is involved in the case? You never do that. Thought it was one of your rules."

"Comes under the heading of undercover work. Any messages?"

"Cooper Boone called while you were out. He wants you to call him back when you get a chance."

"Damn. I've been trying to duck him. He's going to lean on me to attend his wedding in a couple of weeks."

"Stop fighting it, boss. He's an old friend. You have to go. There's no way around it."

Trig was right. He had been friends with Cooper Boone for over a decade. They had some stuff in common when it came to weird talents. Boone was now the head of the Aurora Springs Guild. In a couple of weeks he was going to marry Elly St. Clair, the daughter of a prominent Aurora Springs Guild family. The wedding was certain to be a huge formal Covenant Marriage affair with all the trimmings. Davis would have preferred to go to the dentist.

"I'm too old to be going to weddings," he said. "You know how it is if you show up without a date at my age. Everyone immediately starts trying to set you up with their sister's friend's second cousin."

"Tell me about it. Pressure city. Hey, I'm in the same boat, remember? I've got three invitations this week, so far. Face it, it's the wedding season. What are ya gonna do?"

Davis nodded glumly. "Anything else?"

"Yep, your brother called. Says to warn you that your mother is plotting to introduce you to another candidate."

A sense of gloom pressed down on him. "My lucky day."

"The lady's name is Nola Walters. According to your brother, her family's third-generation Guild from Crystal City. Your mom met her through a friend."

Just what he did not need, Davis thought. Another attempt at matchmaking by his mother.

"Where's the mail?" he asked.

"There wasn't much today. Couple of bills." Trig handed him a crisp white envelope. "And this."

Davis took the letter and glanced at the return address. He recognized it immediately. It was the third letter he'd had from the Glenfield Institute in the past three weeks.

"I'll be in my office." He held out his hand to Max. "Let's go, partner."

Max scurried up his arm and resumed his position on Davis's shoulder.

Davis went through the door of his office, dropped the briefcase beside the desk, and sat down. Max bounced down onto the desk and went straight to his favorite source of amusement, the green quartz vase that held a mound of paper clips. He settled down on the rim of the vase and began rummaging through the shiny heap.

Davis leaned back in the chair and stacked his heels on the corner of the desk. He tapped the envelope against the arm of the chair a couple of times, debating whether to rip it up without reading it or read it first and then rip it up. Decisions, decisions.

Eventually he reached for the letter opener, slashed the envelope, and removed the sheet of letterhead inside. The message was the same as the previous two letters.

Dear Mr. Oakes:
It has come to my attention that you have missed all of the follow-up appointments that were scheduled for

*you after you left the Institute. I urge you to call my of-
fice as soon as possible. . . .*

The signature at the bottom was the same, too: Gordon R.
Phillips, DPP. The initials stood for doctor of para-psychiatry.

He leaned over the arm of his chair, shoved the letter
and the envelope into the shredder, and rezzed the machine. There was a high-pitched hum as the device turned
the paper into confetti.

He settled back into the chair again. Trig was right. Dating someone involved in a case was against all the rules.

"Probably a mistake, Max."

Max selected a shiny paper clip, removed it from the
vase, and carried it across the desk to Davis.

"Good choice," Davis said.

He attached the paper clip to the chain of clips that dan-
gled from the reading lamp. Satisfied, Max hurried back to
the vase and started searching for another suitable clip.

Davis thought for a while. Then he took his feet down
off the desk and rezzed up the computer. There hadn't been
an opportunity to do any research on Celinda Ingram this
morning. Things had been moving too fast, what with finding the body, contacting the police, and tracking down the
new owner of the relic.

It was time to take a closer look at his date.

Within a couple of minutes he found himself reading
the first of a number of lurid headlines in the Frequency
City tabloids.

**LOCAL GUILD COUNCIL MEMBER'S SECRET MISTRESS
IS MATCHMAKER TO CITY'S ELITE**

The next one was similar in tone.

**HIGH-RANKING MEMBER
OF THE FREQUENCY CITY GUILD
INVOLVED IN AFFAIR WITH SOCIETY MATCHMAKER**

There were several more in the same vein. They all included grainy photographs of Celinda. In several she was seen leaping out of a rumpled hotel room bed. The photos had been cropped in a bow to good taste, but it was clear that she was wearing only a filmy negligee. There was a man in the background. He had a towel wrapped around his waist. In two other shots Celinda was shown in a white spa robe running barefoot across a parking lot.

He checked the dates. The salacious news stories were all dated four months earlier. The scandal had taken about ten days to run its course. After that there was no further mention of Celinda Ingram or her business, the Ingram Connection.

He tried the online Frequency City Directory, found a number, and dialed it. Someone answered almost immediately.

"Ruin View Pizza."

"I was given this number for the Ingram Connection," Davis said.

"Yeah, we get that a lot. The Ingram Connection had this number before us. It went out of business a few months ago."

"Thanks," Davis said. He ended the call.

Max had selected another paper clip. Davis attached it to the chain and then settled back to read some of the tabloid pieces in greater depth. The sensational story about the matchmaker who had run the most elite marriage consulting agency in Frequency City had obsessed the papers. That wasn't surprising. Illicit sex always sold well. Add a powerful man and a woman whose personal reputation was one of her most important business assets, and you had the ingredients for a perfect scandal.

> . . . Benson Landry, a high-ranking member of the local Guild Council, is reported to be involved in a torrid affair with noted matchmaker Celinda Ingram. The two were photographed to-

gether in intimate circumstances at the exclusive
Lakeside Resort & Spa last weekend. The couple
was registered under false names in an obvious
attempt to avoid prying eyes.

Miss Ingram, whose exclusive matchmaking
agency, the Ingram Connection, handles only
Covenant Marriages, is the most sought-after
marriage consultant in the city. There is specula-
tion that Benson Landry will soon be tapped to
head the Frequency City Guild when current
chief Harold Taylor steps down. . . .

He did a quick search on the Ingram Connection and
learned that the agency had quietly closed its doors less
than a week after the photographs at the Lakeside Resort &
Spa had been taken.

No wonder Celinda had been so anxious not to get involved in Guild business. She'd been badly burned by a
high-ranking Guild man.

He did a quick search on Benson Landry. It was no surprise that Landry fit the profile of most of the ghost hunters
at the top of the Guilds: a strong dissonance-energy para-
rez talent, extremely ambitious, hints of ruthlessness, and
enough gaps in the record to indicate that he had some secrets.

Davis looked at Max. "Wonder what the hell she saw in
him."

Chapter 4

HE HATED THIS GREEN HELL, BUT IT WAS THE PERFECT HIDING place for the gun. He pushed it inside the small grotto and covered it with a few leaves and palm fronds. The foliage was green, but not the natural-looking green you saw on the surface. Everything down here in the underground rain forest was a weird shade of iridescent green, like the luminous quartz that had been used to construct the catacombs. Even the artificial sunlight was an eerie green.

It wasn't just the colors in the jungle that were strange. Most of the flora and fauna bore a vague resemblance to the plants and wildlife on the surface of Harmony, but down here evolution, modified by the underground environment, alien engineering, and the constant presence of a lot of ambient psi had produced several startling twists and turns.

The experts theorized that the aliens had engineered the belowground ecosystem because the one aboveground was toxic to their kind. It was clear that the aliens had never been at home on the surface of Harmony. They had evidently lived most of their lives in the vast maze of tunnels and chambers they had built beneath the surface. When they had fashioned cityscapes aboveground, they had surrounded them with massive green quartz walls. It was believed that the psi energy given off by the quartz and by something here in the jungle had been an antidote to whatever it was that had been dangerous to them aboveground.

He surveyed his handiwork and was satisfied. The gun was well-concealed, but it would be easily available if he needed it again in the future.

He hurried quickly through a stand of tall fern trees. It made him nervous to get out of eyesight of the gate. He had an amber-rez compass with him, but they were not infallible down here where vast currents of psi energy called ghost rivers could distort the delicate devices. He had a great fear of getting lost in the jungle.

The hot, humid atmosphere was almost smothering. It would rain soon.

A large green bird took flight directly in front of him, startling him so badly he cried out. The creature flapped madly, shrieking its annoyance, and then disappeared into the heavy green canopy overhead.

The constant din of birdcalls and mysterious rustlings in the undergrowth rattled his nerves. He was terrified of snakes and insects. While thus far no species down here had been identified as lethal to humans, that didn't mean they didn't exist. Exploration of the jungle had barely begun. The Guilds were still in the process of trying to find the special kind of psi talents who could open gates to the rain forest. To date only a handful had been discovered.

The gate he used was not one that had been opened under the auspices of the Guild. It was not listed on any official chart. The six-foot-tall hole had been created for him by one of his street clinic patients who happened to possess the unusual type of para-rez talent needed to access the rain forest. The junkie had suffered a most unfortunate overdose once he had finished the job. But what could you expect of an addict?

He hurried through the opening, breathing easier once he was outside in the green quartz corridor. It always amazed him that nothing from the rain forest followed him through the gate. There was not so much as a stray leaf or twig or insect on the glowing green floor of the tunnel. The gates all seemed to generate invisible and, to most humans, undetectable energy barriers that kept the jungle contained.

He walked quickly toward a quartz staircase, adjusting the cuffs of his immaculately tailored white shirt. Even if the police did somehow manage to connect him to the shooting and even if they figured out that he had concealed the weapon in the rain forest, they would never be able to find it. There was no way it could ever be used as evidence against him in a court of law.

Of course, that still left the Cadence Guild. Alvis Shaw had warned him that Mercer Wyatt had hired an investigator to search for the relic. It was no secret that the Guilds did not always feel it necessary to honor the legal niceties when it came to hunting down those who stole from their vaults.

But he was safe. He had been careful. And he was infinitely more intelligent than any Guild man.

Nevertheless, he now had a serious problem. Things had gone terribly wrong last night. He was a brilliant parapsychiatrist, an expert on reading people, but for some reason he simply hadn't expected a low-end, drug-addicted thief like Alvis Shaw to double-cross him. The bastard had actually threatened to set up an auction and sell the relic to the highest bidder. He'd had no choice but to kill Shaw. It wasn't as if he hadn't intended to get rid of him anyway, once he took possession of the relic.

The realization that he had a disaster on his hands had hit when he searched the dying man. Shaw hadn't had the relic on him.

Even as Shaw lay dying, his blood running across the alley bricks, the bastard had laughed.

"Hid it in the antique shop last night. Seemed like the

perfect place. Didn't think anyone would notice it, not with all that other junk piled around it. But it's gone. You're screwed, man. You'll never find it now."

He had torn the antique shop apart, hoping that Shaw had lied to him when he had claimed that the relic was gone. But in the end he had been forced to conclude that the thief had told him the truth.

He had no choice now. Against his own professional judgment he would have to use another patient from the street clinic. The man he had in mind was a former ghost hunter who had been badly psi-burned and was now heavily medicated. The patient was extremely fragile, but that condition had the advantage of making him easier to control than Shaw had been.

He climbed the staircase, aware that he was still shivering. It was a perfectly normal reaction to a highly stressful situation, he assured himself. He was a doctor. He should know.

Chapter 5

ARAMINTA WAS WAITING FOR CELINDA WHEN SHE GOT back to her apartment. The dust bunny was sitting on the railing of the small balcony that overlooked the Old Quarter. She was fully fluffed, with only her innocent blue eyes showing. There was no sign of the red artifact.

Celinda yanked open the sliding glass door, scooped her up, and looked her in the eye.

"Where have you been? Are you all right? You scared the you know what out of me. You've never acted like that before."

Araminta chattered cheerfully and hopped up onto her shoulder. Celinda reached up to pet her. "Don't ever do that again, okay? It's very hard on the nerves."

Araminta muttered reassuringly.

"You hid that relic somewhere, didn't you? I hope you realize that Davis Oakes isn't going to leave us alone until he gets his hands on that thing."

Araminta displayed a vast amount of unconcern. She made hopeful little noises. Celinda recognized them immediately.

"You're hungry again, aren't you? Well, this time I'm not surprised. No telling how long you've been running around. Probably worked off lunch. Let's go see what's left in the refrigerator."

Dusk had begun to overtake the Old Quarter. The Dead City wall was starting to glow faintly. When darkness fell, the ambient luminescence would infuse the surrounding neighborhoods with a pale emerald radiance. Celinda thought of it as a permanent nightlight.

She gave Araminta another pat. Together they went back inside the apartment and into the little kitchen. Most of the apartments in the Old Quarter were small, and this one was no exception. The buildings had all been constructed during the Colonial era. The First Generation colonists had built their original structures in the shadows of the ancient walls that surrounded each of the four Dead Cities that had been discovered: Old Cadence, Old Resonance, Old Frequency, and Old Crystal.

Over the years, as the new human cities had grown and expanded into the surrounding countrysides the Old Quarter had fallen into decay and disrepair. Many of the neighborhoods with their tight, cramped streets and dark, looming buildings had become home to derelicts, prostitutes, and the down and out.

Although gentrification had begun in certain sections, you could still get a cheap apartment in the Quarter. That fact had figured heavily into Celinda's decision to rent in the neighborhood. She had been on a very tight budget when she moved to Cadence to start over. But it wasn't cost alone that had brought her to the Quarter. Like most strong para-rez talents, her senses responded pleasantly to the gentle ambient psi that leaked out of the ancient city.

She opened the door of the refrigerator. Together she and Araminta surveyed the contents. There was a large wedge of leftover lasagna, some salad greens, a carton of milk, and a half-empty bottle of wine.

Araminta displayed great interest in the lasagna.

"Well, I was going to have that for my dinner, but since it looks like I'm eating out tonight, whether I like it or not, you can have the lasagna," Celinda said.

She spooned the lasagna into Araminta's plate on the floor and then went into the bedroom and opened the closet. Her social life had been nonexistent since the debacle in Frequency. She hadn't been inspired to shop for anything more interesting than extremely conservative business suits.

Her choices tonight were limited to two possibilities. The very pink dress sheathed in clear plastic did not count. She was quite certain that once she wore it for her sister's wedding, she would never wear it again. Pink was not her color.

She contemplated instead the classic little black dress hanging at the back. It was long-sleeved and had a demure neckline. The last time it had been worn was at a funeral. She pondered it for a long moment. According to *Ten Steps to a Covenant Marriage*, black was always safe. Furthermore, on a first date *elegant* was the watchword, not *provocative*.

On the other hand, there was a fine line between elegant and dull, and as Davis had made clear, this wasn't exactly the start of a Covenant Marriage courtship.

She pushed aside a couple of jackets and studied option number two, a sleek, dark violet number with a deep, off-the-shoulder cowl neckline that could only be described as provocative.

Number two was probably not a good idea. Regardless of how it had started out, this was not a real date.

But a strange recklessness seemed to have replaced her usual good sense. What the heck, the relic was his problem, not hers. This was the first time she'd been out to dinner with a man in months, and she intended to enjoy it, even if she was breaking all the rules.

She headed for the shower, stripping off her clothes.

*   *   *

AN HOUR LATER SHE INSERTED THE SECOND OF A PAIR OF
amber earrings into her ears and stood back to survey the
results in the mirror. In spite of the stern lecture she had
given herself in the shower, she could not suppress the little thrill of anticipation that shivered through her.

"Think the neckline is too low?" she asked Araminta.

Araminta was perched on the dresser in front of the mirror, playing with a shiny tube of lipstick. She looked up at
the sound of Celinda's voice and made what Celinda took
to be an approving noise.

"I'm not sure." Celinda leaned forward, studying the
drape of the fluid fabric of the cowl neckline in the mirror.
There were lots of deep shadows and some cleavage, but
on the whole, everything still looked decent.

"The earrings may be a little too much," she said to
Araminta. "If there's a fine line between elegant and boring, the line between sexy and slutty is even thinner. What
do you think?"

The doorbell rezzed. Araminta bounced up and down,
dropped the lipstick, and hopped up onto Celinda's bare
shoulder. Celinda could feel four of the dust bunny's six paws
gripping her bare skin.

"Watch the claws," she said. The warning was probably
unnecessary. Araminta had never scratched her, not even
by accident.

The night was warm and humid. There was no need for
a wrap. She stepped into a pair of high-heeled sandals and
went down the short hall to answer the door.

Araminta was chortling exuberantly now, scarcely able
to contain herself.

"Sheesh," Celinda muttered. "If you like Oakes so much,
why did you run off with his relic?"

Araminta ignored the question, of course. But her ea-
gerness was plain.

Celinda stopped in front of the door to check the security peephole.

Her pulse kicked up immediately at the sight of Davis

standing on the other side. He looked as if he had just walked straight out of the heart of midnight in a pair of black trousers, an elegantly casual black jacket, and a black shirt undone at the collar. The only touches of color were his amber cuff links and the amber face of his watch.

But the really startling accessory was the big ball of blue-eyed lint sitting on his shoulder. That explained Araminta's excitement. She had sensed the other dust bunny.

Astonished, Celinda opened the door. "No wonder you know so much about dust bunnies," she said.

"This is Max," Davis said.

Max and Araminta made small, welcoming noises at each other and blinked their daylight eyes.

Celinda stood back to allow Davis and Max into the tiny front hall. Her astonishment gave way to deep suspicion. "Did you bring Max because you think he can find the artifact that Araminta hid?"

"No," Davis said. "That's not why I brought him along tonight."

"Why, then?" she asked, still wary.

He smiled faintly. "Thought that since you and I are going to be busy, he might like to make friends with Araminta. I doubt if Verdigris welcomes critters. Figured we could leave these two in the car while we eat."

Araminta made more small, squeaky sounds. Max responded in kind.

"Well, they do seem to like each other," Celinda said, still a little uneasy about the situation. "How did you find Max?"

"He found me. Started coming around my back door a few months ago after I got out of the—" Davis broke off abruptly. "Made the mistake of feeding him. Next thing I knew, he had moved in."

"That was pretty much how it was with Araminta and me. Got a hunch dust bunnies choose the people they want to attach themselves to for reasons we'll probably never figure out."

"Mysterious dust bunny thing," he agreed. He surveyed the cowl neckline with masculine approval. "Great dress."

She blushed a little. "Thanks. Nice jacket."

"Thanks."

There was a short pause. Celinda tried to think of what to say or do next. Now that the rules against wearing a provocative dress and allowing a date to pick you up at your home had been broken, things were getting murky fast. She was definitely on a slippery slope, but she had to admit it was exciting.

"Ready?" Davis asked.

"Yes." She picked up the small clutch purse on the hall table and followed him out onto the landing. She paused to rez the lock and then dropped her key into the purse.

They went downstairs into the tiny front hall. Mrs. Furnell's front door snapped open right on cue. Betty Furnell peered out. She was dressed in a pair of pink sweatpants and matching top, snappy pink running shoes, and a lot of oversized jewelry that she had purchased from the shopping channel. Her white hair was severely permed into a helmet shape, and her round face was illuminated with avid curiosity.

She gave Davis a not-so-discreet once-over before pinning Celinda with feigned innocence.

"Oh, hello, dear." She hoisted the small plastic sack she held in one hand. "I was just on my way to empty the garbage."

"Good evening, Mrs. Furnell." Celinda hesitated and then decided she had no option but to introduce Davis. "This is Mr. Oakes."

Davis offered his hand. "A pleasure, Mrs. Furnell."

Betty shook his hand vigorously. "I see you've got one of those little dust bunny beasts, too. Cute little devils."

"Yes, ma'am." He looked at the plastic sack. "Would you like me to take that out to the trash bin for you?"

"Heavens no, wouldn't dream of it, not with you all dressed up so nice like that."

"Then, if you'll excuse us, we'll be on our way. We've got reservations."

"Have a lovely time," Betty said.

"We will," he assured her.

Celinda was startled by the unmistakably possessive way he took her arm, opened the front door, and escorted her outside onto the sidewalk.

"I'm guessing that's your alibi for last night?" he asked, sounding amused. "The landlady who can vouch for the fact that you were at home alone between midnight and three AM?"

"Mrs. Furnell doesn't miss a thing that goes on around here."

"Yeah, I got that impression. Does she greet all your dates that way?"

"I have no idea. You're the first date I've had since I moved here to Cadence."

"Hard to believe."

She wasn't sure how to take that, so she let it go.

"How long have you been in town?" he asked, opening the door of a sleek, black Phantom 3000.

"Four months." Celinda got into the car. Now, why did her intuition tell her that he already knew the answer to that question? Maybe it was that subtle little pulse in his psi waves.

The passenger seat cradled her like a leather-clad lover. Araminta hopped from her shoulder onto the back of the seat. Davis closed the door and went around the front of the vehicle.

Surreptitiously, Celinda inhaled the unmistakable smell of expensive car and tried not to appear impressed. The security consulting business obviously paid well, she decided. Whatever else he was, Davis was no ordinary PI.

When he got in beside her, however, she was suddenly very aware of just how close and intimate the interior of the Phantom was.

"Where did you live before you came here?" Davis asked, rezzing the engine.

No doubt about it, she was being interrogated. Well, he was a private investigator after all. She must not forget that.

"Frequency City," she said, cooling her tone a little.

"I'm just making conversation. That's what you're supposed to do on a date, isn't it?" He eased the Phantom away from the curb. "Correct me if I'm wrong, but I'm getting the impression that you would prefer not to talk about your life in Frequency."

"Sorry. Didn't mean to be rude. The thing is, I have to go back to Frequency tomorrow to attend a wedding, and I am not looking forward to it."

"Whose wedding?"

"My sister's. Big Covenant affair. You know the drill, I'm sure."

"Oh, yeah."

She noticed that his jaw had gone very rigid.

"I'm the maid of honor," she said.

"I would have thought that a professional matchmaker would enjoy attending weddings."

This was a first date, and there was a very real possibility that there might never be another. No need to put a damper on things by dredging up her sordid past. She gave him a high-rez smile.

"You'd understand if you saw the dress," she said.

"What dress?"

"The one I have to wear."

He flashed her a quick, curious glance. "What's wrong with it?"

"It's pink. The whole wedding is going to be pink. It's my sister's favorite color."

"Got it. Other than the fact that there's a major pink theme going, you're okay with the wedding? This isn't one of those nightmare scenarios where your sister is marrying your ex-boyfriend or anything, is it?"

"Absolutely not. My sister is marrying a wonderful man. I matched them, myself. It's just that it's going to be a little awkward going back to Frequency."

"Why?"

"The usual story," she said, trying to sound at ease. "I don't have a date for the wedding. You know how it will be. Everyone will start trying to play matchmaker. It's particularly awkward when you're the expert."

It was true as far as it went, but it was a long way from the full story. With luck maybe he wouldn't notice.

"Trust me, you have my full and complete sympathy," he said, sounding grim. "I've got a few weddings to attend myself this summer."

"Alone?" she hazarded.

"Looks that way."

"Well, it's the season. Not like you have a lot of options. There aren't many excuses for ducking a Covenant Marriage if the people getting married are friends or family."

Max and Araminta were sitting very close together on the back of the seat, chattering enthusiastically.

"What do you think they're talking about?" Davis said, turning a corner.

"Who knows?" Celinda turned her head to look at the pair. "I've never watched dust bunnies interact with each other. In fact, until Araminta adopted me, I'd never seen one in person, just in pictures."

"Same here. After Max moved in, I talked to a biologist friend of mine at the university. He told me that very little is known about dust bunnies. They've never been considered destructive pests, so there's never been any funding to study them."

"Thank heavens." Celinda shuddered. "I don't even want to think about what could happen if some scientists decided that dust bunnies should be studied in a laboratory."

"Something tells me that bunnies are smart enough to avoid that fate."

"They do seem to be able to disappear whenever they

wish. Sometimes Araminta slips out at night and doesn't come home until dawn. I have no idea where she goes or how she even gets out of the apartment."

"Max does the same thing occasionally." Davis slowed for a streetlight. "Just another dust bunny mystery."

Conversation stopped. Celinda tried to think of a safe way to restart it.

"What's it like being a security consultant?" she asked.

He shrugged, watching the light. "It suits me. Can't think of anything else I'd be good at. What's it like being a matchmaker?"

Her profession was something else she did not want to talk about tonight. When you were a matchmaker who specialized in Covenant Marriages, you were always focused on the long-term. This was her break-the-rules date with the most interesting man she had ever met, and she was pretty sure the relationship was doomed. On the other hand, she had already shut down one conversational topic tonight, and she *had* asked him about his job.

"It's very satisfying when things go well," she said. "Depressing and frustrating when they don't."

"You mean when you can't find a match for someone?"

"Finding a match usually isn't the problem." She hesitated, thinking of the disaster in Frequency City. "True, there are cases where it is impossible to match a client, but those instances, thankfully, are rare. The real problems start when people don't like the results I come up with and refuse to even meet a potential match."

He threw her a quick look, brows raised. "Does that happen a lot?"

"More often than it should. Unfortunately, when it comes to Covenant Marriages, a lot of people have very fixed ideas of what they want in a mate. In many instances those notions are flat-out wrong. There are occasions when I can't convince a really stubborn client to give one of my recommendations a try."

"What do you do when that happens?"

"Terminate the client's agency contract and refund the fees that have been paid. Marriage consultants try to avoid being responsible for bad matches at all costs. It's not good for business in a field where referrals are everything."

"I can see that. Until the marriage laws get loosened up a little more, getting stuck in a bad CM is the equivalent of a jail sentence."

Spoken with great depth of feeling, she thought. It was going to be a very long time, if ever, before Davis was ready to trust a matchmaker again.

Chapter 6

SHE HAD TO KNOW THAT THE DRESS LOOKED SEXY AS hell on her, Davis thought. She must have chosen it deliberately to make an impact on him.

He decided that might or might not be a good thing. If Celinda had set out to tantalize him because she was attracted to him, that was excellent. But in all likelihood she was playing him in order to distract him from the missing relic. Either way, though, it made for an intriguing evening, just as he had anticipated. Frustrating as hell, though. He had been half-aroused ever since he'd picked her up at her door.

They managed to get through a couple of glasses of wine and dinner without discussing the artifact. In fact, three hours later, when the check arrived, Davis was a little stunned to realize how much they had talked about without even straying toward touchy subjects like relics and Guilds.

Either Celinda was an expert when it came to the feminine art of distraction, or else she really did feel some of the sizzle he was experiencing.

She looked up as the waiter came back with the plastic box that contained the uneaten portion of her grilled fish.

"Thank you," she said, taking the box.

Davis got to his feet. "Is that for you or Araminta?"

"Araminta. I told you, she's been eating like a very large farm animal lately. I'm a little worried, to be honest. Does Max eat a lot?"

Davis shrugged. "Seems like a reasonable amount for an animal that size."

"What do you feed him?"

"He seems happy to eat whatever I'm eating." He smiled a little. "Or drinking. Whenever I open a bottle of beer, he insists I give him some."

"Wonder what they eat in the wild?"

"Probably better not to ask."

Outside, the air was a warm, silken cloak. The night was luminous with the faint green glow of the nearby Dead City wall. Parking around restaurants and nightspots was always at a premium in the Quarter. He'd been forced to leave the Phantom a block and a half away in a narrow side lane.

"Why don't you wait here," he said to Celinda. "I'll get the car and bring it around."

"That's all right," she said. "I love the energy here in the Quarter, especially at night."

She felt it, too, he thought. The energy of the night was all around them. Screw the damn relic. He'd worry about it later. Next year, maybe.

He looked at her. "You're right. Great energy."

She smiled.

He took her arm, savoring the feel of soft, bare, female skin under his fingers. In a heartbeat his senses opened wide to the night and the woman beside him. *Take it easy; you don't want to scare her off.* But she didn't look scared.

He managed to wait, just barely, until they left the main street and walked a short distance into the shadowy lane where the Phantom was parked. He stopped in front of the vestibule of a darkened doorway, turned Celinda toward him, and pulled her into his arms. She did not resist. Her hands went to his shoulders.

In the faint, green glow that emanated from the towering quartz wall at the far end of the lane, he could see that her eyes were deep and mysterious, and her lips were slightly parted. Definitely not scared.

He wrapped her close and kissed her hard, letting her feel the rush that was heating his blood.

She made a soft, urgent little sound. Her hands slid from his shoulders, moving up around his neck. She opened her lips just a little and gave him a taste of the sultry heat that awaited him.

Kissing her was a little like going down into the catacombs and getting a dose of alien psi, only better. This high swept through him with the force of an oncoming summer storm. It was sexual and highly physical, but it was something more, something that caught him by surprise. There was a sense of mind-bending *rightness* about kissing Celinda. She was just what he'd been needing for longer than he could remember.

She whispered something he did not quite catch against his mouth. Her fingers tightened in his hair. He could feel her soft breasts crushed against his chest.

He felt his control start to slip. That hadn't happened in longer than he could remember either. Instead of making him uneasy, he suddenly felt free in a way he hadn't for years.

The hunger inside him grew more intense. He dragged Celinda deeper into the vestibule and pushed her up against the stone wall, bracing her. She nibbled on his left earlobe. He almost climaxed then and there. He couldn't believe she was using her *teeth* on him.

He moved his hands downward on either side of her body, savoring the contours of breast, waist, and thigh. She did not try to stop him. In fact, he could feel one of her elegantly curved calves gliding up the side of his trousers. She shuddered a little in his arms.

He found the hem of her dress and shoved it up to her waist. Then he gripped her buttocks and started to lift her off her feet so that she would have no choice but to wrap her legs around him and squeeze tightly just to hold on.

She gasped and pulled her mouth away from his.

"Wait," she managed breathlessly. "Hold on a minute. I think things are getting a little out of control here."

He groaned. "Celinda—"

"We should both cool down a bit," she said, taking several deep breaths. "I mean, this isn't even a real date, is it? More like a business dinner."

He came back to his senses with a disorienting jolt.

What the hell was he doing? He'd only met her this afternoon, and he'd been about to take her up against a grimy wall. He'd never taken a woman against a wall in his life. He caught her face between his hands and rested his forehead against hers.

"Don't know how it is in your line," he said, "but I gotta tell you my business dinners don't usually end like this."

She gave him a tremulous smile. "Neither do mine."

He opened his mouth to apologize. The sound of footsteps stopped him cold. There were plenty of other people out on the streets of the Old Quarter enjoying the warm summer night, but until now he and Celinda had been alone in the tiny lane. He listened closely.

"What's wrong?" Celinda whispered, going very still.

"Probably nothing." He spoke directly into her ear.

"Oh, jeez. First date I've been on in four months, and I'm going to get mugged, right?"

Very gently he put his hand over her mouth to silence her. He turned her slightly so that he could watch the mouth of the lane from the cover of the shadowed vestibule.

A figure stood silhouetted against the brighter lights of the main thoroughfare behind him. He was tall and spindly, a scarecrow of a man. The outline of a loose-fitting windbreaker was visible. He had a cap pulled down low over his eyes.

The figure hesitated a few seconds longer, as though seeking his quarry. After a while he moved warily forward, heading toward the Phantom.

Davis put his mouth close to Celinda's ear again.

"Stay here."

He made it an order, not a suggestion. He could tell that she didn't like it, but he was pretty sure she was too smart to sabotage him at this critical juncture by making a scene.

He released her and moved quietly out of the doorway.

The figure in the cap had reached the Phantom. He leaned down to peer through the window into the darkened interior.

"Looking for something?" Davis asked behind him.

The scarecrow froze for an instant. Then he jerked upright and whirled around. Davis got a brief glimpse of haggard, death's head features, and then the lane exploded in a raging inferno of green ghost light.

Not one but two wild, acid-colored balls of alien psi energy flared and pulsed on other either side of him, trapping him.

Doppelganger light, Davis thought. There weren't many hunters who could generate a dopp, especially outside the tunnels. He had some immunity—he was descended from a long line of hunters, and almost all ghost hunters could sustain a brush with ghost light—but no one, hunter or not, could survive a close encounter with this much raw energy.

Chapter 7

CELINDA WATCHED THE EVENTS IN THE LANE FROM THE doorway, horrified. Some of her brother's friends were ghost hunters. She had seen them generate small UDEMs on occasion but nothing of this size and certainly not two at a time. In the blazing green energy given off by the twin ghosts she could see Davis pinned against the brick wall.

She had always heard that the only thing that could stop a ghost was another ghost. Davis had told her that he came from a hunter family. Why wasn't he fighting back with a ghost of his own? Then she remembered something else he had told her: *"I turned out a little different."*

Maybe he couldn't generate a ghost. If that was the case, he was in mortal danger. She knew enough about ghost-hunting to be aware that the person who generated a UDEM had to concentrate hard to keep it going. The only thing she could think of to do was to try to distract the man in the cap.

She rushed out of the vestibule, heading toward the fiery spectacle. But before she had gone more than a few steps, the twin ghosts suddenly began to spin chaotically. In the next second they winked out of sight.

The man in the cap appeared to panic. He ran back toward her. Davis pounded after him.

A car engine roared nearby. A split second later, a dark vehicle shot out of an alley, nearly running her down. She scrambled back barely in time. The very high heel of her evening sandal twisted out from under her. She went down, landing hard on her rear.

The car slammed to a halt less than two feet away from where she sat on the ground. The window on the driver's side was down. She could just make out a dark profile. Instinctively, she opened her senses. She was close enough to pick up the highly agitated psi energy patterns emitted by the man behind the wheel.

She heard the door on the passenger side open. The man in the cap tumbled headfirst into the front seat. The driver floored the accelerator, aiming straight for Davis.

As Celinda watched, Davis leaped out of the way with only inches to spare.

The vehicle turned down another alley and disappeared, tires shrieking.

Chapter 8

HIGH HEELS CLATTERED ON THE PAVEMENT.

"*Davis*. Davis, are you all right?"

He turned to see Celinda hurrying toward him. How did women run in high heels? One of the great mysteries of nature.

"I'm okay."

That was a flat-out lie. She had nearly been run down before his eyes, the bastards had gotten away, and he had generated enough silver light to melt amber, which meant that he was headed for the usual burn and crash. He was not okay with any of that. But given that the situation could have been a hell of a lot worse, he figured he was entitled to a little prevarication.

"Thank heavens." She halted in front of him, surveying him anxiously. "I was terrified that you'd been singed, at the very least. I've never seen so much ghost light. It looked like a scene out of a horror movie."

"They're called doppelgangers. Twin ghosts. Not many hunters can generate them, especially such big ones and aboveground at that. The guy is good."

"Are you sure you're all right?"

"Yes," he said through set teeth. "What about you?"

"I'm fine." She brushed at her shapely rear with one hand. "But this dress is ruined."

She was safe. He was suddenly, overwhelmingly pissed. "What the hell did you think you were doing? That son of a bitch nearly flattened you. I told you to stay in the doorway."

She blinked, startled at his tone, and then angled her chin, clearly annoyed. "From where I was standing, it looked like you needed some help. I thought maybe I could distract the hunter. I've always heard that the ghosts break up if the person generating them loses focus."

"Next time you do what I tell you, understood?"

There was a beat of silence.

She cleared her throat very delicately. "Does this sort of thing happen a lot when you go out on a date?"

"You know, a question like that is a real conversation stopper. Come on, I'll take you home."

"You're angry."

He started walking back toward the car. "You scared the hell out of me back there when you came flying out of the doorway and nearly got clobbered by that guy's getaway driver."

"Do you think that man in the cap wanted to mug us or steal your car?"

"Doubt if there are many garden-variety muggers or car thieves around who can pull that kind of heat. Any thug that strong should be running a whole damn criminal empire."

"Davis? What's wrong? You're not just mad at me because I didn't stay put. There's something else going on here. Are you sure you aren't hurt? And what happened to those two ghosts, anyway? I didn't see you generate any counter-ghosts. Did the guy just get scared and run off?"

"No." He reached the car and gripped the door handle on the passenger side very tightly. He debated how much to tell her and then decided to go with a sanitized version of the truth. "I told you I'm from a family of hunters."

"Yes, I know." She searched his face. "But you said you turned out different."

"I did. But I'm still a hunter. Sort of."

She stared at him. "Are you telling me that those ghosts disappeared because you de-rezzed them?"

"Yes."

"With what? I didn't see any ghost light."

"I work ghost energy from a different end of the spectrum. It's almost invisible to the naked eye. They call it silver light."

"I didn't know that ghost energy could be generated from more than one point on the spectrum."

"It's a rare talent, and the Guilds tend to keep it quiet."

"Why?"

"Tradition, mostly," he said, deliberately vague. He was not up to any more explanations. He studied the interior of the Phantom. "Looks like Max and Araminta are gone."

"What?" Distracted, Celinda whirled around and peered into the shadowy front seat of the vehicle. "Oh my gosh, they *are* gone. What happened to them?"

"Must have squeezed out through the window I cracked for them."

"Maybe they got scared when they saw the twin ghosts and ran off." She straightened and looked anxiously toward the nearest dark alley.

"Araminta?" she called.

There was no response.

"Have you got a flashlight?" she said to Davis.

He glanced at the midnight-dark mouth of the alley. The faint acid-green glow of the Dead City wall did not even begin to penetrate its ominous depths.

"Sure, but we're not going to use it to go into that alley. I've had enough excitement for one night. Get in the car, Celinda."

"But if Max and Araminta were badly frightened, they might not come out on their own."

"Don't know about Araminta, but I can tell you that

Max wouldn't have run away just because of a couple of ghosts. Not if he knew I was in the vicinity. My guess is they took off for reasons of their own while we were at dinner, long before cap guy showed up."

He took her arm and gently but firmly stuffed her into the passenger seat. She slid reluctantly into the car. He got a fine, fleeting glimpse of a nicely rounded thigh. As an added bonus, the tear in the violet dress revealed a sliver of lacy black panties. Everything inside him tightened another notch. It wasn't like he hadn't already been thoroughly aroused before the confrontation in the lane. The burn was hitting him hard.

She looked up from the seat, brows scrunched together a little. "But why would they go off like that?" Alarm widened her eyes. "Good grief, do you think that Max lured Araminta away because he has designs on her? Maybe he's out there somewhere right now seducing her."

It dawned on him that from this vantage point he had an excellent view into the inviting shadows of the front of her dress. He sighed. Wrong time and definitely the wrong place. Just his luck.

"They're dust bunnies, Celinda, not a pair of star-crossed lovers. They'll come back when they're ready."

"If that bunny of yours takes advantage of Araminta, I am going to hold you personally responsible."

He said nothing, just looked at her.

She winced. "Sorry. That does sound sort of dumb, doesn't it? I mean, it's not like either of us knows how dust bunnies think, let alone what their mating habits are like."

"Can't be much worse than mine," Davis muttered.

"What did you say?"

He pretended he hadn't heard the question and closed the door very deliberately.

When he got in beside her and rezzed the engine, she turned in the seat, studying him with a concerned expression.

"You look sort of strange," she said.

"Thanks for the compliment."

"Are you going to faint or something?"

"Or something," he said deliberately. "But not for a while yet."

"Maybe I should drive."

He gripped the wheel very tightly and pulled away from the curb. "I'm still capable of driving."

She did not appear entirely reassured, but she turned to look at the alley one more time.

"What about Max and Araminta?"

"They know their way home. The Quarter isn't all that big. Your apartment is only about a half mile from here. My condo is just as close in the opposite direction."

She did not respond to that, but she shifted back around in her seat and clipped her seat belt. He had the uneasy feeling that she was doing a lot of thinking. That probably meant trouble ahead.

He made himself concentrate on his driving, working his way back to Celinda's neighborhood via the maze of narrow streets and lanes that laced the Quarter.

"About this business of you being a sort of hunter," Celinda asked in a suspiciously unconcerned tone of voice.

It had been too much to hope that she would let his earlier explanation go, he thought.

"It's not a business for me." He stopped for a light. "Oakes Security is my business. I'm not a Guild man."

"But you can de-rez ghosts."

"Yes. But as I told you, the ability to work silver light isn't the usual kind of talent. That's one of the reasons I never joined the Guild."

"But you are a type of dissonance-energy para-resonator," she pressed, cautious but determined.

"Yes."

She cleared her throat again. "Can I assume that you're now in that phase they call afterburn?"

The conversation was deteriorating rapidly. It was like watching a slow-motion train wreck.

"That's one term for it," he said.

"It's an adrenaline and testosterone thing, right?"

"I'm not a teenager, Celinda. I can handle my hormones."

"I've heard about the postburn syndrome," she continued in the same polite, too-neutral tone. "A big testosterone rush."

"Seems like just about everybody has heard about the syndrome."

"Yes, well, I hate to break this to you, but women talk."

Right, and he could pretty much guess what women said about hunters who were in the grip of an afterburn. The rumors were true, and they contributed heavily to some of the long-standing negative social attitudes toward the Guild.

There was no getting around the fact that there was nothing like pulling a little ghost light to slam a man into a state of full-blown sexual arousal. The bigger the ghost, the stronger the physical response. Which explained why mothers warned their daughters to stay clear of hunters and why the bars and taverns in the Old Quarter that catered to Guild men were popular with adventurous women, coeds looking for excitement, and bachelorette parties.

"Don't worry, I'm not going to jump on top of you," he said.

"You can't blame a lady for wondering."

Startled, he gave her a quick, searching look. In the amber glow of the dash lights he could see that the corner of her mouth was curved upward, maybe twitching just a bit.

"A word of advice." The light changed. He snapped the sensitive twin mag shift into gear. "This is not a good time to tease me."

"Got it."

"You're not scared?" he asked.

"Of you? No. You're in full control."

He contemplated that briefly. "How do you know I'm in control?"

She raised one shoulder in a tiny shrug. "I just know it."

"You sound very sure of yourself."

"I am."

He wanted to ask her what made her so damned certain that he wasn't going to pounce, but he decided it would probably be a good idea to stop talking about anything even remotely related to sex.

"I melted amber dealing with that dopp," he said quietly. "Do you know what that means?"

"That after the rush, you're going to have to sleep for a few hours?"

"Right. I need to get you home and then get back to my place before I crash."

"I understand."

He turned a corner and drove along another cramped street. Only three more blocks. He could do this.

It seemed like an eternity before he eased the Phantom into an empty parking space at the curb in front of Celinda's apartment. He de-rezzed the engine, unfastened the seat belt, and opened his door.

"Never mind," Celinda said quickly. "You don't have to walk me upstairs. I'll be fine."

"I'll see you to your door."

"The clock is ticking on your afterburn. You'll need the time to drive back to your place."

He set his back teeth together. "I said I'll see you to your door."

She sighed. "Okay, be that way."

"What way?"

"Stubborn, hardheaded, and difficult."

"Hey, give me some credit. I'm good at all those things."

"I guess it's true what they say. Everyone has a talent."

She was out of the car by the time he got around to her side of the vehicle. He took her arm.

He realized his mistake immediately. He never should have touched her. The physical contact had an effect similar to sending power through tuned amber, except in this instance it wasn't just his psi energy alone that was suddenly very, very focused. It felt like every cell in his body was riveted by the woman beside him, clamoring to get closer, to get inside her.

He was drunk on her unique scent, a mix of herbal shampoo and the essence of pure Celinda. He didn't want to merely touch her; he wanted to stroke every part of her from her toes to her ears. He wanted to drag her down onto the pavement and claim her in the most elemental way.

The force of his response caught him off guard. He was not in a standard postburn. He knew that condition, knew how to handle it. This was different. He didn't just want to get laid; he wanted Celinda. No other woman would do tonight. If he couldn't have her, he didn't want anyone else.

You're in deep trouble. Just get her upstairs and get the hell out of here before you do something that will really screw things up.

Betty Furnell's door popped open when they entered the downstairs hall. Betty looked out, beaming.

"Oh, hello there, you two," she sang out cheerfully. "Did you have a nice evening?"

"Lovely," Celinda said.

"Gracious, what happened to your dress, dear?"

"There was a slight accident," Celinda said.

"It's ruined."

"Yes," Celinda agreed, "I'm afraid it is. Good night, Mrs. Furnell."

"Good night. Sleep tight." Betty closed the door with obvious reluctance.

"Be prepared to be cornered again when you go back downstairs," Celinda warned softly.

"I'll be ready," he promised.

He walked her upstairs to her apartment door and waited while she dug out her key.

"I hope Araminta is home," she said.

"If not, I'm sure she'll return by dawn. When Max takes off, he's always back for breakfast."

He took the key from her, rezzed the lock, and opened the door.

Celinda stepped into the hall. And stopped, stiffening.

"I've been burglarized."

He looked past her into the small space. The two drawers in the hall table had been removed, the contents dumped on the floor. From where he was standing, he could see a portion of the living room. The sofa and chairs were overturned. Damp night air wafted in from the open balcony door. The point of entry for the intruders, Davis thought.

"My *stuff*," Celinda wailed. She started to rush into the apartment.

Davis grabbed her arm. "Hold it. You're not going in until I make certain there's no one else inside."

"But—"

"This is what I do, remember? I keep telling you, I'm in the security business." He moved into the hall. "Wait here."

"I hesitate to interfere with a professional doing his job, but what, exactly, are you going to do if the guy has a gun?"

"I'll show him mine." Davis leaned down and drew the small pistol out of his ankle holster.

Celinda looked at the weapon with an enigmatic expression. "That looks like a mini mag-rez."

"It is. Latest and greatest technology."

"It's illegal for private citizens to own mag-rezes," she said very primly.

"Yeah, I've heard that."

He moved into the apartment and made a quick, thorough survey and then went back to the front door.

"All clear," he said. "Looks like they came and went through the balcony door."

"Oh, dear, the *dress*."

He went blank. "What dress?"

"My bridesmaid dress," she said, slipping past him. "If the burglars stole it or destroyed it, I'm doomed. Rachel will never forgive me if I don't show up with that dress."

"Fancy pink thing covered in plastic? I saw it when I checked the closet. Looked fine to me."

"I've got to be sure."

She rushed down the hall to the bedroom.

Something didn't add up, he decided. She didn't even like the pink dress. Why all the fuss?

Intrigued, he watched the mirror above the hall table. From this angle he could see her hurrying into the bedroom. She didn't go to the closet. Instead, she went down on her knees and peered under the bed.

Davis went on into the living room and started righting the furniture.

Celinda returned a short time later, noticeably calmer.

"Dress okay?" he asked politely.

"Yes, it's fine," she said. "I've got to call the police." She picked up the phone.

"Forget it."

"What do you mean?" She stopped, whipping around to face him. "I know the cops probably won't be able to do much. I've heard that when it comes to home burglaries, there's not a lot they can do. But I should at least file a report."

"Celinda," he said wearily, "the reason you're not going to call the cops is because this is Guild business."

Very slowly she replaced the receiver.

"Damn," she whispered. "I was afraid you were going to say that."

Chapter 9

"OKAY," SHE SAID, SINKING DOWN ONTO ONE OF THE kitchen stools, "I agree, this break-in on top of that bizarre scene in the lane with that man in the cap is probably not a coincidence."

Davis had removed his jacket and was methodically straightening the room.

"No, it isn't," he said. "Someone is looking for the relic."

Glumly she watched him right an armchair. "I still don't understand why we can't call the cops."

"Because they aren't very good at handling this kind of thing." He picked up a small drawer and put it back into the end table beside the chair. "They'll treat this as just another routine break-in, and that won't get us anywhere. Also, they don't have the manpower to provide you with twenty-four-hour security, which is what you're going to need."

Shock rolled through her. "What are you talking about?"

"I'm talking about a bodyguard."

She stared at him, feeling as if the wind had been knocked out of her.

Her new career was doomed. Mrs. Takahashi had been

very understanding about the fiasco in Frequency City, but she would almost certainly draw the line at one of her marriage consultants showing up for work with a bodyguard. To say nothing of the wedding, she thought. Another wave of alarm hit her. Dear heaven, her family would be horrified if they found out that the Cadence Guild had thought it necessary to supply her with a bodyguard.

"That's . . . that's impossible," she managed.

Davis swept out one hand to indicate the vandalized apartment. "Whoever did this obviously knows that you were the last person to have the relic in your possession. We have to assume that you are in some danger until we get the thing back."

"But that might be never. There's no telling what Araminta did with it."

"I think we can count on Araminta showing up with that damn artifact sooner or later."

She folded her arms very tightly beneath her breasts, hugging herself. "Just long enough for me to lose my job."

"The Guild will see to it that you aren't fired."

She shuddered. "Don't even think about asking Mercer Wyatt to make a phone call to Mrs. Takahashi. The last thing I want is for her to keep me on the payroll because Wyatt threatened her. It would be utterly humiliating."

"He's not a mob boss, Celinda."

"Okay, so maybe the Cadence Guild isn't into the traditional gang businesses like drugs and prostitution. That doesn't make it an upstanding, respectable business corporation."

He was starting to get irritated. "You've really got a thing about the Guilds, don't you?"

"Yes." She unfolded her arms and gripped the edge of the stool seat on either side of her hips. "And there's something else. I'm leaving town tomorrow for a couple of days. I told you, I have to be in my sister's wedding. I'll be taking Araminta with me, assuming she ever shows up again."

"With any luck, she'll bring that relic back by morning."

"But what if she doesn't? I can't go to my sister's wedding with a bodyguard. How will I explain that to my family? They'll panic if they think my life is in danger."

"Your bodyguard will be male." Davis took out his personal phone. "You can tell everyone he's your date for the wedding."

"My *date*. Are you crazy?"

"If your family is anything like mine, they'll be thrilled that you're not alone."

"You don't understand." She was getting desperate now. "My life back in Frequency got a little complicated before I left town. I can't just arrive with a strange man in tow. There will be questions. Lots of them. Everyone will wonder why I haven't mentioned him during the past four months."

"New job here in Cadence. New boyfriend. No big deal."

"It is a big deal," she shot back. "At least it is for me."

"There's a good chance that you're in real danger here, Celinda," he said quietly. "Are you willing to risk your neck just to avoid a little social awkwardness at the wedding?"

She caught her lip between her teeth and then sighed. "Well, when you put it like that—"

"That's exactly how I'm putting it. I'm also betting you're too smart to argue about this any more tonight."

She frowned. "Where does one get a bodyguard, anyway?"

"From a topflight investigative agency like Oakes Security."

"Oh." She thought about that. "Bodyguards are probably expensive."

"They are if they come from Oakes. But don't worry about the cost. The Guild will pick up the tab."

"Damn. Just what I need, another Guild connection."

He punched out a number on the phone. "You know, it's a good thing I'm such an easygoing, open-minded kind of guy. Otherwise I might start to take offense at all these swipes at the Guild."

"I thought you said you weren't a Guild man?"

"I'm not. But I come from a fourth-generation Guild family. I've got my loyalties." He broke off to speak into the phone. "Trig. Wake up. I need a babysitter to look after a friend tonight while I crash."

There was a short pause.

"No." He turned away to speak into the phone. "I didn't burn a lot of silver, but it was a dopp ghost. I ended up melting a little amber. It's just the usual postburn thing. I'll tell you the whole story when you get here, assuming I can stay awake. If I'm out, the client will explain."

There was another short pause. Davis looked back over his shoulder at Celinda with an unreadable expression. "Right. She's a client now. But we'll be billing the Guild for all expenses."

He ended the call and dropped the phone into the pocket of his trousers.

"I assume this Trig person is going to be my body-guard?" she asked warily.

"Just for tonight." Davis yawned and rubbed the back of his neck. "Someone else will take over tomorrow and stay with you until the case is concluded."

"Who?"

"Me."

She was still dealing with that announcement when the doorbell rezzed a short time later. Davis answered it. When he opened the door she saw a short, stocky man with a shaved head. Elaborate tattoos decorated the thick arms exposed by a black T-shirt. He looked like he could juggle large vehicles without breaking a sweat.

"This is Trig McAndrews," Davis said.

Trig nodded politely. "Miss Ingram."

"Mr. McAndrews."

He grinned. "Call me Trig."

"All right." She inclined her head. What did one say to a bodyguard? "Would you like some coffee?"

He gave her a smile that lit up the room. "That sounds like a truly splendid idea, ma'am."

It also gave her something constructive to do. She slid off the stool and went around the counter into the small kitchen.

While she made the coffee, she listened to Davis give Trig a brief rundown on what had happened. The part that sent a little chill down her spine was the bit about how Davis had been forced to melt amber in order to deal with the twin ghosts. Everyone knew that amber didn't actually melt when someone pushed too much para-resonating psi energy through it, but it did lose its delicate tuning if it was over-used. The thing was, the vast majority of people couldn't generate enough paranormal energy to melt amber. Only someone with a lot of power could do it.

Whatever else he was, Davis was a very strong psi talent. But, then, she already knew that, she reminded herself.

"Tomorrow I'm going to escort Miss Ingram to Frequency for a wedding," Davis concluded. "While we're gone, I want you to see what you can find out about a para-rez who can pull a dopp aboveground. Can't be that many of them running around."

"He shouldn't be too hard to find," Trig agreed. "Guy like that probably has some past connection to the Guild. Wyatt's people will help. You know what they say: The Guild polices its own."

"Hah." Celinda did not look up from spooning coffee into a pot.

"Miss Ingram is not what you'd call pro-Guild," Davis explained.

"Yeah, I got that impression." Trig didn't sound the least bit offended. "Not like she's the only one who has a few doubts about the sterling qualities of the organizations."

Celinda rezzed the coffeemaker and turned around. "But I'll bet the Guilds make excellent clients, right?"

"Oh, yeah," Trig said cheerfully. "They pay right on time, and their checks always clear. We at Oakes Security take that sort of thing real seriously."

"I guess a client is a client," she admitted. "I can't say that I haven't had a few in my time whose chief redeeming quality was the fact that their checks cleared." She surveyed her tiny living room. "Where's everyone going to sleep?"

"Don't know about the rest of you," Davis said, dropping heavily onto the edge of the sofa. "But I'm sleeping right here." He reached down to take off his shoes.

He looked as if he was holding himself together through sheer willpower, Celinda thought. But, then, he had a lot of that. Maybe more than was good for him.

On impulse, she went around the counter and down the short hall to the linen closet. "I'll get you a pillow and a blanket."

When she returned to the living room, pillow and blanket in her arms, Davis seemed vaguely surprised but not ungrateful.

"Thanks." His voice was low and drowsy with the rush of oncoming sleep.

He took the pillow from her, turned on his side, and closed his eyes.

Celinda waited a couple of seconds. When she realized that he was already sound asleep, she unfolded the blanket and covered him with it.

She turned to find Trig watching her with a carefully veiled expression. The room seemed suddenly very quiet.

"Does he do this a lot?" she asked, for want of anything else to say.

"Run up against a doppelganger ghost and melt amber? Nope, can't say that's a real common occurrence for the boss." Trig hesitated. "But he's had his share of unusual cases. Guess you could say that's our specialty at Oakes Security."

"Unusual cases?"

Trig nodded. "That's why Mercer Wyatt called us in on

this one. He thinks there's something weird about that relic that went missing, and Oakes Security does weird."

She saw an opening and seized it.

"Davis said that he was from a Guild family and that he's a hunter of sorts." She kept her tone very casual.

"Right."

"He told me that he doesn't pull ghost light from the usual point on the spectrum."

"He said that much, did he?" Trig looked impressed. "That's more than he tells most people."

"I didn't realize that there were different kinds of ghost light."

Trig lifted massive shoulders in a shrug. "Very few people realize that there's a wide spectrum of dissonance energy leaking out of the catacombs. But most hunters can only work the green stuff."

"He also told me that he was never employed as a regular ghost hunter."

"Ghost hunters tend to be real traditional," Trig said. "Hunters who don't work standard ghost light make other hunters nervous underground."

"So, Davis went into the PI business, instead."

"Uh-huh."

She got the feeling that pushing Trig wasn't going to gain her any more information, so she reluctantly dropped the subject. "I have another extra blanket and pillow you can use."

"Don't worry about me, Miss Ingram. I won't be sleeping tonight." He held up a book. "Brought some reading material with me. With this and some coffee, I'll be fine."

"You're sure?"

"Yep."

She looked at the book. "What are you reading?"

"Espindoza's *History of the Era of Discord*. I'm on the last volume. Almost finished."

She tried not to show her surprise. "I see."

He smiled benignly. "I know, heavy reading for a guy like me, but I'm managing to wade through it."

She grinned. "You're doing better than I did. I never got past volume one." She looked at Davis. "He'll be okay?"

"Sure. Just the normal burn-and-crash thing. He'll wake up in a few hours feeling good as new."

SHE TUMBLED INTO BED A SHORT TIME LATER AND GAZED out the window into the night. She hadn't slept well in four months, but tonight she had a whole bunch of new anxieties to keep her awake. A Guild relic had gone missing and everyone involved held her more or less responsible. There were not one but two men spending the night in her apartment. She had a date for her sister's wedding that was going to take some explaining, and Araminta was out there somewhere in the night running around with a stranger she had only just met.

Sleep was going to be even more elusive than usual tonight.

Chapter 10

❧

ARAMINTA AND MAX RETURNED SHORTLY BEFORE DAWN. The sound of the sliding glass door being opened woke Davis. He watched Trig let the dust bunnies into the apartment.

"Any sign of the relic?" he asked.

"Afraid not," Trig said.

"Damn. Guess that would have been too easy."

Max tumbled across the floor to greet him. Araminta drifted down the hall in the direction of Celinda's bedroom.

Trig stretched. "You need me any longer, boss?"

"No, I can take it from here." Davis sat up and discovered that there was a blanket covering him.

"Miss Ingram put it over you after you conked out last night," Trig said.

"Huh." The thought of Celinda bending over him in what must have been a fairly solicitous manner, ensuring that he didn't get cold during the night, made him feel much better than he had a moment ago.

He pushed the blanket aside and contemplated a shower.

He needed one. Experimentally, he rubbed his jaw. He also needed a shave.

Before he could decide how to proceed, rapid footsteps sounded in the hall.

Celinda appeared. Her hair was a tangled cloud around her face. She wore a dark blue robe secured with a sash and a pair of matching slippers. Araminta was perched on her shoulder.

Davis looked at her and realized that he was getting aroused all over again. He liked Trig a lot, trusted him completely, but right now he wished his friend was anywhere else but here in Celinda's living room. He didn't like the idea of Trig or any other man seeing her like this, all warm and soft and flushed from sleep. The surge of possessiveness caught him by surprise.

"Araminta's back," Celinda announced excitedly.

"Yeah, they both rolled in a couple minutes ago," Trig said, angling his head toward Max.

Celinda turned to Davis. She seemed oddly startled at the sight of him sitting there on her sofa. It dawned on him that, what with his crumpled black dress shirt and trousers and the morning beard, he probably looked as if he, too, had spent the night out on the tiles.

Celinda's hopeful expression dimmed. "No one looks very cheerful. Can I assume that means they didn't bring back the relic?"

"It's still missing." Davis got to his feet. "Mind if I use your shower?"

The request seemed to floor her. Her eyes widened. "Uh." She recovered quickly, blushing a bright pink. "No, no, of course not. Go ahead. I'll, uh, start breakfast. Or something. I think I've got some eggs." She turned quickly to Trig. "Will you stay?"

"Appreciate the offer, but if you'll excuse me, I'll be on my way," Trig said. "I need to start working our contacts on the street and inside the Guild, see if we can find the guy who generated those twin ghosts last night."

"Oh. Yes, of course." Celinda paused, looking first at Trig and then at Davis. "What about the second man?"

"The getaway driver?" Davis nodded. "We'll look for him, too. But we haven't got much to go on there."

"Well," Celinda said, "if it helps, I can tell you that he's got a rather twisted parapsych profile. I would advise extreme caution if either of you happen to run into him again."

They both looked at her.

"Are you saying that because he's involved in a criminal enterprise and, by definition, most outlaws probably have twisted profiles?" Davis asked evenly.

"No." She seemed to hesitate, then come to a decision. She reached up to pat Araminta. "I'm saying that because I can read psi profiles if I get close enough to a person. Last night, for a few seconds, I was very close to the getaway driver."

Davis looked at Trig and then turned back to her.

"Are you telling us that you can sense other people's psi energy patterns?" he asked.

"At close range, yes." She shrugged. "It's one of the reasons why I'm so good at my job. I can match people psychically as well as in the usual ways."

Trig whistled softly. "Whoa. Talk about a nonstandard talent. Ever been tested?"

"Yes. My parents suspected I was a little different. They took me to a private lab. The ability to read psi patterns is extremely rare, so I don't advertise my talent for obvious reasons. But Davis is a strong and evidently rare para-rez himself, so I assume neither of you gets nervous around nonstandard talents."

"How strong are you?" Davis asked.

She hesitated again. "Very."

He raised his brows. "Are we talking off the charts?"

"Well, yes," she admitted, "but I'm sure that's only because the talent is so rare in the population the testing labs don't have a good basis for comparison."

Davis rubbed his jaw again. *Something in common,* he thought. "How much can you tell about a person based on what you pick up from his or her psi energy patterns?"

She gave him a very somber look. "Often a lot more than I really want to know. There are some very strange people out there."

"I've always heard that psi patterns are unique to individuals," Trig said.

Celinda nodded. "In my experience that's true. No two people produce precisely identical psi wave patterns, not even twins."

"Could you recognize the driver of that car if you got close to him again?" Davis asked.

"Yes," she replied. "But I would have to be fairly close. No more than a few feet away at most."

"Oh, man," Trig said. He looked eagerly at Davis. "That kind of talent would sure be useful in our business, boss."

"Sort of like having one of those dogs they use to detect drugs in suitcases," Celinda said dryly.

Trig turned red. "No way, ma'am. I never meant to imply that you're a dog." He went almost purple, clearly mortified. "Or anything like that," he finished weakly.

Celinda gave him a wry smile. "It's okay, I understand."

"Your talent," Davis said, diplomatically emphasizing the word *talent*, "for picking up another individual's psi patterns would certainly be useful when it comes to identifying the driver, but it won't help us locate him. Unfortunately, that's going to take old-fashioned detective work."

Trig grimaced. "Which means I'd better get moving." He looked at Celinda. "Would you mind if I borrowed a book?"

She looked taken aback by the request. "What book?"

"That one." Trig indicated a volume on the table beside a chair. "I started it after I finished Espindoza's *History* last night. Found it on your bookshelf. Hope you don't mind."

She looked at the book on the table. So did Davis. From

where he sat he could just make out the title. *Ten Steps to a Covenant Marriage: Secrets of a Professional Matchmaker.*

"Oh, that one." Celinda suddenly rezzed a dazzling smile for Trig. "Certainly. Help yourself."

"Thanks," Trig said. "I only got through chapter one." He walked back to the table, picked up the volume, tucked it under his arm, and returned to the door. "Nice to meet you, Miss Ingram. Have a good time at the wedding."

"Thanks," Celinda said. Her smile faded.

Trig let himself out into the hall and went downstairs, making very little noise for such a solidly built man. Davis listened closely, but he did not hear Betty Furnell's door open.

He got to his feet. "That book that Trig took with him."

Celinda raised her brows. "What about it?"

"I assume you've read it?"

"I wrote it."

HE WAITED UNTIL HE HEARD THE SHOWER RUNNING BE-fore he went into her bedroom. He stood there for a couple of seconds, inhaling the scent of her space and thinking of how she had made a great fuss about checking to be sure the bridesmaid's dress was safe. But she had not even glanced into the closet. She had looked under the bed.

He crouched beside the bed. There were no telltale lines indicating a hidden floor safe beneath the wall-to-wall carpet. He ran his fingertips along the baseboard. A section felt loose. He tugged gently.

A ten-inch length of the baseboard popped free. Behind it was a dark opening in the wall.

He reached inside and pulled out a gray sack. The object it contained felt heavy in his hand. It also felt familiar.

He untied the sack. The missing relic was not inside. Something else was, though.

He retied the sack, tucked it into the wall, and replaced the baseboard.

He went back down the hall wondering why a professional matchmaker would have an illegal mag-rez gun hidden under her bed.

A woman who lived alone and worried about intruders would probably keep the gun in a place where she could get at it in a hurry, the drawer in the bedside table for instance. But Celinda kept hers stashed in a very inaccessible location.

The mag-rez had been concealed for some serious purpose. Evidence of a crime committed in the past? Or evidence of one that had not yet been committed?

Chapter 11

HE WAS STILL FEELING UNNERVED THE NEXT MORNING when he walked into his office. Everything had gone wrong again last night. First, they had been unable to find the relic in the woman's apartment, and then Brinker had nearly been caught when he tried to search Oakes's car. It had been a very close call.

Ella Allonby, seated behind the reception desk, looked up from some papers.

"Good morning, Dr. Kennington," she said in her crisp, well-modulated, businesslike way.

Everything about her was crisp, well-modulated, and businesslike. She was forty-three years old and astonishingly good at her job. But he hadn't hired her for her office management skills. He had chosen her because she was secretly enamored of him. That made her extremely easy to manipulate.

He paused in front of her desk and gave her a warm smile. "How does my schedule look today, Miss Allonby?"

The impact of the smile brought color to her cheeks just as he had known it would. As always, the wielding of power over another human being, even in such a small way, gave him a pleasant little rush.

"Busy, as usual, sir," she said. "You have three patients this morning and two this afternoon."

"Excellent. Thank you, Miss Allonby."

He went into the inner office, closing the door behind him, and set his briefcase on the desk. He hung the hand-tailored gray silk jacket on the coat rack and then sat down behind the desk.

He looked around the office and felt the old anger rise inside. How had it come to this? He should have been president of the Society of Para-Psychiatrists by now, with a lucrative private practice on the side. He should be publishing papers in the most esteemed journals. He should be giving lectures at the university.

Instead, he had been reduced to changing his identity and starting over as a so-called *dream therapist*. It was humiliating for a man of his power and brilliance. He might as well hang out a shingle advertising himself as a meditation guru or offering to read astrological charts and tea leaves.

A year ago his life and career had been on track. He had been headed straight to the very top of his profession. But the narrow-minded fools at the institute had failed to comprehend his genius. Instead, they had fired him. *Fired him.* His hand clenched in a fist. Not only that, but the administrator had made it clear that he would never get a decent reference. For all intents and purposes, the bastard had destroyed his career.

Admittedly, there had been some unsatisfactory outcomes among the subjects, but that was the nature of the experimental process. It was no reason to fire him. The truth was that it was professional jealousy that had led to his dismissal.

No matter. One day soon they would all pay.

But first he had to find the other relic. Luckily at this point the Guild had no inkling that there were two of the ruby amber devices. The psi-burned hunter who had found them down in the catacombs had turned over only one of the artifacts to the Guild. Sensing that the relics had great value, he had concealed the other one.

Fortunately, the para-trauma the hunter had experienced had brought him to the hospital where Kennington had been working. He had discovered the man's secret in the course of an experiment. It had been no trick at all to pull the location of the concealed relic out of the patient. The man had, of course, died soon thereafter. It had been suicide, according to the records. It was true the hunter had been severely depressed. Kennington had made sure of it with a carefully measured dose of psi meds.

It had taken months to find a thief capable of stealing the second artifact from the Guild vault.

The other bit of good news was that it was obvious that the Guild had no clue as to the nature of the kind of power the artifacts could generate when they were operated by an individual who possessed the right type of psychic talent, *his* type. Those with his brand of psi abilities were statistically quite rare. The odds were excellent that no one else would realize that the relic was anything other than an alien curiosity. Nevertheless, he wanted it in his possession as quickly as possible.

One thing was clear now: Davis Oakes was a problem. Any ghost hunter capable of destroying a doppelganger without generating green fire had to be taken seriously. More crucially, Oakes appeared to have Celinda Ingram in his control. That meant that she was the key to the missing relic.

He rezzed the computer and searched for everything he could find on Celinda Ingram, professional marriage consultant. Everyone had a weakness.

He discovered Celinda's in less than five minutes.

Chapter 12

MRS. FURNELL WAS WAITING AT THE FOOT OF THE STAIRS. Celinda, preparing to lock her door, looked down and got a queasy feeling in the pit of her stomach. Luck had been with her earlier when Trig had left. Mrs. Furnell had evidently not heard him descend the stairs. But she was lying in wait for Davis. It was too much to hope that she would not know that he had spent the night.

Davis was halfway down the stairs, a suitcase in either hand, Max perched on his shoulder. He nodded pleasantly at Betty when he reached the front hall.

"Good morning, Mrs. Furnell," he said.

"I thought I heard someone coming down the stairs." She chuckled. "I meant to tell you both that I had the oddest dream—" She broke off, wincing in pain. She touched her temples with her fingertips. "Oh, dear, I seem to have a headache coming on. Probably that new pillow."

It wasn't like Betty to complain about aches and pains, Celinda thought. Worried, she started down the stairs, the plastic-covered pink dress draped over one arm.

"Are you all right, Mrs. Furnell?" she asked.

"What?" Betty blinked. Her face cleared miraculously. "Yes, dear, I'm fine. Just a bit of a headache. But it's easing up already. I'll take something for it in a minute. I just wanted to wish you a safe trip to Frequency City."

"Thank you," Celinda said.

Araminta stuck her head out of Celinda's oversized tote and chortled happily at Betty.

Betty laughed lightly, reached into the pocket of her purple track suit pants, and took out a small, paper-wrapped candy. "There you go, Araminta."

Araminta accepted the gift with polite greed and downed it with two or three efficient crunches of her sharp little teeth.

Betty beamed at Celinda. "Give my regards to your sister."

"I'll do that," Celinda promised. She tried to edge surreptitiously toward the front door. Unfortunately, Davis was standing in the way, and he showed no signs of moving.

Betty smiled archly at Davis. "I see you're going to attend the wedding with Celinda."

"Wouldn't miss it," Davis assured her.

"You know, I don't believe Celinda has had any overnight visitors in the four months she's been here except for her sister, who came to visit her last month."

Davis gave her a wicked grin. "You can't know how happy I am to hear that, Mrs. Furnell."

Betty laughed. "Go on, you two. You've got a long drive ahead of you."

Celinda yanked open the front door and hurried outside to the Phantom. Davis followed at a more sedate pace. He opened the small trunk and put the suitcases inside. She arranged the pink dress very carefully on top of the suitcases and then stood back and watched him close the trunk.

"You do realize that it will be a miracle if my reputation survives the week," she said.

He shrugged. "What's the big deal about having a man spend the night?"

"A marriage consultant's reputation is her most important asset. In fact, the vast majority of successful consultants are in Covenant Marriages. It sends a subtle signal to the clients, you see."

"That the matchmaker knows what she's doing?"

"Exactly. Mrs. Takahashi took a big chance when she hired me. If word gets out that I let men I barely know spend the night, she'll probably ask me to leave."

For some reason that observation seemed to irritate Davis. "I spent the night on the sofa, remember?"

"Yes." Celinda started toward the passenger door. "But appearances are everything in my business."

He went around to the driver's side and looked at her over the Phantom's low roof. "Don't worry, if your reputation gets damaged because of this case, the Guild will take care of it."

She didn't know whether to laugh or grit her teeth. "Got news for you; there are some things even the Guild can't fix."

Chapter 13

THE DRIVE TO FREQUENCY CITY USUALLY TOOK A LITTLE over three hours, but Celinda had a feeling that with Davis at the wheel they would make it in considerably less time. It wasn't just that the Phantom was a fast car, it was the way Davis drove it, efficiently and with exquisite control.

Araminta, who had been perched on the back of the seat with Max since the start of the trip, hopped onto Celinda's shoulder and made little encouraging noises. Celinda gave her another cookie from the bag of snacks she had brought along.

Cookie in her paw, Araminta returned to the back of the seat and huddled close to Max. She broke off a bit of her treat and offered it to him. He took it as though it were a rare and valuable offering.

"Araminta and Max seem to be getting awfully cozy together," Celinda observed, more to break the silence than anything else. Davis had said very little thus far. After the quick stop by his apartment to pick up an overnight bag and his tux, he had seemed content to concentrate on his driving.

His mouth curved a little at the corner. "Dust bunny love, you think?"

"Whatever it is, I doubt that it can be dignified by the term *love*," she replied. She winced a little, aware of the primness in her voice. "They only met yesterday, and they spent the night together last night. We in the matchmaking profession refer to that as a one-night stand."

"I'm getting the feeling that's probably against one of the rules in that book you wrote."

"It certainly is," she said.

"They're still together this morning. Doesn't that bode well for true love?"

She watched Araminta and Max move a little closer to each other on the back of the seat.

"A brief affair, maybe," Celinda said. "Not love."

"Mind me asking where you got all those rules you put into your book?"

"I made 'em up."

He gave her a quick, sidelong look. "That's a joke, right?"

"Of course it is." She turned serious. "The rules in my book are based on my own experience as a marriage consultant and the combined experiences of several of my colleagues whom I interviewed. Over time you see what works and what doesn't."

"One-night stands don't work, I take it?"

"Nope."

"Good thing we stopped where we did, then, last night, huh? Means there's still hope for us."

She stiffened and stole a quick look at him, wondering if he was teasing her. But Davis looked calm, even thoughtful.

She, on the other hand, was pretty sure that she was probably blushing all the way down to her toes. It was the first time the subject of that scorching kiss in the doorway had come up. She had begun to believe that they were both going to continue to pretend nothing had ever happened, that it might be better that way, given that the relationship was such a crazy mix of business and the personal.

"Last night was a little weird," she said very carefully. "I'm not sure we should draw any conclusions from it."

"You're calling that kiss weird?" He sounded interested, not offended.

"Well, yes."

"In what way?"

"I don't know about you, but I've never gotten half naked in a doorway before." She was suddenly incensed for absolutely no logical reason. "I mean, *anyone* could have walked past."

"Someone did walk past. A guy capable of summoning a doppelganger ghost. And another guy drove past, as I recall. Nearly flattened you."

Back to business, Celinda thought. *It's better that way. Don't let this get personal again.*

They both fell silent for a moment. After a while, Celinda fed Araminta another cookie and thought about the hasty repacking she had done this morning before letting Davis take her suitcases down to the car. On a mad, inexplicable whim she had yanked the plain cotton nightgown out of a case and replaced it with the new, sexy green satin gown she had found on sale a month ago. She hadn't even worn it yet. What had she been thinking?

Twenty miles later she stirred in her seat. "You know," she said, "I'm not sure your theory about Araminta not wanting to be parted from her relic for long is going to hold up. We're almost a hundred miles out of Cadence, and she isn't showing any signs of agitation about being in a car that is driving very rapidly away from wherever she stashed that relic."

"Who knows how a dust bunny's sense of time and distance works?" he said. "She may have no concept of how far away from your apartment we are."

"Hmm." Celinda turned in her seat to take a closer look at Araminta. "You may be right. I think she's sort of distracted."

"By Max?"

"Yes. If you don't get your relic back anytime soon, blame your Lothario of a dust bunny."

"Max is not that kind of bunny." Davis seemed genuinely insulted. "Trust me when I tell you that Araminta is the first female he's shown any interest in since I met him six months ago. Furthermore, Max isn't the only one who's had a long dry spell."

"You're saying that you haven't had a date in six months? I find that a little hard to swallow."

"My engagement ended about six months ago," he said quietly. "My business took a downturn at about the same time. I've been concentrating on rebuilding."

"I see." In spite of herself she felt a sharp pang of sympathy. Having a Covenant Marriage engagement end at the same time that your business hit some difficulties would have been tough for anyone. "I just assumed from the car and your clothes that Oakes Security was doing well."

"The car and the clothes are left over from before things hit the skids."

"Trust me, I know what it is to have everything you've worked for suddenly go south," she said quietly.

The Phantom ate up a few more miles of near-empty highway.

"What about you?" he asked after a while. "Last night you said something about not having had a date in four months?"

"I've been busy, too. It wasn't easy finding a new job, and after I got one, I devoted myself to proving to my new boss that she hadn't made a huge mistake by hiring me."

"Leave anyone special behind in Frequency?"

She thought about Grant Blair, the very nice lawyer she had been discreetly dating at the time of the disaster. "There was someone. It seemed promising for a while, but it ended badly."

"Mr. Perfect?"

"No," she said. "He was not Mr. Perfect."

"What happened?"

"I told you, it ended." She glanced at him. "Look, are you sure you want to get any deeper into this conversation? I thought men didn't like to talk about old relationships."

Davis shrugged. "I like to know what I'm dealing with. This guy you were seeing, would that have been Benson Landry, the hunter who's slated to take over the Frequency Guild?

She was shocked speechless. It took her a few seconds to find her tongue. "You know about Landry?"

"I'm a detective, remember?"

She pulled herself together with an effort of will. "Benson Landry is not the man I was dating back in Frequency. Landry is a manipulative bastard. He also has a very scary parapsych profile."

Davis's eyes tightened at the corners. "Like the driver of the getaway car last night?"

Celinda blinked and then shook her head ruefully. Just like that, they were back to business again. "No," she said, thinking about it. "Both men give off unwholesome vibes, but they aren't the same vibes. The getaway driver is a powerful psi talent with an obsessive streak a mile wide, but he is sane."

"Landry isn't sane?"

"The last time I saw him, he was teetering on the edge of insanity. But the most frightening thing about him is that he passes for normal."

"So there's no chance that Landry was the getaway driver?"

She shuddered. "Absolutely none."

"What about the other man, the one in the cap who fired up the twin ghosts?"

She shook her head. "Definitely not Landry. I didn't get close enough to read his psi, but I could see enough of him to be certain. That man was tall and gaunt. Landry is built much differently."

"Okay, so much for that angle."

She looked at him. "What made you ask if one of those men might have been Benson Landry?"

"Just occurred to me that if one of them was Landry, we would have had an obvious connection to work with."

"The obvious connection being me?"

"Yes."

She made herself exhale slowly and evenly. She would not take it personally, she told herself.

"Don't take it personally," he said.

"Too late. I think I am taking it personally."

"Look at it this way; it would have made things easier."

"You mean from an investigative point of view?"

"Right." He paused. "Okay, I can see where you might not want to be a connection in this case."

She shivered. "Especially if it means being connected to Benson Landry. Look, as long as we're talking about the case again, I want to go over the details of our cover story."

"What about them?"

"I get that I'm supposed to pass you off as my date for the wedding," she said, "but I don't think you realize just how curious my family is going to be."

"I'm not a big fan of fake details in cover stories," Davis said, his attention on the highway. "They tend to trip you up. Keep it simple is my motto."

"How simple?" she asked warily.

He moved one hand on the steering wheel in a slight, negligent gesture. "We met recently, hit it off immediately, and now we're getting to know one another."

"I assume you have parents?" she asked patiently. "Siblings?"

"Oh, yeah."

There was an ominous ring to the words, a man admitting he had a nemesis.

"If you showed up at a family event with a mysterious girlfriend that you hadn't ever mentioned, wouldn't everyone demand to know more about her?" she asked pointedly.

"There shouldn't be any problem if we just stick to the truth as much as possible," he said, calmly insistent. "They want to know what I do for a living? Tell them I'm in the security business."

"How did we meet?"

"In the course of an investigation. I came to your office to ask you some questions regarding a case I was working on. There was an instant attraction. We both felt the thrilling frissons of energy resonating between us. I asked you out, and you said yes. Simple."

She looked at him in disbelief. "Thrilling frissons of energy?"

"I thought it had a romantic ring."

She took another deep breath and tried again. "Look, my sister has arranged for everyone from both families to stay at a hotel in the Old Quarter tonight. The rehearsal dinner will be held there this evening, and after the wedding tomorrow, the reception will take place in the hotel ballroom."

"So?"

"So, you do realize that you cannot share a room with me, don't you? My father would come unhinged. My mother would cry, and my sister would be worried sick. No telling what my brother might do."

"Your family doesn't think you're all grown up yet?"

"It's not that." She hesitated. "It's because of what happened with Benson Landry."

"The hotel room photographs?"

"Damn. I should have known. You found those, too?"

His mouth curved with wry apology. "I keep telling you, I make my living as an investigator. Finding out stuff is what I do."

She wrinkled her nose. "I doubt that you had to dig too far to find those awful pictures. They were all over the tabloids in Frequency City. Benson Landry is a very powerful man in that town. The news that he was involved in an affair with me made headlines for nearly two weeks. It destroyed my reputation as a marriage consultant."

"In other words, your family feels protective of you after what happened."

"Yes."

"Don't worry about the hotel room situation," Davis said easily. "I'll take care of it."

"How?" she demanded.

"It is precisely for situations such as this that the hospitality industry invented the concept of connecting rooms."

She absorbed that. "I see."

The landscape had altered dramatically. The rich, agricultural region around Cadence City, fed by the mighty Cadence River, had given way to the over one hundred miles of stark desert that separated Cadence from Frequency. The long haul was broken by the occasional truck stop where drivers could recharge the flash-rock engines of their vehicles and grab some really bad food.

Here and there along the highway, dirt roads veered off into the desert. Most of them were unmarked. Celinda assumed they led to abandoned ranches or homesteads. A couple were identified with faded signs indicating roadside attractions.

Her personal favorite attraction was the one located halfway between the two cities. It was announced every twenty or thirty miles by a series of billboards that had once glowed in the dark but had long since faded to a dull, pea green. The first one had appeared just outside of Cadence: Only a Hundred and Fifty Miles to the Haunted Alien Ruins. The one they were passing now advised, Thirty Miles to the Haunted Alien Ruins.

"Mind if I ask you a personal question?" Davis said after a while.

"Yes," she said, aware that probably wasn't going to stop him.

"What made you, a professional matchmaker, think that Benson Landry was worth the risk to your reputation?"

The question blindsided her.

She hesitated, on the verge of her customary answer.

Just one of those things. Swept off my feet by a big Guild man. Landry was good-looking. Powerful. You know what they say about Guild men being good lovers. Thought I'd find out. It was a reckless fling that went bad when the tabloids got hold of the story, blah, blah, blah.

But for some reason she found herself wanting to tell him what had really happened. After four long months of keeping the secret to herself, of thinking that she could and would keep it for a lifetime, she was suddenly overcome with the urge to confide in a man she had only just met.

It was his psi-vibes, she thought. She trusted Davis in a way she had never been able to trust any man.

Still, there was danger in revealing her secrets.

"Yesterday you told me that one of the things you offered your clients was confidentiality," she said cautiously.

"Yes."

"Does that extend to other people involved in a case that you happen to be investigating?"

"Depends. My policy is to protect the privacy of everyone involved unless it conflicts with my number one priority."

"Solving the case?"

"It's what I do, Celinda."

She twisted around in the seat to look at him. "What about me? Can you guarantee that you'll keep my secrets?"

"Yes. Unless it keeps me from doing my job."

"What happened to me in Frequency City has nothing to do with recovering the relic."

"Then I'll keep your secrets, Celinda."

She watched him for a moment longer and then settled back into the seat. She believed him, she thought. But what if he didn't believe her? She would look delusional, at the very least. Worst-case scenario, he might conclude she was a pathological liar.

Ice trickled down her spine. She folded her arms very tightly around herself. Araminta suddenly hopped down onto her shoulder and made small comforting noises. Celinda unwound her arms, reached up, and patted her gently.

"I never for one moment believed that Benson Landry was worth the risk to my reputation," she said eventually. "Just the opposite. I think of him as a man out of a nightmare."

Davis gave her another one of his enigmatic looks. "So how did you wind up in bed with him?"

"That's easy. He drugged me."

Chapter 14

DAVIS FELT AS IF HE'D TAKEN A BODY BLOW. "WHAT THE hell?"

"I knew he was dangerous the moment he walked into my office," Celinda continued in that same too-even tone.

"He was a client?"

"No. I never accepted him as one. Never signed a contract. Never took his money."

"He wanted you to match him, and you refused?"

"Landry's positioning himself to take over the Frequency Guild when the current Guild boss retires. There's the usual power struggle going on. As I'm sure you're aware, very few Guild chiefs retire willingly. Most of them have to be forced out of office by their Councils. Harold Taylor has been in ill health for some time. It won't be long before he either dies or has to step down. He can't hold on to his power base much longer."

"And Benson Landry is waiting to make his move," Davis said.

"He's not just waiting, he's actively preparing. Part of

that preparation is finding himself a suitable wife. Guild bosses are almost always married."

"Old tradition," Davis agreed. "There are reasons."

"Landry wanted me to find him a match for a Covenant Marriage. Being the arrogant SOB that he is, he had a long list of requirements, of course."

"Let me hazard a guess," Davis said. "He wanted someone who was beautiful, rich, and who came from a wealthy, well-connected Guild family."

"If that was all he wanted, I'm sure he would have done his own matchmaking. Everyone knows that the members of powerful Guild families usually marry people who are also from other high-ranking Guild families. The marriages aren't based on compatibility and love. They're more like old-fashioned political alliances designed to cement power. You don't need a professional matchmaker for that. You use lawyers, accountants, and personal connections."

"You're right." Davis considered that for a moment. "As the guy in line to take over the Frequency City Guild, Benson Landry could have his choice of brides from among the most powerful Guild families."

"Unfortunately, Landry has set his long-range objective on more than just control of the Frequency Guild. He wants to move into politics. I think he plans to use the Guild resources as a power base to fund and operate his campaigns. He wants to become a senator."

"Are you serious?"

"Entirely."

"No Guild boss has ever been able to get elected to such a high office. I don't think any Guild exec has ever gotten further than a position on a city council."

Celinda's smile was very cold. "Probably because by the time a man gets to a position of power within the Guild, he has acquired the kind of record that would not stand up to close scrutiny by the media. It would be like a mob boss deciding to run for public office. Too many dead bodies buried around town. Guild bosses usually have to be content to manipulate powerful men from behind the scenes."

Davis told himself he was under no obligation to defend the Guilds. But, damn it, his ancestors had fought at the Last Battle of Cadence when Guild ghost hunters had been all that stood between the megalomaniac Vincent Lee Vance and his hordes of crazed followers. People tended to forget that the desperate, struggling colonies would have fallen under the tyrannical rule of an insane despot if it hadn't been for the Guilds. Pride ran strong in his blood.

"I won't deny that a certain amount of power brokering goes on in the Guilds," he said. "But that's true of the rest of society as well. People who have power tend to use it. Sort of goes with the territory. And it takes a certain degree of ruthlessness to get to the top of any organization. You don't really believe that any of the city-state senators or the other members of the Federation Council, let alone the president and vice president, are as pure as untuned amber, do you?"

"Of course not, but they don't usually come to the job with all the baggage that a Guild boss would bring to it. Even if a high-ranking Guild exec was a model of respectability, he'd still have to overcome the public image of Guild CEOs. Let's be honest here. They have some long-standing PR problems."

"Can't argue that," Davis admitted. "All right, so Benson Landry wants to become a senator."

"Yes. And that's why he came to me. To achieve his objectives, he needs to marry outside the Guild, preferably the daughter of a wealthy business family or someone from an elite political family. He requires an alliance that can help him build strong connections outside the Guild."

"He wanted you to find him that perfect wife," Davis concluded.

"Yes."

"You told him no."

She touched Araminta again, lightly. He was coming to recognize that small action.

"I tried to do it carefully," Celinda said. "Professionally. I knew Landry was dangerous. I made it clear that I only worked on Covenant Marriages based on sound parapsych principles of personal compatibility, et cetera, et cetera. I told him that I did not believe that marriages based on political connections and financial issues stood much chance of achieving long-term happiness for either party."

"What did he say?"

"He said he wasn't interested in all that, quote, garbage, unquote, about happiness and that I could ignore the compatibility aspects. I was to concentrate on finding him a wife from a good, socially connected family, and he would take care of the rest. He even had a couple of names for me to start with."

"Why didn't he do his own courting, in that case?"

"He assumed, quite rightly, that most non-Guild families would discourage their daughters from marrying a Guild man, even one who was set to become the head of the organization."

No surprise there, he thought. The social divisions between Guild and non-Guild weren't as strong as they had been in the old days, but they still existed, especially in upper-class circles. Landry's decision to try to marry into a socially prominent family outside the Guild was testimony to his determination to achieve his objectives.

"I think I see where this is going," he said. "Landry figured that if the most exclusive matchmaker in Frequency City recommended a match between himself and one of the women on his list, the woman and her family might be willing to consider the match. Is that it?"

"Yes. I suspect he also planned to apply other kinds of pressure as well, once he had made his selection. The dirty little secret of most of the socially prominent families in Frequency or any other city is that chances are they've had some mutually beneficial dealings with the Guild in the past. A lot of them owe the Guild a favor or two. And just as the Guild always pays its debts, it has a reputation for collecting them as well."

"Let's not go into that again." He flexed his hands on the steering wheel, holding on to his patience with an act of will. "All right, I've got the picture. You refused to accept Benson Landry as a client. What happened next?"

"He didn't take being declined well." Celinda's fingertips tangled in Araminta's scruffy fur. "I knew he was furious, but I hoped that, given his enormous ambition, he would focus on finding another way to achieve his objective."

"But that wasn't how it went down?"

"For a while I thought I was safe. He never came back to my office. Then, one evening I had an appointment that didn't finish until quite late. After the client left, I stayed at the office for another hour, doing some paperwork. When I finally went downstairs, the garage was almost empty."

She stopped talking. Davis glanced at her. She was staring straight ahead at the highway, her expression stark and frozen. Her hand was still on Araminta. The dust bunny was huddled very close on her shoulder.

"Go on," he said quietly.

"I walked past a pillar." There was no emotion at all in her voice now. "Landry leaped out and grabbed me from behind. He plunged a needle into my arm."

Cold fire burned in Davis's veins. He gripped the steering wheel so hard he wondered that it didn't shatter in his hands.

"Bastard," he said very softly.

"I tried to scream for help, but the stuff worked fast. Within seconds I was numb all over. I couldn't even stand. But I didn't go out. I realized later that he didn't want me unconscious, just unable to move or speak. He put me in the trunk of his car. I'm claustrophobic. It was . . . a nightmare."

He thought about the weeks he had spent at the Glenfield Institute. *Been there, done that.* He said nothing. He knew better than anyone that there wasn't anything he could say to erase the trauma.

Araminta made a small, anxious sound.

Davis fought his freezing rage in silence.

"He carried me to that hotel room," Celinda continued, still speaking without any trace of emotion in her voice. "He let everyone think I was drunk. When we were alone, he stripped off my clothes and pulled a nightgown over my head."

He had to ask the question, had to know how bad it had been for her. "Did he rape you?"

"No."

But an odd note had crept into her voice.

"He left me in the bed at the hotel. I later found out that he was due at a civic function that evening. He had to make an appearance there."

"What about the photographers?"

"The drug Landry gave me had just started to wear off when he returned to the room. The first thing he did was pick up the phone and call someone. I heard him say, 'Bring the champagne up now.'"

Again he detected the curious flattening in her voice. He was no psi-reader, but in his business he'd heard a lot of people tell a lot of lies. He usually recognized them when he heard them. She wasn't exactly lying now, he decided. But he was certain that she was leaving out something important. Perhaps Landry had raped her, and she did not want to talk about it. He could understand and respect that.

"After he made the phone call, Landry changed into a bathrobe," she continued. "I could move a little by then, but I kept very still, hoping he would think I was still immobile. I knew that my only chance was to shout for help when room service arrived."

"What happened?"

"Room service was very prompt," she said. "The problem was that the man pushing the cart wasn't the only person who showed up. There were also a couple of photographers."

"The tabloid paparazzi guys?"

"Yes. I staggered to my feet and screamed at them, but no one paid any attention. Evidently, 'Help me, this man kidnapped me,' isn't a universally recognized cry for assistance. The photographers took the photos and ran off. The room service person started to leave."

"I doubt if that was room service. More likely someone Landry paid to stage the scene."

She glanced at him in surprise. "I hadn't even considered that, but it makes sense."

"What did you do?"

"My only thought was to get out of the room before the door closed behind the guy with the cart. My head was spinning. I had a terrible headache, and I thought I might throw up. But at least I could move again. I made it out the door. Landry didn't even try to stop me. He laughed and said something about this being just the beginning. One of the last things he said to me as I left was, 'I'm going to destroy you.'"

"Bastard," he repeated, softer this time.

"*Sick* bastard. I told you, the man is not right in the head. He's scary crazy, because he's able to conceal his craziness from others."

"I believe you. What did you do next?"

"I went down a back staircase and found a hotel linen closet. There were some spare spa robes inside. I grabbed one and left through a back door. But the two photographers were waiting in the parking lot."

"The bathrobe photos."

"Yes."

She stopped talking. He knew she was wondering if she had just made a major mistake by confiding in him.

"Got one more question," he said.

She shook her head slightly, not saying no, more like pulling herself out of the past and back to the present. She was still petting Araminta.

"Can I assume you didn't go to the cops because you

didn't think they would take your word over that of a member of the Guild Council?" he asked.

"No," she said, visibly regaining her fortitude and iron-willed determination. "I kept quiet because his threat to destroy me was not the very last thing he said."

He went even colder inside. "He threatened to kill you?"

She shook her head again, a clear negative this time. "Oh, no. The last thing he would have wanted was a murder investigation, especially with me as the victim. There were too many clues that would have led back to him. He had made it clear to the press that I was his mistress, after all. There was a record of the appointment he made to meet with me at my office. I had left notes about my decision not to take him as a client and so on. No, he didn't threaten to kill me."

"What *did* he threaten?"

"He said that if I went to the police he would destroy my family."

"Did he say how?"

"He was very specific. He said he'd see to it that my father lost his job at the company where he has worked for over thirty years and that my mother would be forced out of her position at the library. He said he'd make sure my brother never got accepted as a member of any of the new rain forest exploration teams. He even went so far as to promise that he'd make sure my sister's marriage was called off."

"Does your family know the truth about what happened?"

"No, absolutely not," she said, sinking a little into the seat. "I didn't dare tell them the truth. They would have insisted that I go to the police and damn the consequences. I just couldn't risk it."

"They think what everyone else in Frequency thinks? That you fell hard for Landry, and when the affair was exposed in the press, you had no choice but to close your business and leave town?"

"Yes." She gave a tiny shrug. "Part of it was true. I didn't have any choice but to leave Frequency. I decided that it would be safer for everyone. Besides, my business was doomed, anyway, after the scandal broke."

"Do you really believe that Landry could have carried out his threats?"

"For the record, I don't think he could have stopped Josh Santana from marrying my sister. I don't think there's any force on the planet that could keep those two apart. But Landry has more than enough power to make life hell for both of them as long as they live in Frequency City."

"The Guilds aren't all-powerful, in spite of what you seem to think."

"Give me a break. Back in Cadence, if Mercer Wyatt set out to get a librarian and a midlevel executive fired, don't you think he could call in some debts and get it done?"

He exhaled slowly. She was right, he thought. Mercer Wyatt had spent years playing the IOU game in Cadence. He could do a lot of damage if he chose.

"Yeah, probably," he admitted.

"And he certainly would be able to keep a young, newly minted research scientist like my brother off an exploration team. The Guilds have enormous control over who goes into the rain forest."

"Okay, I'll give you that. The big difference is that Wyatt doesn't operate that crudely."

"You mean, he wouldn't cash in a lot of valuable debts to the Guild just to carry out a personal vendetta against a matchmaker."

"Be a waste of assets," Davis said. "Wyatt is too smart to go in for that kind of petty manipulation."

"You mean he's not crazy."

"No," he agreed. "Wyatt is not crazy."

"Trust me, Benson Landry is."

Chapter 15

MIDWAY THROUGH THE REHEARSAL DINNER, CELINDA'S great-aunt, Octavia, who was on her third green ruin martini, leaned over to whisper in her ear. "I like your new boyfriend." Octavia winked. "He's hot. Ghost hunter by any chance?"

Celinda felt the heat rise in her cheeks. Her only consolation was that it was highly unlikely that anyone else had overheard the comment. The large, private hotel dining room was packed with various members of the Ingram and Santana families as well as assorted bridesmaids and groomsmen. Two long tables, decorated with a sea of pink flowers, pink napkins, pink tablecloths, and pink favors, had been set up to accommodate the crowd. Pink champagne and cocktails had been flowing freely all evening. Things were getting loud.

"Not exactly," Celinda whispered back.

"You sure?" Octavia asked. She looked skeptical.

Octavia was a small, dynamic woman who, after she had a few martinis in her, tended to veer toward the unpredictable and outrageous. Tonight she wore one of the blonde big-hair wigs from her vast collection and sparkled under the weight of what must have been a couple of pounds of glittery costume jewelry.

There were certainly those in the Ingram clan who were of the opinion that Aunt Octavia's skirts were too short and her heels were too high for a woman of her age, but Celinda was not one of them. She usually found her aunt wonderfully entertaining. But tonight she was starting to get a little worried.

Everyone had been polite and friendly this afternoon, but, as she had warned Davis, her arrival at the hotel with a strange man had sent shock waves through the family. Fortunately, what might under normal circumstances have been an overwhelming flood of pointed questions had been drastically tempered by the fact that the focus of attention was on the bridal couple.

Celinda had concluded that she and Davis just might be able to pull off the deception if they could escape early from the reception tomorrow evening.

But now Octavia, fueled by the martinis, was starting to get dangerous.

Octavia leaned back in her chair and squinted a little to get a better look at Davis, who was seated on the other side of Celinda. At the moment Davis was deep in conversation with Celinda's brother, Walker. They were talking about the rain forest expedition team that Walker planned to join next month.

Octavia chuckled. "Your Davis reminds me of a hunter I knew when I was your age." She fanned herself theatrically with a napkin. "Talk about hot. *Ooh-hah.* I'll never forget that night we went down into the catacombs, just the two of us, with a sleeping bag. He worked a little ghost light, and I'm telling you, talk about setting fire to the sheets." She paused reflectively. "Actually, he did set fire to the sleeping bag. It was an accident, of course. The ghost he pulled got a little too close and—"

"Aunt Octavia, please," Celinda interrupted, a little

desperate. "I told you, Davis is not a ghost hunter. He's in the security business."

"Don't care what line he's in, I'm sure that man must be some kind of hunter." Octavia peered at Davis again. "Not the usual type, though. Whatever he is, he's strong. Yes, indeedy, I can feel some real psi energy there."

The problem was that Octavia probably did sense Davis's energy. It was no secret in the family that Celinda had inherited at least certain elements of her particular psi talents from her.

The difference between them was that, although Octavia could sense energy in others, she could not read the waves and patterns the way Celinda could. She would never have been able to distinguish between the clean, strong currents that came from Davis and the twisted, scary patterns given off by a man like Benson Landry. She did, however, recognize raw power when she picked up the vibes.

"I'd appreciate it if you wouldn't mention your theory to anyone else, Aunt Octavia," Celinda said in a very low voice. What was it Davis had said? Something about sticking to the truth as much as possible. "Davis is nonstandard. Like you and me. He tries to downplay his talent. You know how it is; if it got out that he's a little different, it could hurt his business."

"Of course." Octavia assumed a sage air and took another swallow of her martini. "Perfectly understandable. Mum's the word."

"Thanks." Celinda picked up her wineglass and took a healthy swallow. It was going to be a very long night.

At the far end of the table, her father, Newell, and the groom's father, Anthony Santana, rose to toast the bridal pair.

Newell Ingram was of medium height, wiry and compact. His green eyes were lit with intelligence and good humor. He picked up a spoon and gave Celinda's mother a private smile. It was the sort of smile that only two people who have known each other for a very long time could exchange.

Gloria Ingram reached out and briefly touched his hand.

Celinda looked at her lovely, vivacious mother and thought how radiant she was tonight.

Newell used the spoon to strike a water glass lightly. The room fell silent.

He smiled proudly at Rachel and launched into a small, fatherly speech that had every woman in the room reaching for tissues.

"Ever since you were born, I've known this day would come," he said quietly, as though speaking to her alone. "I used to lie awake at nights worrying about it, dreading it. And yet, more than anything else in the world, I wanted you to find the kind of happiness that your mother and I have known."

Celinda looked at her sister through a film of happy tears. Rachel was glowing. Her pale blonde hair was cut in a graceful curve, framing her delicate features and beautiful eyes. Tomorrow in her wedding dress she was going to look like a princess out of a fairy tale, Celinda thought.

Beside her, Josh Santana, dark-haired and dark-eyed, held her hand. He looked handsome and so very proud.

Celinda smiled a little to herself. A perfect match.

". . . And so, Josh, I welcome you into our family," Newell concluded. "I know that you will make my little girl very happy. That is all I ask."

Everyone rose to drink the toast. A cheer went up.

Davis leaned in close to Celinda. "Nice family."

"Yes, I know." She dabbed at her eye with her pink napkin. "I've been so worried that moving away from Frequency might not have been enough—" She broke off abruptly, not wanting to spoil the moment.

"You were afraid that moving away might not have been enough to protect them from Landry?"

She nodded wordlessly.

Everyone sat down again. Mr. Santana launched into his toast.

"Joshua, I also knew this day was coming from the moment of your birth. Your mother and I worried about it more

than you will ever know. But when you introduced us to
your beautiful Rachel, we knew that we could relax and rejoice. You have chosen well, my son."

Celinda and the other women seized more tissues.

At the end of his father's speech, Josh surprised everyone by rising to his feet and picking up his glass. He smiled
straight at Celinda.

"There is one more toast to be made tonight. Celinda,
Rachel and I want to thank you from the bottom of our
hearts for giving us the gift of a perfect match. We like to
think that fate would have brought us together somehow,
some way. But the truth is, this is a big city. We might never
have found each other if it hadn't been for your matchmaking talents. Tomorrow we will enter into a Covenant Marriage knowing that we have made the best decision of our
lives. We will always be grateful to you."

Everyone leaped to their feet again. A round of applause
went up.

Celinda could hardly see her sister's smiling face through
her tears. She grabbed another tissue.

THE DINNER ENDED A LONG TIME LATER, THE GUESTS
drifting away into the hotel bar or upstairs to their rooms.
Davis put an arm around Celinda's waist and guided her toward the door. He could feel the tension that tightened her
whole body. She had done a great job of acting during the
dinner, even managing to look as if she were enjoying herself. But he could tell that the whole wedding scene was an
ordeal for her instead of the happy celebration it should
have been. All because of a bastard named Benson Landry.

"Had an interesting conversation with your brother," he
said in an effort to ease her fragile mood. "He's sure excited about joining one of the jungle teams."

Before she could respond, Newell and Gloria Ingram
stepped directly into their path. Both were smiling, but he
could see the implacable determination in their eyes.

"I warned you this wasn't going to be simple," Celinda whispered. "Prepare to be grilled."

"Take it easy," he said softly. "Just follow my lead."

"Sorry we haven't had a chance to chat, Davis," Gloria said warmly. "Things have been so busy. We're delighted that you're here, though. So nice to know that Celinda is making new friends in Cadence."

"Have a nightcap with us in the bar?" Newell said in a tone that left no room for refusal.

Celinda looked more uneasy than ever. *Panicky* would not have been too strong a word, Davis thought.

"It's late," she said on a tone of false regret. "Big day tomorrow."

Davis smiled at Newell and Gloria. "Sounds like an excellent idea."

They took a booth at the back of the dimly lit bar. When the small glasses containing the after-dinner drinks had been served, Gloria looked directly at Davis.

"How did the two of you meet?"

"Luck," he said. "I was investigating a case involving a stolen artifact. The trail led straight to Celinda's office."

Celinda's fingers froze around her glass.

Newell narrowed his eyes. "You thought Celinda was a suspect?"

"No," Davis said calmly. "The missing artifact wound up in an antique shop. Celinda happened to purchase it. She didn't know it was stolen, of course. I offered to buy it back from her and return it to my client. We made a deal." He paused to smile at Celinda. "The next thing I knew, I was asking her out to dinner. One thing led to another, and here we are."

Newell seemed satisfied with that. "Just one of those chance meetings, then."

"Right," Davis said.

Gloria looked at Celinda. "In other words, you didn't meet through a matchmaker."

"Good grief, no, Mom." Celinda rezzed up a reassuring

smile. "Neither of us is looking for a permanent match at the moment. I mean, we're both so busy with our work. We're just enjoying each other's company. Nothing serious."

She didn't have to make it sound that casual, Davis thought, irritated.

"I see," Gloria said. She did not appear greatly relieved, but there was not much she could say.

"Was the relic valuable?" Newell asked with genuine curiosity.

"The shopkeeper only charged me five dollars for it," Celinda said quickly.

Newell frowned. "Someone hired a private investigator to track down an artifact worth only five bucks?"

"It has a lot of sentimental value to my client," Davis said smoothly.

Celinda nearly choked on a sip of her drink. She lowered the glass and grabbed a napkin. Davis decided she was probably having a tough time imagining a sentimental Guild boss. He had to admit it was a bit of a stretch.

"How long have you two known each other?" Gloria asked.

"A while," Davis said before Celinda could speak.

"And you're not serious about each other," Gloria said, coolly polite, "yet she brought you to a family wedding."

"Celinda is the one who said we weren't serious." Davis sipped his drink and lowered the glass. "I'm hoping to change her mind."

On the other side of the table, Celinda's eyes widened in shock. "No, really," she got out weakly. "We're just friends."

"Yeah, really," he said. He turned back to Gloria. "Don't worry, though, I plan to give her plenty of time to get to know me."

Gloria cleared her throat in a very meaningful way. "If the two of you do get serious, I'm sure you will, of course, consult a marriage consultant."

It was not a suggestion, Davis thought. More like a parental demand.

"Definitely," Celinda said, bobbing her head up and down very quickly. "Don't worry, Mom. You know me; I wouldn't dream of doing something stupid like getting married without the advice of an expert. Goodness, no one knows more than a marriage consultant just how important it is to get professional help. I'm sure Davis agrees. Don't you, Davis?"

"Right," Davis said neutrally, "professional help. It worked so well for me last time. Why wouldn't I want to repeat the experience?"

Celinda glared at him.

Newell's brow crinkled. He looked vaguely baffled.

"I beg your pardon?" Gloria said, rounding on Davis in sudden suspicion. "Are you *married*, Mr. Oakes?"

"No, Mrs. Ingram." He watched Celinda over the rim of his glass. "Had a close call a while back, though."

"Davis had a somewhat negative experience with a marriage consultant," Celinda explained in icy accents. "He employed a matchmaker who evidently did not know what she was doing. Fortunately, he and his fiancée discovered that they were not right for each other before the Covenant Wedding took place, so there was no harm done."

"No harm done," Davis repeated thoughtfully. "Now, there's an interesting way of looking at it. I, however, take a somewhat different view."

Celinda's glare grew more stern. "What is that supposed to mean?"

"As far as I'm concerned, my experience with a marriage consultant can pretty much be summed up as nonrefundable," he said.

Celinda and Gloria were both looking mystified now, but an expression of deep sympathy appeared on Newell's face.

"Nonrefundable." Newell shook his head with a grave air. "Not good. Not good at all."

Celinda and her mother switched their attention to him and then back to Davis.

"What are you two talking about?" Gloria demanded.

"Nonrefundable honeymoon cruise tickets," Davis said. "Nonrefundable deposits on the caterers' bills and the rental of the hotel ballroom and a few thousand bucks worth of flowers. Did you know that flowers are not returnable? And then there was the champagne. Didn't open one damn bottle, but I still got charged for most of it."

"Wait a second," Celinda said, "the cruise tickets I understand. Are you saying you got stuck with the rest of the expenses, too?"

He gave her a steely smile. "My fiancée had always dreamed of a full-blown Covenant Marriage, but her family didn't have enough money to pay for it. So, thinking I was making a long-term investment, I picked up the tab."

Celinda winced. "Oh, dear."

Newell shuddered. "When I think of what I would have been out if Rachel and Josh had called off their marriage at the last minute, I get cold chills down my spine."

"Nevertheless," Gloria said, exuding womanly wisdom, "far better to find out that things are not going to work out before a Covenant Marriage takes place than afterward."

"I won't argue that point," Davis said. "I'm just saying it was an expensive lesson about the fallibility of professional matchmakers."

Celinda fixed him with an air of grim challenge. "Surely you don't mean that you would rather trust your own judgment than use a professional consultant the next time?"

He shrugged. "I don't see how I could do any worse."

"Oh, for Pete's sake," she shot back, "that's like me saying I'd rather do my own detective work rather than hire a professional investigator."

"It's not the same thing at all."

"It is, too. There is solid statistical evidence and a number of parapsych studies proving that people who follow the advice of a properly trained matchmaker are far more likely to contract happy, fulfilling marriages than those who don't use a professional."

"Sounds like you're quoting from that book of yours again."

"Maybe you should read it." She folded her arms on the table and narrowed her eyes. "The statistics and the citations for the studies are all in the appendix."

"Wow," he said, deadpan. "It has an appendix? You know, I'm really going to have to take a look at that book one of these days."

"If you ever get around to actually buying a copy," she said, acidly sweet now, "I'd be happy to sign it for you."

Out of the corner of his eye, Davis saw Newell and Gloria exchange an odd look. Newell slid out of the booth and reached back to help Gloria to her feet.

"If you two don't mind, we're going upstairs to our room," Newell said genially. "Been a long day, and it will be an ever longer, busier one tomorrow."

Davis got to his feet and shook Newell's hand. "Thanks for the drink, sir."

Gloria leaned down and kissed Celinda on the cheek. "Good night, dear. See you in the morning." She straightened and looked at Davis. Amusement sparkled in her eyes. "I'm so glad we had this little chat, Davis. I feel I know you much better now. See you at the wedding."

"Good night, Mrs. Ingram."

Newell and Gloria disappeared into the hotel lobby, heading toward the elevators.

Davis sat down and looked at Celinda.

There was an acute silence.

He cleared his throat. "I think that went well, don't you?"

Chapter 16

CELINDA WAS TOO STUNNED TO RESPOND. THEN THE AB-surdity of the situation struck her like a flash of ghost light.

She put her head down on her folded arms and started to laugh.

"Damn, are you crying?" Davis slid around the curve of the booth and patted her awkwardly on the shoulder. "It's okay. I know trying to pretend that I'm your new boyfriend isn't easy, but you're doing just fine."

She dared not raise her head. She was laughing too hard. Maybe she was sinking into hysteria.

"Your parents didn't seem too upset when they left," Davis said, apparently having decided to take an encouraging tack. "Look on the bright side. Whatever they're thinking right now, it's a good bet that they don't have a clue that I'm here as your bodyguard. That was the whole point, remember?"

She managed to get herself under control with an effort of will. She raised her head, aware that her eyes were damp and her face was probably flushed.

"Sorry," she mumbled. She used a napkin to wipe her

eyes. "I don't know what came over me. Blame it on the stress."

"You were laughing," he said, sounding deeply relieved. "I thought—never mind."

"I can't believe we got into that stupid argument in front of my parents." She felt the odd laughter start to well up inside again and swallowed hard to suppress it. "Probably all the champagne at dinner. What were we thinking?"

"Don't know about you, but I was thinking that I was getting damned tired of hearing you tell everyone I was just a casual friend."

She stilled, astonished. "Well, it's not like there are a lot of useful terms to describe a man in your position. I was doing my best to make our relationship sound normal."

"But it's not normal, is it?"

"Listen, you're the one who said this little charade was going to be simple, remember? 'Just stick to the truth as much as possible,' you said. If you will recall, I wanted to discuss our cover story in detail on the drive here, but you insisted on blowing off that plan."

A suspicious gleam of amusement darkened his eyes. "Are we arguing again?"

She sat back, slouching in the seat. What was wrong with her? It was the stress.

"No. I think I've had enough quarreling for one evening," she said very politely. "It's time I went to bed. I'm going to be wearing pink tomorrow. I need my sleep."

DAVIS OPENED THE DOOR OF HER ROOM USING HER KEY A short time later. She switched on the lights. Max and Araminta were sitting side by side on the table looking out at the night through the sliding glass window.

"We're back," Celinda announced.

Araminta and Max tumbled down off the desk, rumbling greetings. Celinda reached down, scooped up Araminta, and plopped her on her shoulder. Araminta immediately began making little cooing noises in her ear.

"I think she wants another snack," Celinda said. Morosely, she eyed the empty dishes on the table. "Looks like she and Max went through everything I ordered from room service for them before we left. I'm going to have to break open the minibar. Do you know how much they charge for the stuff inside a minibar?"

Davis picked up Max. "Keep a record. I'll put it on the Guild's tab. Wyatt can afford a few snacks out of a minibar, trust me."

"I believe you. Problem is, how eager is he going to be to pay for things like minibar snacks if he doesn't get his relic back?"

"Well, he won't be thrilled," Davis said.

She groaned. "You know, I could do without having the head of the Cadence Guild annoyed at me. I'd have to leave town. Again. It was bad enough pulling up roots here in Frequency because I pissed off a para-psycho member of the local Guild."

His expression hardened. "Regardless of the outcome of this case, you're not going to be forced to leave Cadence."

"Hah. Easy for you to say." She crouched down in front of the minibar and de-rezzed the little seal. "You don't know what it's like living in a town after you've made a high-ranking Guild person mad, trust me."

"I do trust you," he said quietly. "But I think it's time you tried trusting me."

Something in his words froze her in place. She looked up at him. It was a long way, given her current position close to the floor. When she finally got to his face, she saw that his features were set in grim, implacable lines.

"Great," she said evenly. "Now I've annoyed you, too."

"Uh-huh."

She rose to her feet, chagrined. "Sorry. Things have been a little stressful lately. I really do need a good night's sleep."

He inclined his head, coldly polite. "I'll say good night, in that case."

He walked to the connecting door. "I'll open this again after you're in bed."

He went into his own room, Max on his shoulder, and shut the door very quietly.

She stood looking at the closed door for a long moment. This was clearly one of the downsides of hanging around with a bodyguard. They were in the habit of giving a lot of orders.

Araminta made encouraging little noises in her ear.

"Right." Celinda said. She went back down on her knees in front of the minibar again. "First things first. A girl's gotta eat."

SOME TIME LATER SHE TURNED OVER IN BED FOR WHAT was probably the thousandth time and finally gave up trying to sleep. She pushed herself up on her elbows and glumly studied the door that connected her room to Davis's. It was open, but the crack was no more than a couple of inches wide.

It was impossible to see into the other room, but she had been listening for quite some time, and things were awfully silent on the other side of the door. Evidently Davis wasn't having any trouble sleeping.

At the foot of the bed, Araminta's blue eyes glittered in the moonlight. She was awake.

"Don't tell me you're hungry again," Celinda whispered.

Araminta scampered across the covers, batted her blue eyes, and made hopeful sounds.

"Okay, all right, I wouldn't want you to starve." Celinda got out of bed, pulled on her robe, and padded across the room to reopen the minibar. There was enough green light to illuminate the contents. "What's it going to be? Cookies or nuts?"

Araminta dithered briefly and then fixed her attention squarely on the nuts.

Celinda plucked the nuts out of the bar, straightened, and tore open the package. She dumped the contents into the dish on the table. Araminta hopped down and began munching daintily.

"At least you're not out there in the dark running around with Max in a strange city," Celinda said softly. "What did you do with that stupid relic?"

Araminta ate a nut.

"Do you have any idea how much trouble we're in?"

Araminta displayed no sign of concern. She selected another nut.

Celinda went to the window and looked out at the view of the night-darkened city. The hotel was located in the heart of the Quarter, which was suffused with the pale glow of Old Frequency.

She opened the sliding glass door and moved out onto the balcony. The air was warm and balmy. Resting her elbows on the iron railing, she savored the gentle rush of alien psi and contemplated the night.

The intriguing aura of some very familiar energy pulsed nearby.

Startled, she stepped back and turned quickly, pulling her robe more tightly around her.

Davis was lounging against the railing of his balcony. He was wearing only his trousers. His feet were bare and so was everything else above his waist. Moonlight and the faint glow of the green wall's radiance gleamed on his shoulders. He looked at her with eyes as mysterious as the night. Max sat beside him on the railing.

"Couldn't sleep?" Davis asked.

"Araminta was hungry again."

"Well, sure. It's been at least an hour and a half since you last fed her. What did you expect?"

"I swear, it's as if she's been possessed by the spirit of a teenage boy." She paused. "What are you doing out here?"

"Thinking."

"About the case?" she asked cautiously.

"And other things." He paused a beat. "Mostly other things."

She wanted to ask him what other things he was thinking about, but she reminded herself that she didn't know him well enough to push into his private space.

Max chose that moment to hop across the three-foot span that separated the two balconies, showing no fear of the three-story drop to the ground, and landed on the railing next to Celinda. He chortled politely to her and then tumbled down to the floor. He disappeared into the room to join Araminta on the desk. Celinda heard more crunching noises.

"Bet I could do that," Davis said, studying the distance between the two balconies.

"Do what? Jump from your balcony to mine?" She shuddered. "Don't even think about it."

"Why not?"

"Because it would be a dumb-ass risk to take, that's why not. Good grief, you might miss, and then I'd be stuck having to explain to Mercer Wyatt why he's never going to get his relic back."

Davis's teeth flashed in a brief, wicked grin. "Nice to know you care."

"Yeah, well, I've got a vested interest in you. The way I look at it, you're all that's standing between Araminta and me and the boss of the Cadence Guild. I want you to stay safe. No taking chances. Got it?"

"Got it. Hang on a second."

He vanished into his room. She waited for him to reappear, wondering what was going on.

A moment later he walked out onto her balcony.

"Made it," he said. "Rest assured, no extreme risks were taken."

She shivered but not from the cool night air. He was standing very close to her, so close that she could detect a lot more than his psi power. She was intensely aware of every aspect of him. Her pulse was already thrumming faster, and she could feel the now-familiar flutter in the pit of her stomach.

"Good to know," she whispered. "Because I really don't want anything to happen to you."

He smiled slowly. "I appreciate that, even if the only reason you want me around is because I'm your shield against the Cadence Guild."

The intimacy of the night and Davis's own uniquely compelling aura enveloped her, affecting all of her senses. Sensual excitement effervesced through her veins. Mr. Almost Perfect.

She was suddenly sure that she could not only leap from one balcony to the next, she could probably tap dance along the railings. Who cared about the risk?

"That's not the only reason I want you around," she said.

She was amazed by the sound of her own voice. It was downright sultry. She was positive that she had never sounded sultry before in her entire life.

Davis gripped the lapels of her robe with both hands and tugged her closer. "You're sure?"

She was having trouble breathing now. But in a good way. A thrilling way.

"I'm sure," she managed.

He tightened his grip on her robe and kissed her.

Impossible as it was, she was certain that Davis's energy and her own somehow came together in a resonating pattern that set fire to the night. She was suddenly swept up in a delirious cascade of invisible psi.

Just like last night, she thought. She should probably call a halt to things before they went too far. Just as she had last night. One-night stands were against all the rules.

But with this man she no longer cared about the rules. She didn't want to waste time planning for the future because, given Davis's attitude toward matchmaking and Covenant Marriage, they probably didn't have one. Tonight might be all they had together, and she intended to seize the moment.

That realization alone was enough to tip the scales of common sense.

She closed her hands fiercely around his shoulders, glorying in the feel of sleek muscle and warm male skin. He responded with a heavy groan and deepened the kiss.

When she sighed a little and parted her lips, he shifted his hands, tightening them around her waist. He was heavily aroused. She could feel him and knew that he wanted her to be aware of the effect she was having on him.

Exhilaration arced through her. She suddenly felt incredibly sexy and wildly feminine.

Boldly she broke free of the kiss to press her lips to his throat. A shudder went through him. Without warning he scooped her up into his arms, high against his chest, and carried her into the darkened bedroom.

She thought he was going to put her down on her bed. Instead, he took her through the connecting door into his room and stood her on her feet. She saw that the covers had been kicked down to the foot of his bed. Davis had obviously had as much difficulty sleeping as she had.

She was so intoxicated with the heady, exuberant wonder of what was happening that she almost lost her balance.

Davis caught her with one hand, undid the sash of her robe, and peeled the garment off her shoulders. It pooled around her bare feet, leaving her in her pale green satin nightgown.

Davis smiled slowly at the sight of the gown. He ran his fingers under the edge of the tiny straps, just touching her skin.

"Nice," he said. "Very nice."

"I got it on sale last month," she confessed, before stopping to think. "I've been saving it for a special occasion."

He looked pleased. "Like tonight?"

She smiled. "It certainly looks that way."

His laughter was sexy and incredibly intimate. "Looks like this is my lucky night."

He picked her up and put her on the rumpled bed. Straightening, he stripped off his trousers and tossed them aside. He wasn't wearing anything underneath.

A tremor of unease went through her. But before she had a chance to reconsider the wisdom of what was about to happen, Davis came down beside her on the bed. He leaned over her, trapping her between his braced elbows, and began to kiss her hungrily.

The kisses rained down, dampening her mouth, her throat, heating her blood. Hot energy pulsed, Davis's and her own, resonating once again in a pattern that drove both of them to a higher level of excitement. It had never been like this with any other man, she thought. *Perfect.*

She forgot her momentary misgivings. Eagerly she explored him, savoring the muscular contours of his back and hips. When her fingers closed around him, he sucked in a deep, shuddering breath.

"I won't last long if you keep that up," he warned, his voice low and husky.

Thrilled, she tightened her fingers a little, challenging him. This time his low laugh sent small, exciting chills up and down her spine.

He slid the satin straps off her shoulders and eased the gown down her body, all the way to her ankles. He dropped it onto the floor beside the bed.

He found her breast with his mouth, and she forgot all about teasing him. She gasped and sank her nails into his back. Her entire body ached with need. Every inch of her skin was shatteringly sensitive.

Davis's big, warm hand slid down her waist, across her stomach. He curled his fingers into the hair at the juncture of her thighs.

She kissed his shoulder, licked him, and then, on impulse, tested his skin with her teeth. He made a soft, hoarse sound and then he caught her nipple very gently between his own teeth His fingers slid lower, seeking secrets.

She stopped breathing. Everything inside her tightened to an unbearable degree. She could feel her own slickness and knew that his hand must be covered with the moisture.

When he moved on top of her a short time later, she was trembling with anticipation and desire.

He positioned himself, and then he started to ease his way into her.

"You're so tight," he said, his voice ragged. "Relax for me."

"I'm trying," she gasped. "You're too big."

"No. You just need to take it easy."

She took several deep breaths. "Okay. I'm relaxed."

"You're sure?"

"I'm sure."

Instead of pressing forward, he withdrew. She caught him closer, panicked that he had changed his mind.

"No," she said, clutching at him. "Don't leave me."

"I wasn't going anywhere. Trust me."

He found the little nubbin hidden between the protective folds of flesh and stroked it again. Almost immediately she felt herself begin to soften and open.

"Yes," she said. "Oh, yes, *please*."

He continued to stroke her until her pleas turned to demands. Then he rolled onto his back, taking her with him.

She sprawled on top of him, knees on either side of his thighs. He found her again with his hand, using thumb and forefinger to drive her mad.

The climax struck out of nowhere. She was unprepared for it because she had never felt anything like it in her life. Pulsing waves of exquisite energy swept through her, releasing a burst of sheer euphoria.

She heard someone scream softly in the shadows. Belatedly she realized that she was the screamer.

Davis gripped her buttocks and pushed himself into her in one smooth, relentless move. He thrust twice, three times and then he went quartz-hard all over. She opened her eyes to look down at him and saw his mouth open in a grimace that could have been either great pain or unbelievable pleasure.

He roared.

There was no other word for it. It was the cry of an exultant male claiming his mate.

She had time to thank her lucky amber that none of her relatives were in the room next door before she collapsed along the length of him.

A LONG TIME LATER HE ROUSED HIMSELF, ROLLED AWAY from her, and flopped back onto the pillows. There was enough emerald-tinted light coming through the sliding glass door to show her that he was smiling with masculine satisfaction.

"You always do that?" he asked.

"Do what?"

"Scream."

She blushed furiously. Well, at least with all the shadows he couldn't see her turning bright pink.

"I don't know," she mumbled.

He levered himself up on one elbow and looked down at her. "Why don't you know?"

"I've never done that before."

"Screamed?"

"Had an orgasm."

He was clearly taken back. "Are you sure?"

"It isn't the kind of thing you make a mistake about, is it?"

"No, it's not."

"Trust me, I've never felt anything that delicious before in my life. I'd have remembered."

"Sorry you had to wait this long, but I have to tell you I'm very glad I was around when it finally happened."

"Me, too." She wound her arms around his neck. "You

think maybe we could try it again? Make sure it wasn't a one-time thing?"

"My pleasure."

He bent his head and covered her mouth with his own. Energy flared once more in the shadowed room.

A LONG TIME LATER, SHE AWOKE WITH A START, AWARE that she was being carried in a man's arms. Fear lanced through her, bringing with it memories of the terrible night that Benson Landry had carried her into the hotel room, pretending to the staff that she was intoxicated.

"No." Instinctively she started to struggle.

The arms that cradled her tightened, imprisoning her against a hard male chest.

"Take it easy," Davis said gently. "You're okay. You're just dreaming."

The reassuring sound of his voice and the familiar pulse of his psi waves drove out the brief panic. She opened her eyes and looked up at him.

"What are you doing?" she asked, still disoriented.

"Taking you back to your bed."

That didn't sound promising.

"Why?" she asked, bewildered now.

"I like to sleep alone," he said quietly. He put her down onto her bed and straightened. "Don't take it personally."

She was mortified. He might be perfect for her, but in spite of what they had just shared, the feeling was not reciprocated. It was not as if he had not warned her that he was not interested in long-term relationships, she reminded herself. And it was not as if there were rules against one-night stands for very good reasons. Still, kicking her out of his bed before the night was over seemed a little extreme.

She felt humiliated. She was also furious.

"Got news for you," she said. "I *am* taking it personally."

She pulled the covers up to her chin, rolled onto her side, and turned away from him.

He did not leave immediately. She could feel him standing there, looking down at her. She held her breath, wondering if he would change his mind.

"Good night," he said very quietly.

He went back into his own room. She lay awake for a long time, looking out the window at the glowing green spires and towers of the Dead City. Araminta hopped up onto the bed, cuddled close, and made soft little sounds.

He's Mr. Almost Perfect, Celinda reminded herself, *not Mr. Perfect. Get used to it.*

She finally went to sleep.

Chapter 17

BENSON LANDRY'S PHONE REZZED LOUDLY. HE HAD JUST disengaged from the luscious, energetic, extremely inventive blonde, and he was enjoying the pleasant ennui of the aftermath. He was in no mood to take the call. But there weren't many people who had his private number. When someone used it, there was always a reason.

He rolled away from the blonde, sat up on the edge of the bed, and reached for the phone.

"Landry," he said. "This had better be important."

"If you will give me five minutes of your valuable time, I think you will find what I have to say very interesting, Mr. Landry."

The voice was cultured, resonant, authoritative. It was also unfamiliar. That was enough to rez a slew of alarm bells.

"Who is this?" he asked sharply.

"My name is Dr. Titus G. Kennington. I believe you and I have an acquaintance in common. A woman named Celinda Ingram."

His insides went cold. He reached back and gave the blonde a hard shove.

She got the message. It wasn't the first time he had sent her away immediately after he had finished with her. Expressionless, she got out of bed, picked up her things, and went into the bathroom to dress.

"What about Celinda Ingram?" he said into the phone, suppressing the urgency that had suddenly consumed him. He had thought that problem had been settled four months ago.

"We'll get to her in a moment. First, let us discuss our partnership."

"Why in green hell should I take you on as a partner?"

"Because I am prepared to give you something you want very badly in exchange."

"That would be?"

"I can ensure first that you become the new boss of the Frequency Guild. I am also prepared to go further. I will help you achieve your other goals: a bride from a wealthy, high-ranking, non-Guild family and a shot at a senate seat."

I'm dealing with a real nutcase, Benson thought. But since this particular whack job had gotten close enough to obtain his private number, he had to pay attention. The only thing he could do was keep the guy talking as long as possible so that he could get enough information to find him.

"Sounds promising," he said. "Out of curiosity, how are you going to go about fulfilling your end of the bargain?"

The blonde emerged from the bathroom, fully dressed. She went to the door without a word and let herself out into the hall. Benson ignored her. His security staff would escort her off the estate.

"You will soon see," Kennington said. "Now, then, as a member of the Frequency Guild Council, I assume you've heard the rumors about a certain alien relic that went missing from the Cadence Guild security vault?"

This was getting more interesting by the second. Maybe the guy wasn't a total whack job after all.

"There's talk going around that an artifact was stolen,"

he said carefully. "Wyatt is keeping the whole thing quiet, but they say he's looking hard. He wants it back."

"He wants to recover it because it is extremely unusual," Kennington said. "It's made of a type of amber that no one has come across before. But not even Wyatt knows about the relic's unique properties."

"What properties?"

"You wouldn't believe me if I told you, so I suggest a demonstration, instead."

"If you think I'm going to waste my time—"

"I assure you, Mr. Landry, once you have seen what the ruby amber device can do, you will be extremely eager to form a partnership with me."

"How are you going to demonstrate the damn thing if it's missing?"

"I'll let you in on a little secret, sir, something that no one else knows. There are two ruby amber artifacts in existence. I've got the other one."

"In that case, why do you want a second one?"

"It is simply too powerful and too valuable to be left in the hands of people who have no idea what it can do."

"Why make a deal with me?" Benson asked.

"I think, given the course of recent events, that your odds of recovering the second relic are much better than mine," Kennington said.

"Why?"

"A variety of reasons. First, the person who knows the location of the other relic is currently in Frequency City. That is your town. As a Guild Councilman you can operate freely without inviting unwanted scrutiny. And last, but certainly not least, you have an intimate acquaintance with Celinda Ingram."

The old rage welled up out of the dark pit inside Benson.

"How does that bitch come into this?"

"I do not believe that she currently has the relic in her possession, because if that were true, the Cadence Guild would have forced her to return it. But it appears that she knows where it is."

Should have killed her when I had the chance. Four months ago he had realized that Celinda had somehow sensed the deep well of darkness that was the source of his power; sensed it and feared it. For years he had been able to conceal the churning black pit from the rest of the world, but when she had refused to take him on as a client, he had known that she was aware of his secret. There was no other explanation for her actions. He was a member of the Guild Council, after all, the most powerful ghost hunter in town. No one turned him down.

But getting rid of her permanently four months ago would have been too risky, he reminded himself. The murder of the most exclusive matchmaker in Frequency would have launched a high-profile investigation. The police would have demanded Guild cooperation, and that old fool Harold Taylor would not have protected him.

"Let's say I agree to recover the second relic for you," he said. "Why would I give it to you? If it has some valuable properties, as you claim, I'd want to keep it for myself."

"You are, of course, free to do so," Kennington said in that same smooth, annoyingly urbane tone. "But it won't do you any good. Even assuming you understood its unique properties, you would not be able to rez it."

"Why not?"

"It requires a special type of psi talent: *my* kind. But in exchange for the recovery of the artifact, I will agree to employ the device on your behalf."

"You really think you can use it to make sure I become the next boss of the Frequency Guild?"

"And everything else you want, Mr. Landry." Kennington was practically purring. "Everything else. I trust that you will think of this arrangement as a mutually beneficial one. In your position as a man of increasing power and influence, you can help me in many ways. I, in turn, will use the device to take you as high as you wish to go. Do we have an agreement?"

"First I'll need to see what the relic can do."

"Of course. I suggest we perform the demonstration immediately. You may choose the venue. There is just one stipulation."

"What's that?"

"Like ghost light, the power of the relic is quite weak unless it is accessed underground or close to a source of alien psi."

"My office is in the Old Quarter," he said. He was getting jacked up. His instincts told him he was onto something important. "It sits directly over a hole-in-the-wall."

"That should do it. Also, for purposes of this demonstration, we will need an experimental subject."

"Who?"

"It doesn't matter to me. One of your men, perhaps, or a member of your household staff."

"Hang on." Benson rezzed the bedside security intercom.

The guard at the gate answered immediately.

"Yes, Mr. Landry?"

"Has the woman left yet?"

"Miss Stowe? She's here now. One of the men is getting ready to drive her home."

"Bring her back to the house. I'm not quite finished with her after all."

Chapter 18

"GOT NEWS FOR YOU, I AM TAKING IT PERSONALLY."

Davis gazed up at the ceiling. He was screwed. It had been too much to hope that she wouldn't wake up when he carried her into the other room, too much to hope that she might not have a problem with the fact that he wanted to sleep alone.

He didn't want to sleep alone. He wanted to spend the rest of the night with her curled tightly against him. He wanted to wake up in the morning and find her in his arms.

But he didn't dare take that risk.

It was a long time before he fell asleep. When he did, he dreamed.

He held the child tightly in his arms. The kidnappers were not far behind. They were still invisible in the maze of catacombs, but it wouldn't be long now before they closed in. They were homing in on the frequency of the amber he wore in his watch.

He had just ditched the watch in a nearby tunnel. He had backup amber set at a different frequency, but

*he could not risk using it yet. It would not take the
men who were following them long to pick up the second signal and realize that he had switched amber.*

There was only one chance left.

*"Close your eyes and don't move, Mary Beth. I
promise you that if we both stay absolutely still for
the next few minutes, the bad men won't even see us."*

"Okay," Mary Beth whispered.

*She clung to him, one arm wrapped around his
neck, and regarded him with the solemn trust that
only a six-year-old child could give. It was a miracle
that she had any confidence in him at all after what
she'd been through. She had never met him before in
her life. But forty-five minutes ago he had rescued
her from the kidnappers, and she had believed him
when he told her that he had come to take her home.*

*The sounds of the approaching men were closer
now. They were using a sled. There was no way a man
carrying a six-year-old kid could outrun one.*

*Not much longer, he thought. Maybe thirty sec-
onds. He had to get the timing right, or he and Mary
Beth would never make it out of this chamber.*

*Mary Beth closed her eyes and pressed her face
against his chest, a child trying to hide from the mon-
sters under the bed.*

*The sled was very close now. He could hear the
sound of the simple amber-drive motor. Only the most
primitive kinds of engines worked underground.*

*"He's close," one of the men said, excited. "We've
got him. Can't be more than a hundred feet away."*

*"Move it," another man said. "If he gets out of
here with the girl, we're all dead."*

*"Stay very, very still, Mary Beth," he whispered.
She froze in his arms.*

He pulled silver light. A lot of it.

*The sled hummed loudly. It rolled out of one of the
ten vaulted entrances of the underground chamber.*

And then the driver brought the damn thing to a halt, right in the middle of the room.

"Check the frequency," the driver snapped.

He held his breath and his focus, counting the seconds.

One minute.

The second man on the sled studied the amber-rez locator. "Straight ahead."

Two minutes.

"You sure?" the driver demanded, looking at the nine other doorways.

"Positive. I'm telling you, I've got a solid reading."

"I don't like this," the third man said uneasily. "Something doesn't feel right."

Three minutes. The men continued to argue. Mary Beth did not stir, although he could feel her little body shivering with fear.

Four minutes.

"All right, let's go," the driver said, making the executive decision.

The bastard finally rezzed the sled's engine. The little vehicle shot across the chamber. It made straight for the vaulted doorway, zeroing in on the frequency of the amber watch that lay on the quartz floor just inside.

The sled passed within a yard of where he stood with Mary Beth pressed tightly against his chest.

Five minutes. An eternity.

"Ghost-shit," the driver howled. "That's his damned watch. He tricked us."

But it was too late. The driver couldn't stop the sled in time. It plowed straight through the faint shadows cloaking the vaulted entrance of the tunnel, triggering the alien illusion trap.

The men screamed when they were plunged into the trap's psychically generated alien nightmares, but not for long. No human could stay conscious for more *than a few seconds under those conditions. Mary Beth jerked at the sounds.*

He stopped working silver light. He was breathing hard and already starting to shake. He didn't need to test his amber to know that he had melted it. Luckily he now had a fresh supply.

"It's okay, Mary Beth," he said. "The bad men can't hurt you now."

She raised her head and looked at him with big, amazed eyes. "They went right past us, but they didn't even see us."

"No," he said. "They didn't."

He had to move quickly. The clock was ticking. He had maybe fifteen minutes at most to get back to the rendezvous point and turn Mary Beth over to the team. At least they now had the sled. With the illusion trap triggered, it was safe to go through the doorway to get it.

"It was like we were invisible," Mary Beth whispered, watching him kick the three unconscious men off the sled.

"Yeah." He checked the slab's amber-rez locator. It was functioning. "Like we were invisible."

He made the rendezvous point. The last thing he remembered was the face of the hunter who took the girl out of his arms. Then the cold chills swept over him, and everything faded to black.

FIVE DAYS LATER HE AWOKE TO DISCOVER THAT HE *was trapped in a living hell named the Glenfield Institute, dimly aware of what was going on around him but utterly unable to communicate. He could smell the coffee the doctors drank and hear their grim diagnosis.*

"Psi coma. He may never come out of it. Even if he does surface, he's going to be a total burnout case. He'll spend the rest of his life in a parapsych ward."

Chapter 19

TITUS KENNINGTON LOOKED AROUND BENSON LANDRY'S office with amused disdain. Talk about clinging to the past, he thought. Unlike the Cadence Guild headquarters, which under Mercer Wyatt's command had been moved into a gleaming downtown office tower, the Frequency Guild was still located in its original compound in the Old Quarter of the city.

The decision to move the Cadence Guild headquarters downtown had been a public relations bid designed to make the organization appear more mainstream. Here in Frequency, however, the local authorities were apparently not overconcerned with public opinion. The very fact that a man like Benson Landry had risen to such a prominent position in the Guild was proof that the local organization was not all that determined to modernize.

Landry was unstable and very dangerous. The dark energy emanating from him was similar to other para-sociopaths Titus had encountered in the course of his professional career. In addition, the man was obviously clinging to sanity by his fingertips. When this was over, he would have to be dealt with. But right now he was the only tool available for the job at hand.

Landry's office had been built in the period following the Era of Discord when the status and power of the Guilds had been at their height. The room was paneled in spectrum wood and elaborately inlaid with yellow amber. A variety of alien antiquities, including an array of unusual-looking green quartz vases, were arranged around the room. The top of Landry's desk was a smooth slab of quartz. The walls of the Dead City rose right outside the window. At night the office would be suffused with a radiant green light.

Power resonated throughout the room, not just the symbolic power associated with status and authority that one expected to encounter in the domain of a Guild Council member, but the very real paranormal power that emanated from the catacombs below.

Landry looked at him. "I brought Miss Stowe because I thought she would find this interesting."

"Yes, of course." Titus gave the blonde his soothing, *Trust me, I'm a doctor* smile. "A pleasure to meet you, Miss Stowe."

She smiled back, looking baffled but not frightened. She was clearly making an effort to show polite interest, a professional call girl who was accustomed to satisfying the whims of her clients.

"Benson tells me that you want to demonstrate an alien artifact to him," she said.

"That's right." Titus looked at Landry. "Any chance we can do this down in the catacombs? There's a fair amount of ambient psi in here, but the more the better for our purposes."

Landry shrugged. He crossed the room and rezzed a hidden lock. A section of the wall opened up, revealing a flight of steep stone steps that led down into darkness.

Invisible waves of energy flowed up the steps into the room. They were, Titus knew, a sure sign that somewhere down below there was an opening into the catacombs.

"This way," Landry said, picking up a flashlight. "Watch your head."

He rezzed the flashlight and led the way down the steps. The blonde went next. Titus followed.

The staircase ended in a dank, heavily timbered basement that dated from the Colonial era. Landry played the beam of the flashlight on one wall, revealing a modern, mag-steel door secured with a sturdy lock.

Titus watched him rez the lock, wondering how many bodies had disappeared through the door and into the maze of catacombs over the years. There had always been rumors about that sort of thing, especially in the old days. Titus did not doubt the stories and legends associated with them. He was certain that at various times, all of the Guilds had found the endless, largely uncharted alien tunnels convenient dumping grounds. Once a body disappeared into an unexplored section of the ancient underground maze, it was unlikely ever to be found.

The heavy door swung open on near-silent hinges, revealing a scene illuminated in the acid-green glow of alien energy. Titus found himself looking through a jagged opening in a green quartz wall. Beyond was another staircase. The steps, like the endless maze of tunnels and chambers beyond, were constructed of green quartz. They had been designed for feet that were not quite human.

The green quartz that the aliens had used to build everything from urns and vases to the most ethereal aboveground spires and towers was virtually indestructible. Certainly no tool yet fashioned by humans was able to make a dent in the stuff.

The experts did not know what forces had been powerful enough to create the rips and tears in the tunnel walls, but there was no shortage of them beneath all of the Dead City ruins. Some researchers speculated that great earthquakes had, over the years, created the openings. Others suspected that the holes in the walls had been fashioned by the aliens themselves—possibly criminals, rebels, or others who had found the openings useful and who'd had access to the powerful tools that had been used to construct the catacombs.

Over the years the main entrances to the vast underground realm had been excavated by licensed, authorized explorers and researchers. The Guilds controlled access, because they were the only ones who could provide protection from the energy ghosts that drifted at random through the tunnels.

But ever since the arrival of the human colonists, uncharted holes in the walls had been exploited by a wide assortment of people who, for one reason or another, had a reason to go underground without professional protection. Licensed and unlicensed small-time antiquities collectors, entrepreneurs engaged in the manufacture and distribution of illegal substances, criminals fleeing the law, and risk-takers attracted to the adventure of unauthorized exploration all made use of the openings.

A short distance into the glowing green tunnel, Landry came to a halt and looked back at Titus.

"Will this do?" he asked.

"Yes," Titus said. "This will do nicely." He withdrew the ruby amber artifact from his pocket and smiled at Miss Stowe. "This is what I intend to demonstrate."

She glanced at it without much interest. "It's not made out of green quartz. It looks like red plastic."

"Believe me when I tell you that this is no human-made plastic."

He focused on her psi patterns, rezzing energy through the ruby amber. He possessed a great deal of natural talent, enough to read her psi waves and even exert a limited and very temporary influence over them. With the aid of the ruby amber, however, his own power was enhanced to an astonishing degree.

Working swiftly, he pulsed psi through the device, dampening and neutralizing the woman's own paranormal wave pattern. Her eyes widened slightly in shock. She shook her head once and started to step back, as though to flee.

Then she froze, an expression of total blankness on her beautiful features. She stood, unmoving, staring blindly into the middle distance.

Landry frowned. "What the hell did you do to her?"

"I put her into an instant trance by temporarily neutralizing her psi rhythms."

"Huh."

Landry walked slowly around the blonde. He paused behind her and clapped his hands very suddenly. The woman did not flinch. He continued walking until he was back in front of her. He waved one hand before her eyes. She did not blink. There was no sign that she was aware of him.

"Okay, so you can put her into a trance," he said. "What good is that?"

"This is not just any trance," Titus said, assuming a lecturing tone. "With the aid of this relic I have placed her in what is essentially a blank dreamscape."

"She's dreaming?"

"Not yet. She is prepared to dream, however."

"Explain," Landry ordered.

"As you may or may not know, scientific research has confirmed that the dreaming state is the only state in which our psychic senses interact freely with our other five senses without distinction. When we dream, our natural ability to distinguish between the normal and the paranormal disappears."

"So?"

"Most people have had the experience of going to bed with a problem on their minds and awakening the next morning with a solution or at least a new way of approaching the problem. They will tell you that the answer came to them in their dreams. They are correct. During the dreaming state the mind is free to work on the problem with both psi and normal senses in a unique and extremely creative manner that cannot be duplicated in the waking state."

"Skip the academic crap. Get to the point."

Titus suppressed a sigh. It was extremely irritating to be

forced to work with an individual of such limited intellect and education, but he had no choice.

"As I said," he continued, striving for patience, "the dream state provides a very creative environment, but there is a downside."

"What's that?"

"There is a reason why, in the waking state, our normal and paranormal senses are distinct and separate, so much so that many people unknowingly suppress their psychic side altogether." He hurried now. It was obvious that Landry was losing patience. "That is because the dream state is extremely hazardous from a pragmatic point of view."

"Got it." Landry snapped his fingers. "If we went around in a dream state all the time, we wouldn't know if the car coming at us in the intersection was real or just a dream construct."

"Exactly."

Landry was smarter than he appeared, Titus thought. It would be a good idea to keep that in mind.

Landry surveyed the blonde. "All right, you've got her in a waking dream state. Now what?"

"As I said, in this condition she is not able to distinguish between dream and reality. With the aid of this relic I can ensure that when I bring her out of the trance she will believe that everything that has happened during the past few minutes was nothing but a dream."

"You mean she won't remember our conversation?"

"No more than she would any other dream." Titus spread his hands wide. "And what she does recall she will dismiss as only a dream."

"This is getting interesting," Landry said. "But I'm not sure I've got a lot of use for that device."

Titus cleared his throat. "Perhaps I should mention another application."

"What's that?"

"In the dream state many of her natural defenses are down."

"Meaning?"

"Meaning that if you ask her a question, she will give you a completely honest answer. This is all a dream to her. In the dream state one does not lie. Go ahead, ask her something you think she would likely conceal if she were awake."

Landry laughed harshly. "How old are you?"

"Thirty-six," Miss Stowe said. She spoke in a monotone.

Landry frowned. "She told me she was twenty-eight. She sure as hell looks twenty-eight. Must have had some work done."

"Why don't you try something a little more complicated?" Titus suggested dryly.

"She was Senator Rathmorten's mistress for a while," Landry said. "I wonder if she knows what really happened to his wife. There were rumors that he killed her, but they evaporated quickly. There was no proof, and he was a senator, so he would have been able to quash the investigation."

"Why don't you ask Miss Stowe what she knows?"

Landry looked at her. "Do you know how Elizabeth Rathmorten died?"

"Rath murdered her," Miss Stowe said.

"Shit," Landry whispered, fascinated. "How do you know that?"

"I was there that night," Miss Stowe replied in the same uninflected voice. "His wife had gone out earlier. The senator and I had sex in his office. I left the mansion but returned a few minutes later through the side entrance because I had forgotten my earrings. When I got back upstairs to his office, I heard his wife's voice. She had come home sooner than expected. There was an argument. I was afraid they would hear me, so I hid in a hall closet."

Landry glanced back over his shoulder at Titus. "This is fucking amazing."

"I'm glad you think so," Titus murmured. Holding the focus with the ruby amber for this long a period of time was exhausting, but he dared not show any weakness to Landry.

Miss Stowe continued speaking. "I heard sounds of a struggle. And then there was nothing but silence. When Rath came out of his office he was carrying his wife in his arms. I could see that her head was covered in blood. He took her out of the house and drove off with her."

Miss Stowe stopped.

"They found Elizabeth Rathmorten's body in the alley behind an apartment building," Landry said to Titus. "It looked like she had jumped. Shit, with information like this, I'll have Rathmorten in the palm of my hand."

"Have you seen enough?" Titus asked.

"Yeah, sure, let's get out of here."

"One more thing." Titus focused on Miss Stowe. "You have had an unpleasant dream, but that is all it is, a dream. You do not want to remember it because every time you try, you will get a pounding headache. You are not feeling well. You want to go straight home and go to sleep."

He stopped pulsing psi through the relic. Miss Stowe blinked several times, looking confused. Then she collected herself and turned to Landry.

"I'm sorry," she said, her hand on her stomach, "but I'm feeling a little ill. I think I should go home."

"Sure," Landry said. "I'll drive you back to your apartment myself."

BENSON WATCHED KENNINGTON USE THE RELIC ONE LAST time just before the woman got out of the car, ensuring that the events of the past hour would be nothing but a dream to her.

He sat behind the wheel of the big Oscillator 600 and waited until she disappeared through the door of her apartment building. Then he looked in the rearview mirror.

Titus Kennington, sitting in the backseat, looked a little weary but smugly satisfied.

The son of a bitch thinks he's playing me.

"I'm impressed," Benson said. "You've got a deal."

"Excellent." Kennington smiled his patronizing smile. "I'm delighted to hear that, Mr. Landry. It will prove profitable for both of us."

Once he got his hands on the other relic, Benson thought, he sure as hell wasn't going to turn it over to Titus Kennington. Instead, he would get rid of the doctor and take possession of both relics.

Whatever Kennington's form of psi talent was, it was a safe bet that it was not unique. There would be others who could control the relic, others who, in turn, he could control. With the resources of the Guild behind him, he could find the talent he required to take advantage of the ruby relics.

"I suggest we discuss the problem of Miss Ingram and her new bodyguard," Kennington said.

Chapter 20

CELINDA WIPED THE STEAM OFF THE BATHROOM MIRROR
with a washcloth and surveyed her image. She didn't look
any different, she decided. Okay, maybe she was a little
flushed, but that could be attributed to the recent shower.
Surely no one in her family would guess this morning that
she'd spent a goodly portion of the night engaged in hot
sex with her bodyguard.

She looked at Araminta, who was perched on the counter,
grooming herself.

"This is the bride's day," Celinda said. "Everyone will
be focused on Rachel. I'm just the maid of honor. No one
will give me a second glance."

Araminta stopped fussing with her gray fur and batted
her blue eyes.

"Well, it's not as if you spent the night entirely alone,
either, missy."

She scooped up Araminta and went back into the main
room to finish dressing. The door to Davis's room was still
partially ajar. She could hear the shower running. She stood

still for a moment, remembering the night with mixed emotions.

I like to sleep alone. Don't take it personally.

How else could a woman take that kind of comment? she wondered.

She dressed in the black trousers and the dark green top with the three-quarter-length sleeves that she had brought along to wear to breakfast. She heard Davis's shower go off while she was putting on her lipstick.

A knock sounded on the door of her room.

"That'll be room service with the eggs and toast I ordered for Araminta and Max," she called through the connecting door. "I'll get it."

She crossed the room, Araminta on her shoulder, and opened the door.

Waves of dark, twisted psi energy slammed across her senses, making her recoil backward so quickly that she stumbled and almost fell.

Benson Landry, dressed in traditional ghost-hunter khaki and leather, a knife on his hip, lounged in the opening.

"Hello, Celinda," he said, giving her his trademark hunter's smile, the one he thought was so incredibly sexy. "Heard you were in town for a family wedding. Thought I'd drop by and see how you were doing. Been a while."

She heard a soft rumble in her ear. Araminta was growling. Only her daylight eyes were showing, however. She had not gone into full predatory mode, but she was clearly on the edge.

"What do you want?" Celinda asked, astonished that she was able to keep her tone even. Her heart was pounding in her chest, and adrenaline was snapping through her.

"I told you," Landry said, reptilian eyes gleaming. "Just wanted to see how you were getting on."

"You're here for some reason. What is it?"

"Why don't you invite me in, and we'll talk?"

"We have nothing to say to each other. I kept my part of the bargain. Leave me alone."

"Yeah, well, I'm in a mood to change the terms of our deal." He raised his brows at the sight of Araminta on her shoulder. "What is that thing? Looks like something a cat coughed up." He chuckled.

Davis materialized beside Celinda. He had put on a pair of trousers, but he was still nude from the waist up. Max was perched on his shoulder.

"Get out of here, Landry," he said, his voice gravedigger soft.

Landry narrowed his eyes. "Who the hell are you?"

"Davis Oakes. You might want to write that down. We'll be meeting again one of these days. But this isn't a good time. Got a wedding to attend."

The rising tide of male hormones was palpable. Celinda's anxiety level went up several more notches. The last thing they needed was a bad scene with a powerful member of the local Guild.

"Davis is a friend of mine," she said quickly. "We're just here for my sister's wedding. We're going back to Cadence tonight."

"Looks like a real close friend, all right," Landry said, amused. "He know about us, honey?"

"I know all about you and Celinda," Davis assured him in that same frighteningly soft tone. "Don't worry; one of these days I'll get back to you on that. But like I said, this isn't the time or place."

Landry was momentarily nonplussed. Celinda knew that he was not accustomed to defiance of any kind. It took him a few seconds to process Davis's words.

"What the hell are you talking about?" he finally got out. "Are you threatening me, Oakes?"

"No," Davis said, "I don't do threats. That was more like an IOU. I always make good on those."

Celinda could hardly breathe now. There was going to be a fight. She could see it coming like a freight train bearing down on her. There would be a dreadful scene. Hotel security would be summoned. Her family would be embarrassed. Rachel would be upset on her wedding day. There was no telling how the Santanas would react, but having one of the wedding guests engage in a fight with a leading member of the local Guild was not going to go down well, that was for sure. No one here in Frequency wanted to be on the wrong side of a Guild Council member.

"Stop it," she gasped. "Both of you. There's no need for this."

Predictably, Landry paid no attention. "My information says you're a cheap PI who was hired to keep an eye on Celinda because she's got something that belongs to the Cadence Guild."

"Your information is wrong on one significant point," Davis said.

"Yeah? What's that?"

"I'm not cheap."

Landry snorted. "Not a very good PI, either, by the looks of it. Not if you had to resort to screwing Celinda to get the location of the relic out of her. Boring work, isn't it? One night was more than enough for me."

Something very dangerous appeared in Davis's eyes. Lethal psi energy pulsed.

Celinda slipped closer to outright panic. She had to distract both men.

"You know about the relic?" she said to Landry.

"Word travels fast in my circles." He shrugged. "Imagine my surprise, though, when I heard you were the one who has it. Small world, huh?"

"But I don't know where it is," she said. "That's the truth. Believe me, if I had it, I'd turn it over to the Cadence Guild."

"Honey, you're in Frequency now. That means you'll turn it over to me."

"I just told you, I don't have it," she said.

"You heard her," Davis said.

Landry narrowed his snake eyes. "Whoever hired you sure as hell thinks that she knows where it is. That's good enough for me."

"Mercer Wyatt hired me," Davis said. "And he's going to be pissed if you get in my way."

"Screw Wyatt. He's an old man. He may still be giving the orders in Cadence, but he doesn't give them here. This is my town. That means I give the orders."

"I'll have Wyatt confirm that with Harold Taylor," Davis said. He took hold of Celinda's elbow, pulled her back, and started to close the door. "Meanwhile, we've got a wedding to celebrate. Get lost, Landry."

Celinda sensed the change in the vibrations of the tangled spiderweb that was Benson Landry's whacked-out psi energy pattern. She knew at once that somewhere in his mind a trip wire had just been triggered. A monstrous spider was crawling up from the abyss.

"Watch out," she said, edging back instinctively.

But the danger came from behind. Acid green light flared in the room. She whirled around, shocked, and saw a nasty energy ghost coalesce. The core of the fiery ball was fierce and unstable, just like the man who had summoned it.

"I'm going to teach you a lesson, Oakes," Landry said. "You're not going to a wedding today; you're going to a hospital."

Frustration and rage flashed through Celinda. The urge to leap at Landry and go for his eyes with her fingernails was almost overwhelming. How dare he threaten the people she loved?

The people she loved? She had just included Davis on that list.

But there was no time to ponder the implications of that impulsive thought. The rumble in her ear was getting louder. There was another, echoing growl from Max.

With a jolt Celinda realized that both dust bunnies were now at full alert. Their normally fluffy fur was sleeked flat against their small bodies, revealing all six legs and a lot of very sharp teeth. Even more disconcerting was the appearance of their second sets of eyes. The amber ones they used for hunting were wide open, glowing with a predatory light.

It dawned on her that if they attacked Landry, there was no telling what he might do to retaliate. Max and Araminta could certainly inflict some painful wounds, but they were too small to do anything more than draw blood. That would only inflame Landry all the more.

She clutched at Araminta.

"No," she whispered. "Please don't."

"Hold on to her," Davis said quietly. He took Max down from his shoulder and gripped him in one hand. "We don't want them getting singed."

Celinda tucked Araminta safely into the crook of her arm. Araminta resisted, straining to get free.

The green ghost was moving now, closing in on Davis as Landry used his psi energy to manipulate it.

There was no question but that Landry was a powerful para-rez talent. Celinda knew that even a light brush with the flaring radiation at the outer edges of the ball of alien energy would be sufficient to knock a human being unconscious for hours. Sustained contact for more than a few seconds would leave a severe psychic burn.

"This is what happens to cheap PIs who don't know enough to back off when they should," Landry said, vicious eyes alight with an unwholesome excitement. "Time you understood that I'm the boss here in Frequency."

A distraction was needed, Celinda thought. And the only one at hand was Araminta. She started to lower the dust bunny to the floor. Araminta was wriggling eagerly, anxious to be set free. Celinda was sure that she would head straight for Landry's ankle.

Davis studied the ghost as though it were a particularly bad piece of post–Era of Discord art. "You know, Landry, I really don't have time for this today. I keep telling you, I've got a wedding to attend."

All Celinda saw was a faint silvery shimmer in the air. It

was as if she were suddenly viewing Landry's energy ghost through an antique mirror.

The UDEM flared once more, wildly, and then winked out of existence.

Hurriedly she tightened her grip on Araminta, securing her again.

"Some other time," Celinda whispered soothingly.

She looked at where the ghost had been. There was no sign of it. She had witnessed Davis's unusual talent the night before last when he had de-rezzed the twin ghosts. Nevertheless, she was a little awed by what he had just done. No one de-rezzed a Benson Landry ghost.

Her reaction was nothing compared to Landry's. It was clear from his expression that he was stunned. He was also furious.

The dark spiderweb of psi emanating from him quivered dangerously, but the spider had paused. In that instant of crystalline tension she realized that the only thing preventing Landry from attacking Davis physically was fear. It was the one force strong enough to stop a true para-sociopath from doing whatever he pleased. Landry had enough control left to realize that he might not survive the outcome of a showdown.

It was her brother, Walker, who shattered the unnatural silence. He came up behind Landry in the hall, anger blazing across his face.

"What the hell is going on here?" he demanded. "What are you doing in my sister's room, Landry?"

"He is not in my room," Celinda said quietly. "If you will notice he is standing in the hall."

Landry swung around, features set in savage, frustrated fury. Without a word he strode swiftly away, heading for the elevators.

Walker looked from Celinda to Davis and back again. "What was that bastard doing here?"

Celinda pulled herself together. "Nothing. He heard I was in town, that's all. Came by to say hello."

"The hell he did," Davis interrupted mildly. "He came here to threaten your sister."

"Davis." Celinda glared, appalled. "Please shut up. This is none of your business."

"It is now," he said.

"I trusted you," she wailed.

"I know." His expression softened a little. "And you're going to have to trust me again."

Walker frowned. "Someone want to tell me what's going on?"

"Sure," Davis said. "Come on in."

Walker stepped warily through the doorway, still uncertain.

"Oh, no, you don't," Celinda said to Davis. "He's my brother. It's my family that's at risk here. You have no right to interfere."

"You've done your best," Davis said. He closed the door behind Walker. "But the bottom line is that you can't protect your family from the likes of Benson Landry. The only way to stop a guy like that is to kill him."

"I was getting around to that, damn it," she shouted. "Now, you've gone and ruined everything."

Chapter 21

❧

DAVIS WATCHED THE EXPRESSION ON HER FACE AS SHE RE-
alized what she had just said. Suddenly he understood. A mix
of soaring admiration for her reckless daring collided with
a mind-bending fear of what could have been the outcome.

"Should have figured as much," he said. "That explains
a few things."

"Celinda?" Walker was bewildered. "Are you saying that
you were going to try to kill Benson Landry? Holy shit.
Have you gone crazy over there in Cadence?"

"Damn, damn, damn." She walked to the bed and sank
down on it.

Araminta, fully fluffed again, muttered in a concerned
way. Celinda set her free. The dust bunny drifted up onto
her shoulder.

"I had a plan." Celinda stared at the closed door, her
hands small fists in her lap. "I know his weakness, you see.
I was going to try to use it against him."

"Will one of you please tell me what the hell is going on
here?" Walker demanded.

"I will," Davis said. He walked to the window and stood looking out over the Quarter. He was still trying to get his pulse rate back down to somewhere near normal. *She had planned to murder Landry.* "Four months ago Benson Landry drugged your sister and set her up for the tabloids in order to destroy her business after she refused to take him on as a client."

"Son of a bitch," Walker said tightly.

Davis turned around. "But that wasn't enough for him. He also threatened to ruin her whole family if she went to the police. Celinda tried to protect all of you by keeping silent and by moving away from Frequency."

"I *knew* it." Walker rounded on Celinda. "I knew you couldn't possibly have fallen for that bastard. We all knew it. Why did he show up here this morning? To threaten you again?"

"It's complicated," Celinda said. Her jaw was rigid.

Davis crossed his arms and leaned one shoulder against the wall. "Your sister happened to purchase an alien relic that had been stolen from the Cadence Guild vault. I tracked her down and offered to buy it back. But Araminta ran off with it and hid it before we could make the exchange. Someone else back in Cadence is also looking for the artifact. Somehow Benson Landry found out about it, too. That's why he came here this morning."

"What a mess." Walker shoved his fingers through his hair. He peered more closely at Davis. "You're not really Celinda's date for the wedding, then, are you?"

"No, he isn't," Celinda said wearily. "He's my bodyguard."

Davis looked at Walker. "She's half right. I'm also her date for the wedding. It's called multitasking."

"Mom told me this morning that she and Dad thought things looked serious between you two," Walker said.

Celinda's head came up at that. "Good grief, what made her come to that conclusion?"

Walker spread his hands. "Something about the conversation that took place last night when they invited the two of you to have a drink with them, I think."

Celinda blinked. "But we argued in front of them. It was embarrassing."

Walker nodded. "Right. Mom said there weren't many people who could have dragged you into an embarrassing quarrel in a public place. She said that meant that whatever you and Davis had going must be serious."

"I don't believe this." Celinda was clearly flummoxed. "We had a stupid quarrel in a bar, and they assumed our relationship was *serious*? That's ridiculous."

"What's ridiculous," Walker said evenly, "is that you're evidently planning to get rid of Benson Landry all by yourself."

Celinda reached up to touch Araminta. "Davis is right. There's no other way to stop a man like that. Landry's not right inside. The proper parapsych term is para-sociopath, I think. No conscience. He sees everyone else as a form of prey. He enjoys controlling and manipulating others with fear. He feeds on it, in a way."

Walker shuddered. "No wonder you didn't want him for a client. In hindsight, we're probably damn lucky he didn't hurt you physically or even kill you in retaliation." He stopped, fresh alarm making him tense. "He didn't do anything to you when he drugged you, did he? I swear, if he did, I'll kill him myself, now. This morning."

"No," Celinda said quickly. "He didn't touch me, not in the way you mean."

Walker relaxed fractionally. "You've spent the past four months trying to figure out how to get rid of him? Without ever discussing the problem with your family?"

"She was trying to protect you," Davis said. "She wanted to do the job by herself in case things didn't go right. She didn't want the rest of you accused of murdering a high-ranking Guild official."

"Things are dicey enough as it is," Celinda explained.

"What was this big plan of yours?" Davis asked.

She exhaled deeply. "It was based on the assumption that a man like Landry must have made some enemies in his climb to the top. I figured I had a pretty good built-in alibi. After all this time, I didn't think that the Frequency police or the Frequency Guild Council would look twice at a matchmaker who'd had a brief affair with Landry and then moved to Cadence City."

"Go on," he said, morbidly fascinated.

"Two months ago I managed to purchase a mag-rez gun."

"Which explains the one I found under your bed."

Her eyes widened. "You know about my gun?"

He didn't have to answer because Walker was staring at her with the kind of shock only an older brother could comprehend.

"Damn, Celinda," Walker said. "Everyone knows it's illegal for everyone except cops to carry mag-rezes."

She made a vague gesture with one hand. "Turns out it's not that difficult to buy one on the streets in Cadence. It took me a while to figure out how it's done, but in the end all I needed was a lot of cash. The little man who sold it to me showed me how to fire it and included a couple of spare clips in the bargain."

"I don't believe this," Walker said. "My sweet, naive little matchmaker sister bought a hot mag-rez."

"In my spare time I've been driving out into the countryside to practice," Celinda said. "I'm getting quite good."

"Oh, jeez." Walker massaged the back of his neck as though he might be getting a headache. "You were just going to walk up to Benson Landry and shoot him?"

"Not exactly." Celinda looked affronted. "I planned to make it look like he'd been hit by one of his many enemies. I've been studying him for the past four months, charting his movements. I decided it would be impossible to get onto the grounds of his estate. Too much security."

Davis raised his eyes to the ceiling. "Praise be, some common sense, at last."

"The same was true of his office in the Guild compound," she continued, ignoring him. "But he's involved with a lot of civic and political stuff. He attends receptions and fund-raisers every week, and he spends a lot of time at his club. He doesn't surround himself with security when he goes to places like that. It's bad for his image."

"You mean he doesn't use any obvious security," Davis said.

She looked at him, frowning. "You saw him a few minutes ago. He didn't have any bodyguards with him."

"Got a hunch they were waiting for him down in the lobby." Davis gave that some more thought. "My guess is he didn't bring any up here because he believed that he was going to be talking to you alone about the relic. Evidently he didn't want anyone, not even his security people, to hear that conversation. Interesting."

Walker began to pace the small space. "This is a hell of a situation. One thing's for sure, we can't tell Mom and Dad about it today. They'd be frantic. And Rachel's day would be ruined if she found out what was going on."

"Don't you think I know that?" Celinda got to her feet and straightened her shoulders. "That is precisely why you will both keep quiet about this whole thing. Understood? If either one of you upsets anyone else in the family, I will never forgive you."

"Okay," Walker said, raising a hand, palm out. "I agree that keeping quiet about this is for the best. At least for to-day."

Celinda switched her steely gaze to Davis. "Will you give me your word you won't say anything more about this today?"

He contemplated the possibilities and then inclined his head. "Assuming no other factors in the equation are al-tered, I'll keep quiet. I think we've got a better chance of handling this from Cadence, anyway."

Celinda regarded him with deep suspicion. "Factors?"

"What do you mean about dealing with this from Ca-dence?" Walker asked, watching him closely.

"Benson Landry thinks Mercer Wyatt is an old man who's lost his edge," Davis said. "He's wrong." He thought about how Wyatt would react when he learned that Landry was trying to steal the missing relic. "Probably dead wrong."

Chapter 22

"THIS IS THE HAPPIEST DAY OF MY LIFE," RACHEL SAID.

Celinda smiled at her in the mirror. "You look so beautiful. When you walked down the aisle I could tell that Josh couldn't believe his eyes."

They were alone in the mirrored dressing room. Rachel was still in her wedding gown. Yards of white satin and gossamer netting billowed and drifted around her. She was radiant.

The formal Covenant Marriage ceremony, replete with all the ancient vows and customs that the First Generation colonists had brought with them from Earth, had lasted nearly an hour. Now the reception was in full swing in the hotel ballroom. Celinda could hear the muffled strains of the music.

"You're the one who made it all possible." Rachel turned and hugged her tightly. "I don't know how to thank you."

"I'm sure that you and Josh would have found each other without me." Celinda hugged her back. "I speeded up the process a little, that's all."

"I don't believe that for one moment. You made it happen,

and we will always be grateful." Rachel stepped back. "We both owe you so much. Now, it's your turn. Mom says that things look serious between you and Davis Oakes. I'm so glad you've found someone at last."

"Slight misunderstanding, I'm afraid." Celinda made a face. "Davis and I got into an embarrassing little argument in the bar last night, and suddenly Mom decided we were meant for each other."

"Don't discount her intuition. You know it's way above average."

"Trust me when I tell you that Davis and I aren't going to be sending out wedding invitations any time in the near future." She hesitated. "Davis is not keen on the institution of Covenant Marriage."

"You could start with a Marriage of Convenience. Let him get used to the concept."

"You know how I feel about MCs. Not interested."

"I know," Rachel said. "MCs are against your rules. But if Davis isn't ready for a full Covenant Marriage, you might want to consider one."

"Why are we talking about Davis and me?" Celinda rezzed up a bright smile. "This is your day. We're supposed to be getting you changed into your traveling clothes. Got a feeling Josh has had enough of the formalities. He's ready to start the honeymoon."

She put her hands on Rachel's shoulders and turned her firmly around to face the mirror. Then she reached up and carefully unpinned the wedding veil.

"You love him, don't you?" Rachel said, watching her in the mirror.

Rachel had inherited their mother's keen intuition. Everyone in the family knew it.

Celinda went still, the pearl-studded veil in her hands. She met her sister's eyes. "I've only known him for a couple of days."

Rachel smiled. "I knew I wanted Josh the moment I met him. He says he felt the same way about me."

"Wanting and loving are not always connected."

Rachel wrinkled her nose. "You're quoting your own rules again. Know what I think?"

"What?"

"I think you should burn your little book. It's one thing to exercise common sense and discretion. It's another thing to have so many rules that you end up missing out on life altogether."

Celinda said nothing. Just looked at her in the mirror.

Rachel's eyes widened, first in comprehension and then with delight.

She started to grin. "You've already thrown out a few of those stupid rules, haven't you? Which ones?"

Celinda sighed. "I started with the No One-Night Stands rule."

"Hmm. Has there been a second night?"

"No," Celinda said. "There hasn't. Not yet."

Rachel chuckled. "Something tells me there will be."

HALF AN HOUR LATER CELINDA STOOD WITH DAVIS, HER family, and the rest of the wedding guests at the front entrance of the hotel. They all watched Josh sweep Rachel through a hail of pink rose petals and tuck her into the front seat of a gleaming gray Coaster. He got behind the wheel, put the car in gear, and drove away.

There was a great deal of waving and cheering. Celinda realized that her eyes were damp with tears again. She was not alone. Both mothers, Great-Aunt Octavia, and most of the other women were dabbing at their eyes with handkerchiefs.

"I can't believe my little sister is actually married," Celinda whispered to Davis. "It feels almost unreal."

He smiled. "You're the one who matched them."

"I know. But this is my sister we're talking about. I mean, I remember when she went out on her first date, for heaven's sake. I knew he was all wrong for her and told her she was wasting her time."

"What did she say?"

"She said she knew he wasn't the guy she was going to marry, but she wanted to get in some practice so she'd be ready when the right man came along." Celinda smiled fondly, thinking about the past. "Rachel was always the more adventurous of the two of us."

"Could have fooled me." Davis took her arm and drew her back into the lobby. "Plotting the cold-blooded execution of the next boss of the Frequency Guild strikes me as fairly adventurous."

She looked around swiftly. "Good grief, Davis, keep your voice down."

"It's okay," he said, mouth curving faintly. "I like that in a woman."

She felt as if he'd picked her up and dropped her into a pool of glacier-melt water. Reality returned with an unpleasant jolt. Rachel's fairy-tale wedding was over. Now they had to go back to Cadence to face the problems of the missing relic and a sociopath Guild man.

"I didn't think of it as adventurous, you know," she said.

"Yeah? How did you think of it?"

She considered the question closely. "More like a necessity. Just something that had to be done in order to keep my family safe."

"Point taken," Davis said quietly. There was a world of understanding and approval in his eyes.

In the lobby, the wedding guests mingled, exchanging good-byes and offering more congratulations to the parents of the bride and groom. Those who were not spending the night at the hotel prepared to collect their cars and drive home.

Davis checked his watch. "Eight o'clock. Time for us to hit the road. If we leave now, we'll be back in Cadence before midnight."

Celinda saw her mother coming toward them. She had obviously overheard Davis's comment.

"Are you sure you want to make that long drive tonight?" she asked. "You're welcome to come back to the house with us. Or you can stay here at the hotel and go home tomorrow."

"I have to go in to work tomorrow morning, Mom," Celinda said quickly. "I'm still the new person at the agency, you know. I don't want my boss to think I'm unreliable."

"I understand, dear. Well, at least take some of the left-over hors d'oeuvres with you to eat on the road."

"Good idea," Newell said, coming up to join them. "I think I saw a lot of those little cheese and cucumber sandwiches left on the buffet table. Plenty of cookies, too. Hate to think of them being thrown away, given what I paid for 'em."

Walker sauntered over. "There are some crackers and chips left, too." He surveyed Celinda's pink gown and grinned. "I'll bet you never wear that dress again. You look like a big slice of the wedding cake."

Celinda raised her brows. "That might be amusing if it wasn't coming from a guy in a pink cummerbund."

"Shows how much you know," Walker said. "Pink is the new black for men this year."

Davis smiled and tightened his grip on Celinda's arm. "Let's go see what's left on the buffet table."

"I'll come with you," Walker said. "I want some more of those little cheese twist thingys."

"Help yourself to as much as you want," Newell said. "It's all nonrefundable."

They walked back through the lobby and along a wide, paneled hallway. The glittering ballroom was nearly empty. The only people inside were two uniformed members of the hotel staff, a man and a woman, who were starting to pick up the silver serving trays. The cleanup process had begun.

"We'd better hurry," Walker said. "They're starting to take the food away."

A scream rang out, so high and shrill, Celinda was amazed it didn't shatter the glass in the chandeliers. It emanated from the female member of the hotel staff.

"What are those *things*?" the woman shrieked. She dropped her tray and leaped back from the table. "There's one in the cake. *Oh my God*, there's another one in the champagne fountain."

The other staff member stared first at the cake and then at the fountain. "What the hell? They look like dust bunnies."

"I'll go get the manager," the woman yelped. "I don't get paid enough to deal with stuff like this."

She set out at a dead run, heading toward a set of swinging doors at the far end of the room.

Celinda got a sinking feeling in the pit of her stomach. She looked at the buffet table. "Uh-oh."

"Hang on," Walker said, pulling out a small flash-rez camera. "I want to get a picture of this. Too bad Rachel and Josh missed it."

On the buffet table Araminta was deep into what remained of the four-tiered pink and white wedding cake. She was nibbling on a pink icing rose. There was more pink and white icing matted on her fur.

Max was perched on the edge of the multilevel glass fountain that had been used to display and serve the pink champagne. He seemed to be wobbling a little. As Celinda watched in horror, he swayed back and forth and then went headfirst into the fountain bowl, splashing champagne everywhere. He started swimming.

"Little guy can't hold his liquor," Davis explained.

Chapter 23

"I GUESS ARAMINTA RAN OUT OF ROOM SERVICE FOOD,"
Celinda said. "I should have checked on her a couple of
hours ago to see if she needed more."

"Look on the bright side," Davis said. He kept his eyes
on the night-shrouded highway. "They didn't stage their
surgical strike on the buffet table until after the bride and
groom had left. No harm was done to the Great Pink Wedding. After a while you'll laugh about it."

"Araminta ruined that beautiful cake."

"It had already served its purpose."

"But Rachel wanted to keep the top tier as a souvenir.
The hotel staff was supposed to box it up and freeze it.
That's the tier Araminta went after first."

"Look, if you're that worried about it, we can pay to
have another cake made," he said soothingly. "Just that one
tier. The baker can box it up and freeze it, and it will be
waiting for your sister when she and Josh get back from
their honeymoon."

Celinda looked dubious. "It would be expensive."

"So what? We'll put it on the Guild's tab."

Out of the corner of his eye he saw her mouth twitch a little.

"The bill you plan to send to Mercer Wyatt when this is over is going to be very interesting," she said. "I assume you itemize?"

"Sure."

"I can see it now. One single-tier wedding cake decorated with pink roses and, oh, by the way, there's a para-sociopath member of the Frequency Guild Council after your relic."

"Wyatt's been around awhile. He takes these things in stride."

"You know him well enough to be sure of that?"

"I've worked for him before. He won't complain as long as I hand over the relic along with the bill."

Her wry little smile faded. She leaned her head against the back of the seat and appeared to sink into a state of deeper gloom. "I wonder what the odds of that happening are?"

"We'll get it back."

She turned her head to look at him, her face lit a pale gold by the amber lights of the dashboard. "You really think Wyatt will take care of Benson Landry?"

"Landry is ghost bait. He just doesn't know it yet."

She seemed to brighten a little at that.

Night lay heavily on the vast swath of lonely desert between Frequency and Cadence. Silver moonlight gave the landscape an eerie luminescence that was as mysterious and exotic as the glow of alien quartz. He could see one other vehicle in the rearview mirror. Occasionally they passed cars coming from the opposite direction. But mostly they had the road to themselves.

He liked being out here in the desert at night, he thought; he liked being alone with Celinda. And the dust bunnies, of course.

The departure from the hotel had been somewhat delayed due to Celinda's insistence on taking both dust bunnies upstairs to rinse them off in the bathroom sink. By the time Araminta and Max were clean and fluff-dried and the overnight bags, together with the infamous pink brides-maid's dress, had been packed into the trunk of the Phantom, it was close to nine o'clock. But he figured that if he pushed things a little, they would still be back in Cadence by midnight.

The two miscreants were napping. Araminta, stuffed with wedding cake, was stretched out on Celinda's lap, four eyes closed. Max was on his back on the narrow deck beneath the rear windshield. He was sound asleep, all six legs projecting straight up out of his fur. Whenever Davis checked the rearview mirror he could just make out the shapes of six small paws silhouetted against the headlights of the vehicle behind the Phantom.

Celinda looked back at Max, worried. "Do you think he'll suffer any ill effects from the champagne?"

"No. This isn't the first time he's gotten rezzed up on booze. He'll be fine. Dust bunny metabolism seems to be fairly efficient."

Celinda made a face. "I guess it was sort of funny when you think about it."

He laughed. "Glad your brother got the pictures. Twenty years from now, those are going to be everyone's favorite shots of the wedding."

The headlights of the Phantom picked up a faded billboard advertising one of the old roadside attractions they had passed on the trip to Frequency: Only Ten Miles to the Haunted Alien Ruins.

"Dad used to stop there sometimes when we were kids," Celinda said. "It broke up the long drive. Ever seen it?"

"No. I've explored some outpost ruins near Crystal City, though."

"This one doesn't even qualify as an outpost. It was probably more like a restroom stop for the aliens. Whatever artifacts were there originally were carted off years ago by ruin rats. But it was fun to visit."

She fell silent. Davis checked the rearview mirror again.

The lights of the following car were closer now. He could make out the distinctive grill of a powerful Oscillator 600.

The more traditional Guild men favored Oscillators.

As he watched, another big vehicle appeared behind the Oscillator.

An icy tingle of awareness disturbed the intimacy that he had been savoring for the past hundred and forty miles. Experimentally, he rezzed the accelerator.

The two vehicles behind the Phantom fell back for a few seconds. But a moment later they regained the lost ground and then some.

He fed a little more power to the Phantom's finely tuned engine. The car picked up more speed. The two sets of lights in the rearview mirror kept pace.

"Looks like we may have a problem," he said quietly.

"What's wrong?" Celinda said. She saw that he was watching the rearview mirror and turned in her seat to look back. "You're worried about that car behind us?"

"It's been following us since we left Frequency. Now there's a second car."

"What's so strange about that? This is the main highway to Cadence."

"I noticed the Oscillator a few miles outside of Frequency when the traffic thinned out. But it didn't close the distance between us until a few minutes ago. Now the second vehicle has and is moving in fast."

She drew a deep breath and let it out slowly. "You think it might be Landry, don't you?"

"More likely some of his men. I doubt that he'd want to risk being directly involved."

"In what?"

"Getting rid of me and grabbing you."

"I was afraid you were going to say that." She turned back around in her seat and watched the highway very steadily through the windshield. "But this snazzy car of yours can outrun them, right?"

"Sure. Problem is, I think this is probably going to be a pincer move. That's the way I'd set it up if I were Landry."

"I beg your pardon?"

"See the two vehicles coming toward us?"

"Yes."

"They just appeared a few minutes ago. Got a hunch they've been sitting out here in the desert, waiting for us."

She looked at the advancing headlights. "You mean they're trying to ambush us right here on a public highway?"

"I think that's the plan. It's not a bad one, either. Got to give Landry credit for strategy."

"I hate to ask this, but have we got one?"

"A plan?" He watched another faded billboard come up in the headlights: Last Chance to See the Haunted Alien Ruins. "We do now."

"What are we going to do?"

"What everyone does on a long road trip. We're going to visit a roadside attraction. Hang on."

He rezzed the brakes, cranked the wheel, and sent the Phantom into a screaming, smoking turn. They shot down a pitted and pocked dirt road toward the ruin site. The Phantom bounced and jolted violently. Celinda clutched Araminta with one hand and used her other hand to brace herself against the dash.

Max awoke with a start when he was jolted down off the rear deck. He disappeared from view for a few seconds. The next thing Davis knew, he had scrambled up onto the back of the driver's seat to take in the action.

Araminta wriggled free of Celinda's restraining hand and fluttered up behind her. Both dust bunnies suddenly looked very excited. Born hunters, he thought.

"We've got a couple of little adrenaline junkies with us," Celinda said, glancing at the bunnies.

"When you get right down to it, they're predators." Davis maneuvered to avoid a particularly deep crack in the pavement. "Goes with the territory."

The road was bad. The Phantom was catching a little air

at the top of some of the higher ruts. He had no choice but to decrease his speed somewhat.

Up ahead, maybe a couple of miles or more, he could just make out a faint green glow in the night.

"Looks like someone left the lights on for us," he said.

Celinda twisted around in her seat to look through the back window again. "Those four cars are all stopped on the highway. Maybe they won't try to follow us. No, wait, one of them is making the turn. Damn, they're all coming after us."

"Those vehicles are a lot heavier than the Phantom. With luck they'll have to slow down more than we will in order to deal with this road."

"We're headed for the old ruins?"

"Yes. Got a feeling the folks behind us are going to be armed with those illegal mag-rezes that evidently anyone with enough cash can buy on the streets these days. We've only got one between us. Bad odds."

"I should have brought mine."

"In hindsight that would have been a good idea, yes. Next time we go to a wedding, we'll have to remember to pack it."

She ignored that. "We're headed for the ruins so that we can use the quartz wall as a barricade, right?"

"No." Forced to slow down a little more, he reluctantly put the Phantom into a lower gear. "We're heading for the ruins because we need to get underground before the shooting starts."

"What good will that do?"

"Mag-rezes, like most high-tech gadgets that use magnetic resonating technology don't work very well underground. The heavy psi down below screws up their mechanisms. It makes the guns just as dangerous to whoever is rezzing the trigger as they are to the target. That's why ghost hunters don't carry them."

"Oh, right," she said. "Come to think of it, I believe the little guy who sold me my gun did say something about not trying to use it underground. He told me it might explode in my hand."

"Any chance that once we get inside the wall at the site you'll remember where the entrance to the catacombs is?"

"Yes." She kept her attention on the lethal parade of headlights behind the Phantom. "It's inside the tower. There's a staircase that seems to go down forever, and there are a lot of twists and turns in it. When you stand at the top, you can't see the bottom. Really spooky. I think that's why the attraction never made a lot of money for the two men who ran it."

"Too spooky?"

"No. Too many steps. Customers realized that once you got down to the bottom, you had to climb all the way back up in order to get out. It was a very long climb. I remember a lot of people taking one look at that staircase and then demanding their money back."

"Maybe we'll get lucky, and that's just what those guys back there will do," he said, going for a little positive thinking.

"We probably shouldn't count on that."

"No," he agreed, "probably shouldn't. I'm assuming that because it was once a tourist attraction, the stairwell and the adjacent tunnels are clear of illusion traps?"

"They certainly were when it was operating as an attraction," she said. "I can't see any reason why anyone would have reset a trap."

He thought about that. Only someone who possessed a special kind of psi talent—an ephemeral-energy para-resonator, otherwise known as a tangler—could de-rez or reset a trap. Neither he nor Celinda could deal with one.

"We'll have to take our chances," he said. "Not like we have a lot of choice here."

"I couldn't de-rez a trap," she said. "But I can detect them, which means we should be able to avoid any that we come across."

He thought about the night he had taken Mary Beth from the kidnappers. "I've got some ability to sense them, too. Between the two of us, we can do this."

Chapter 24

THE GLOW OF THE QUARTZ WALL THAT SURROUNDED THE ancient outpost grew brighter as they drew near. Davis was aware of the ambient psi energy leaking out of the ruins now. He knew that Celinda sensed it, too.

"Is your talent like that of other hunters?" she asked. "Does it get stronger when it's enhanced by alien psi?"

"Yes."

The wall was coming up fast now. He could see the remains of an old human-made parking lot. Recklessly he increased the speed of the Phantom again.

"They're falling back a little," Celinda assured him. "You're right, they can't take this road as fast as we can."

He concentrated, trying to anticipate problems.

"Did the people who ran the ruins as a concession put up a gate of any kind?" he asked.

"I remember a makeshift wooden gate that they opened for you after you bought the ticket."

"With luck it won't be locked."

"I doubt it. The place has been abandoned for years."

The Phantom slammed to a stop in the parking lot. A

badly weathered sign heralded the entrance: Welcome to the Haunted Alien Ruins. Beneath the sign a large wooden gate hung limply on its hinges.

"Gate's unlocked," Davis said. "One less thing to deal with." He killed the engine and the headlights. "Everybody out. Now."

Celinda already had her seat belt undone. She grabbed Araminta with one hand and opened the passenger-side door with the other.

Davis got out on the other side and stretched an arm back into the interior of the vehicle. Max immediately hopped down onto the offered perch and bounced up onto Davis's shoulder.

The four vehicles were still some distance away down the road, but they were closing fast. Headlights jumped and bounced in the night.

Davis yanked the mag-rez out of his ankle holster.

"Go," he ordered.

Celinda was already moving, running toward the entrance. Suddenly she ground to a halt.

"What?" Davis snapped

"I don't know. Something's wrong. Araminta is upset."

"This isn't the time to worry about her feelings. Move."

Celinda started running again. Davis saw the shadow on her shoulder tumble down to the ground.

"Oh, damn," Celinda wailed. "She's going back to the car. I can't leave her."

"She'll be fine. She can take care of herself."

"No, Davis, I think she wants something from the car."

Celinda rushed after Araminta.

Davis looked at the fast-approaching cars. "Damn."

But it was too late to stop Celinda. She had reached the Phantom. Araminta was on the ground beside the passenger door, jumping up and down and chattering wildly.

Celinda opened the door. Araminta disappeared inside. Celinda reached in after her.

"Come on, Celinda." For the first time Davis felt a tendril

of real panic. If Celinda would not obey, they were doomed. He started back for her. "Get over here. *Now*."

She had already extricated herself from the car. She whirled and ran toward him. He saw that she had her over-sized tote in one hand. Araminta was on her shoulder, seemingly content.

They ran, flat-out, toward the entrance.

"She wouldn't come without the tote," Celinda explained, breathless.

They raced through the opening created by the sagging gate. The interior of the walled compound was illuminated by the glowing quartz that surrounded it. A handful of ancient spires and domed structures loomed, eternally alien and mysterious in their fantastical, ethereal design.

Old, hand-painted, human-made signs loomed over tumbledown concession stands.

Snacks and Sodas.

Get Your Souvenir Photo Here.

It was the last sign that caught his eye. It was posted outside the entrance to an airy, radiant, green quartz spire.

Prepare to Descend into the Underworld.

"That's where the staircase is," Celinda said.

Brakes and tires squealed. He glanced back over his shoulder. The first of the four cars was just pulling into the parking lot. The other three were right behind it.

Celinda dashed through the vaulted entrance of the ruin. He followed.

One look at the glowing quartz staircase, and he understood why the old attraction had lost a few potential customers. The steps plunged downward, twisting and turning in a nightmarish version of a spiral staircase that was vaguely disorienting to human senses.

There was no banister. None of the staircases in the catacombs had been outfitted with them. Evidently the long-vanished aliens hadn't worried about safety violations or liability insurance problems.

Luckily, in this instance, the sides of the stairwell were

close enough to touch. Celinda flattened one palm against the quartz wall on her right and braced herself as she rushed down the strangely twisted steps. He did the same.

The intense paranormal energy that was always present in the catacombs hit his senses in a rush. The stuff had a mildly exhilarating effect on anyone who possessed even an average level of psi ability. For those like Celinda and himself with strong parapsych profiles, the effect was even more intoxicating.

He saw Celinda look up over her shoulder toward the entrance of the stairwell. He did the same. There was no noise from above now. That wasn't surprising. The energy in the quartz walls had a dampening effect on sound.

"I don't see anyone following us yet," Celinda said.

"Keep moving," he ordered.

She plunged down another twist in the stairwell and disappeared from sight.

He paused for an instant before following her and glanced up toward the entrance again. A figure loomed in the opening. As he watched, another man joined the first. They started down.

He rounded the next bend in the stairwell. When he looked back this time, he could no longer see the entrance or the men following them. Below him, Celinda was almost at the foot of the stairs.

He saw her stumble about three steps before the bottom. She managed to catch her balance by reaching out for both sides of the stairwell, but the action caused her to lose her grip on the tote.

The large bag sailed to the foot of the steps ahead of her, spilling its contents. Two clear plastic boxes containing leftover wedding cake and crackers topped with pink cream cheese tumbled out onto the quartz floor. The food was followed by a leather wallet, a package of tissues, a variety of feminine toiletries, including a brush and lipstick, a small note pad, a pen, and a pair of sunglasses.

"Oh, damn," Celinda said.

She bent down and frantically began scooping up the fallen items.

"Forget it," Davis said, reaching the last step. "We don't have time."

"But Araminta—"

"She either stays behind with the tote or she comes with us. Her choice. This isn't negotiable, Celinda."

Mercifully, she did not argue this time. She started to straighten. Then she froze.

"Davis."

"What?"

She scooped up one of the objects that had fallen out of the tote. It was a familiar chunk of what looked like crimson plastic.

"Son of a bitch," he said softly. "The relic."

Chapter 25

"NO WONDER ARAMINTA WASN'T CONCERNED ABOUT leaving it behind in Cadence," Celinda said. "She must have hidden it inside my tote before we left for Frequency. That's why she wouldn't let me leave the tote in the car a few minutes ago."

"Let me have it." Davis reached for it.

Araminta went wild, just as she had last time, bouncing up and down on Celinda's shoulder and chortling fiercely.

"I think I'd better hang on to it," Celinda said. "We don't want Araminta racing off with this thing again. Once was enough."

Davis studied Araminta, who looked adamant. "I think you're right. Okay, let's get going."

Celinda looked around. Seven glowing tunnels, each marked with a high, vaulted entrance adorned with cryptic engravings, radiated away from the round chamber at the bottom of the staircase.

"Which way?" she said.

Davis indicated a tunnel that opened up behind the stairwell. "That one. Those guys will come out of the stairwell facing in this direction. I'll be behind them. It will give me a small element of surprise."

She turned back to him, dismayed. "I thought the plan was to hide in the tunnels until they leave."

"They're ghost hunters," Davis said. "Have to assume they've got the new generation of amber-rez locators that will enable them to pick up any signals from tuned amber, whether or not they have the frequency. You and I are both carrying amber, and we can't risk discarding it. If we got out of sight of that staircase, we might never find it again."

She didn't argue. The legends of people who lost their tuned amber and ended up wandering in the green maze until they died of thirst or went mad were familiar to everyone. To be without tuned amber underground was to be doomed.

Gripping the relic, she moved briskly ahead of him into the tunnel he indicated.

"How do you intend to deal with those men?" she asked.

"Carefully."

"One against lord only knows how many doesn't strike me as good odds. You need help, Davis."

"I've got Max."

"You've also got me and Araminta."

He looked thoughtfully at Araminta. "She might be useful, especially if she thinks she's protecting you."

"Hey, I can be useful, too," she said tightly.

"You can be useful by staying out of sight until this is over."

She was suddenly furious and frustrated. He was right. What did she know about fighting a band of thugs?

He brought his mouth very close to her ear. "There isn't any time left. I can hear them on the stairs. Stay here and swear to me you won't panic, no matter what you think you see."

He did not wait for her to respond to that strange order. Releasing her, he went toward the vaulted entrance with Max on his shoulder. There he stopped, flattening himself against the wall.

She realized that he was still holding the mag-rez gun, but it was reversed in his hand.

She could hear voices and heavy boots on the stairs.

"Put the mag-rez away, you damn idiot," one of the hunters said angrily. "We're underground now. You're more likely to kill yourself or one of us than you are to nail Oakes."

"Remember, whatever happens, we need the woman alive," a second man growled. "If she goes down, Landry will be furious."

"She won't be a problem," the first man said. "Oakes is the only one we need to worry about. You heard Landry, he's no ordinary hunter, but he is some kind of nonstandard freak who can de-rez a ghost without using ghost heat."

"He may be a freak," a third man observed coolly, "but there are five of us. No way he can take down five ghosts at a time. No one can do that, not without melting amber. Once his amber is shot, he's ghost bait."

So it was five against one, Celinda thought. It was definitely not going to be a fair fight. Davis needed help.

"I'm getting a reading," one of the hunters said. "Tuned amber. Less than twenty feet away. They're hiding inside one of these tunnels."

Another raised his voice. "This is over, Oakes. We all know that. Give us the woman, and you're free to go. We don't give a damn about you. Just send her out here. Landry isn't going to hurt her. He just wants some information from her. This doesn't involve you. This is Guild business."

Rage shot through Celinda. *Guild business*. The universal excuse for anyone connected to the Guilds.

She looked at Davis, who was still positioned flat against the glowing green wall, gripping the barrel of the mag-rez gun. Surely he didn't intend to use it, she thought. But perhaps he was desperate enough to take the risk.

She sensed his psi energy pulse in a sudden surge of power.

An instant later, Davis and Max both disappeared.

She stared at the entrance of the tunnel, unable to believe her eyes. The pair had vanished. Literally. Not as in moving so quickly she hadn't been able to follow them. They were both simply gone.

Except Davis wasn't gone. She could still sense his psi pattern resonating as strongly as ever.

She realized that she was having trouble focusing on the place where he had been standing with Max on his shoulder only a second ago. The air seemed to waver and shimmer a little.

The patch of air that was not quite in focus suddenly moved, flowing out into the stairwell chamber. If she had not been looking directly at the slight distortion at the entrance of the tunnel, she would never have seen it.

That was when it dawned on her. Davis had just made himself and Max invisible.

Impossible.

Before she could wrap her brain around the mixed messages her senses were receiving, Araminta uttered a low, rumbling growl and tumbled from her shoulder to the floor of the tunnel.

The dust bunny raced after the silvery, shimmering patch of air. As she ran, she went into full hunting mode, all eyes and teeth.

Celinda hurried after her.

Shouts of anger and surprise went up in the outer room.

"What the fuck?"

"What happened to Reynolds?"

Celinda reached the tunnel entrance in time to see one of the khaki-and-leather-clad hunters crumple to the floor. He sprawled there, unmoving. The other four stared at him, dumbfounded.

She was still several feet away from them; nevertheless, she could perceive their violently pulsing psi energies quite clearly. Her senses were naturally a lot stronger underground.

"Maybe he had a heart attack or something," one of the

hunters said uneasily. "What the hell are we supposed to do now?"

"We came here to get the woman," another hunter growled. "We're not leaving without her."

The man who had been speaking jerked violently and fell to his knees, groaning. His head snapped forward, as if from a blow. This time he crumpled flat on his face. His psychic energy still pulsed, but it was as if everything had suddenly been thrown into neutral. He was alive, she realized, but unconscious.

"What's happening?" one of the hunters shouted. "What's going on here?"

She shivered. *Welcome to the haunted alien ruins, folks. Step right up. You're going to get your money's worth today. There's a real live ghost in the chamber with you.*

For the first time it struck her that Davis, Max, and Araminta might, indeed, be able to handle all five hunters by themselves.

The three men still on their feet were looking around uneasily. One of them was checking a device in his hand.

She retreated a step, putting her back against the wall.

"I'm getting two readings," the hunter said. "Shit. One is right here in the chamber."

"There's no one here but us, you idiot," one of the others barked. "You're probably picking up my amber or Greg's."

A piercing shriek rent the tense atmosphere in the outer chamber. It came from the hunter who had been trying to sort out the readings on his locating device.

Celinda peered around the opening in time to see that Max had rematerialized. As she watched, he launched himself up the pants leg of one of the hunters. Araminta was right behind him, going for the other leg.

The man screamed again and began swiping madly at the front of his trousers.

"Get them off me! Get them off me!"

Max reached the man's waist, heading for the throat.

The terrified hunter swung wildly at Max and managed to connect. Max went flying but not before drawing blood.

The hunter yelled again and batted at Araminta. She leaped away from his khaki-clad leg, but Celinda saw that the fabric was already damp and darkening rapidly.

"Something bit me!" The hunter staggered back, cradling his bleeding hand against his side. Looking haunted, he produced a knife, threw up an energy ghost as a shield, and started to retreat toward the staircase.

The air behind him shimmered. He jerked, but he did not go down. He whirled to confront the unseen menace behind him, knife slicing wildly at the air.

Then he toppled sideways, landing on the floor with a jolting thud. The blood from his wounded hand ran onto the green quartz. The ghost he had rezzed winked out.

Celinda looked anxiously at Max. He had landed adroitly and was already back on his feet, evidently unharmed.

More ghost light flared. The two hunters who were still on their feet had managed to regroup sufficiently to put their backs to each other. They had generated two large, violently pulsing balls of energy to protect themselves and were retreating toward the foot of the staircase. Both had drawn their knives.

Dark, disturbing energy poured off them in sickening waves. *Fear,* Celinda thought. The stuff was so strong it threatened to drown her own senses.

Her first impulse was to try to dampen the psi-based energy before it overwhelmed her. Her fingers tightened convulsively around the ruby amber relic in her hand. Power tingled in her palm.

Suddenly she knew in a way that she could not explain that she had a choice. She could, indeed, suppress the men's fear, or she could enhance it. If she chose the latter, she was also very certain that she could block the intensity of the waves so that she would not be swamped by them.

Acting on instinct, she pushed her own para-rez power

through the ruby amber. Working gingerly at first but with growing confidence, she sent pulses of resonating energy designed to augment the frequency of the waves the men were generating.

The hunters' fear metamorphosed into unholy terror. They both started screaming. The ghosts they were attempting to manipulate ebbed and flared in a pattern that even to her inexperienced eyes looked increasingly feeble and disorganized.

She barely managed to pulse enough additional psi through the ruby amber to protect her own senses from the onslaught. But her mental barricades held, muting the impact of the hunters' over-rezzed response.

On the floor, the leather vest worn by one of the fallen men seemed to open of its own accord, revealing a chunk of amber hanging on a metallic necklace. As she watched, the amber disappeared into thin air.

She realized that Davis was probably close to melting his own amber. He had just confiscated some backup.

Araminta and Max circled the wobbling energy ghosts warily, searching for openings.

The air in front of one of the UDEMs shimmered. The rapidly weakening ghost winked out. A heartbeat later, the second ghost disappeared.

"What's happening?" one of the men shouted.

"How in green hell should I know? Maybe this place really is haunted. Let's get out of here."

"What about Landry?" the first man insisted.

"Screw Landry. We can't fight what we can't see."

Knives in hand, the men fled toward the staircase.

The first hunter stumbled over some unseen object and went down. His head jerked to the side. He lay still.

The second one shrieked and kept on shrieking. Max and Araminta were scampering up his pants leg. He swiped at them with his knife, dancing on one foot.

His legs went out from under him. He fell to his knees and sprawled on the floor.

A deathly silence filled the chamber. Celinda looked at the figures of the fallen men. She sensed psi energy from all five. They were alive, but all were unconscious.

The air shimmered again, bright and silvery.

Davis appeared, standing amid the sprawled hunters. He was breathing hard. Sweat ran in rivulets down his face and saturated his shirt.

He still held the mag-rez in one hand. She knew then that he had used the butt of the gun as a club during the combat.

He looked at her, eyes as hot as a mirror struck by sunlight.

"We need to get out of here," he said. "Now."

"Are you all right?" she asked, too shaken to demand an explanation.

"Yes, but I won't be for long. I only pushed it this far once before. The burn isn't going to last very long. I can feel it fading already. The crash is going to be bad."

"You melted amber?"

"Three times, but that's not the problem. Move."

He was deadly serious. She snatched up her tote, dropped her wallet, the plastic containers of food, and the relic inside, and held her hand out to Araminta.

They followed Davis and Max up the spiral staircase.

"You'll have to drive," Davis said.

"I sort of figured that."

"Ever driven a twin-mag shift?"

"Yes. I learned on Walker's Specter."

Davis was climbing slowly but steadily. It didn't take psychic senses to realize that he was moving forward on willpower alone. *The burn isn't going to last very long. I can feel it fading already.* It was obvious that he was not experiencing the high-rez rush before the crash that hunters normally got when they melted amber. Something was very wrong here.

Panic sliced through her. If he collapsed in the stairwell, she would not be able to haul him out on her own. The personal phones wouldn't work out here in the middle of the desert, so she would not be able to call for help. They would be trapped until Davis recovered. That could take hours. At least some of the men down below in the chamber were bound to regain consciousness before that happened.

She moved up close behind Davis, planted her hands against his back, and started pushing. He didn't say anything, but with the added support he was able move a little faster.

His weight grew heavier as they made their way up the staircase. At one point she nearly despaired. Max looked as worried as a dust bunny could get. He chortled encouragingly in Davis's ear.

At last the tower entrance came into view.

Davis paused, chest heaving. He handed the mag-rez to her.

"Just in case they had the sense to leave a guard outside," he said. "If we need this, you'll have to be the one to use it. In this condition I couldn't hit the broad side of a Dead City wall."

"All right." She took the gun from him. It was lighter than her own older model, but she could see that the mechanism was the same.

"You okay?" he asked hoarsely.

"Don't worry. I'm saving my panic attack for some other time."

"I'm glad to hear that, because you're the only one who can get us out of here before some of those bastards down there come to or someone comes looking for them."

She shuddered. "Rest assured, I've got the big picture here."

A moment later, they emerged from the stairwell. Celinda's pulse was pounding, not just from the physical effort of shoving Davis up the last few stairs but from the fear that someone else was going to jump out at them. She gripped the mag-rez very tightly in her right hand and prayed.

No one accosted them when they left the tower.

"Idiots," Davis muttered. "Should have left a man on guard up here."

"Just be grateful they didn't. I certainly am."

"No problem with gratitude here, either."

He was starting to slur his words, a sign of the physical exhaustion that was rolling over him. But it was the psychic fatigue dampening his senses that worried her the most. The afterburn had not struck him nearly this hard the other evening when he had de-rezzed the doppelganger ghosts in the Old Quarter of Cadence. Whatever he had done to make himself invisible had sapped every ounce of psi power he possessed.

She managed to wedge him into the passenger seat of the Phantom and belted him in place.

Max and Araminta tumbled in after him. Davis leaned his head back against the seat and closed his eyes. Max made anxious little noises.

"Don't worry, Max," Celinda said. "He'll be okay. He just needs to sleep."

Max did not appear reassured. Araminta cuddled close to him, offering silent comfort.

Celinda got behind the wheel, rezzed the high-powered engine, and drove out of the old parking lot, skirting the heavy Oscillators that Landry's men had used.

She worked her way gingerly back toward the highway, afraid of jostling Davis any more than necessary. When she hit an especially high bump a little too hard, she glanced at him quickly. He didn't open his eyes, but in the amber glow of the dashboard lights she was pretty sure she saw him wince.

"Sorry," she said.

"It's not me I'm worried about."

"Oh. Right. The car. Well, look on the bright side. If you need a new one when this is all over, you can just put it on the Guild's tab."

"There is that. Celinda, I want you to listen closely to what I'm going to tell you."

She did not take her eyes off the battered old road. "Okay."

"I'm going to go under before we reach Cadence."

"The burn and crash. Yes, I understand."

"Not like the other night. This will be a major crash. As in, I may not come back out of it."

"*What?*" Horrified, she jerked her eyes off the road long enough to cast him a quick, searching look. "What are you talking about?"

"The last time this happened, I ended up in a parapsych hospital for nearly two months."

"You're starting to scare me here."

"Whatever you do, promise me you won't take me to an emergency room. Call Trig as soon as you can. He'll know what to do."

She could hardly breathe. A fine tremor swept through her. She reminded herself that she had postponed the panic attack. She had to stay calm and in control.

"All right," she said quietly.

"Tell Trig everything. Make sure he knows we've got the relic. He'll take it from there. I want that damn thing back in Mercer Wyatt's hands tonight."

The last few words were so weighted down with exhaustion that she could barely comprehend them.

"You're going to be okay, Davis," she said firmly.

He did not respond. When she gave him another fleeting glance, she saw that his eyes were closed. That was normal, she told herself. But something about his energy patterns didn't feel at all normal. Max huddled closer to him.

It took forever to get to the highway. When she reached it, she pointed the Phantom in the direction of Cadence City and gave the powerful vehicle its head. The reflective white lines on the pavement became a blur.

Ten miles later she realized that Davis was shivering

violently. She took one hand off the wheel and touched his forehead. He was frighteningly cold.

His psi energy waves had faded to almost nothing. He wasn't sleeping, she realized. He was sinking into something that felt much deeper and darker: a coma.

Chapter 26

~

WHATEVER WAS HAPPENING TO DAVIS, HER INTUITION told her that it did not fall into the admittedly flexible category labeled "normal," not even for a hunter.

She was making excellent time, but she was still a good hour away from Cadence. All her instincts were shrieking that she had to do something now to stop Davis's slide into psychic oblivion.

Max looked dreadful. He was crouched forlornly on Davis's shoulder, muttering. Araminta was perched on the back of the seat. She hadn't eaten a thing in the past hour.

"Davis?" Celinda said, glancing across at him. "Can you hear me?"

There was no response. His head hung forward. The only thing that held him upright was the seat belt.

"Davis, wake up," she said, infusing a tone of sharp command into her voice. "Talk to me."

Silence. Davis's psi waves pulsed more weakly.

She thought about the relic in the tote and then she thought about what she had been able to do with it during the fight in the underground chamber. One thing was certain, she couldn't run any psychic experiments while speeding along the highway at thirty miles over the speed limit.

Another badly weathered billboard came up in the headlights. It promised Cold Drinks & Snacks Next Exit.

She slammed the brakes, slowing the Phantom abruptly, and swung off the highway onto the side road. Her headlights picked up the looming shape of a sagging, unlit building. The old roadside snack stand had been closed for a long time.

She drove around behind the deserted stand and shut off the headlights. If any of Landry's men had managed to climb back out of the alien ruins and give chase, they wouldn't be able to see the Phantom parked behind the tumbledown snack stand.

She grabbed the tote from behind the seat, reached inside, and found the relic. The energy emanating from it was reduced to a trickle again. The powerful sensation she had experienced holding it underground was gone.

But energy was energy, and now, thanks to her experience in the alien chamber, she had a sense of how to employ it.

She unbuckled her belt, climbed over the gearshift, and wrapped herself around Davis, trying for as much physical contact as possible. Max retreated to the back of the seat, making way for her. He seemed to understand that she was trying to help.

Davis was shivering violently now. He stirred slightly when she put her leg over his thighs and slipped an arm behind his neck. She sensed that on some level he was aware of her presence.

She gripped the ruby amber relic and hugged him tightly to warm him physically while she concentrated on his cooling psi energy.

The patterns snapped into focus immediately, not as brilliantly clear and distinct as when she was underground but far more so than when she read psi waves with only her innate talent.

She saw that Davis's rhythms were not only weakening rapidly, the waves were losing their elegantly controlled pattern. The normally strong, steady pulses were increasingly erratic. Hot and cold light flashed across the spectrum.

Desperate, she selected the strongest band of pulsing energy she could perceive and then sent her own psi through the ruby amber artifact.

For a few heart-stopping seconds she feared that nothing was happening. Then the ragged band of energy began to resonate with her psi waves in a rhythm that reinforced Davis's normal pattern. The waves became stronger and more regular.

She urged a little more power through the ruby amber, selecting another point on the spectrum. Those wavelengths also began to steady. She shifted to a new point and repeated the process.

The steadying of one or two bands seemed to have a restorative effect on the others. The remaining waves emanating from across the psychic spectrum rapidly strengthened and became regular.

Davis grew warmer to the touch.

Max chortled excitedly.

Davis groaned, raised his lashes a little, and looked up at her with eyes that no longer burned like over-rezzed flash-rock.

"Are we there yet?" he asked.

He still sounded very, very tired, but now it felt like a normal exhaustion.

She was so relieved she almost cried. "Not quite. Another hour or so."

"I feel like I just fell off a cliff into a deep ocean and had to swim back to the surface," he muttered.

"That's probably a pretty accurate description."

He watched her very steadily through half-closed lids. "I didn't get back under my own power. You were there. I could feel you."

"We can talk about it later. I think it's time you got some real sleep. You need it."

He closed his eyes. She waited a tense moment or two, afraid that he might start to slip away from her again. But his psi rhythms, although slowed and gentled by deep slumber, remained steady and strong across the spectrum.

She scrambled back behind the wheel, set the relic on the dash, and rezzed the engine. When she reached the highway, she turned toward Cadence for the second time that night. She called Trig as soon as she could get a signal. He answered on the first ring.

"How was the wedding?" he asked.

"Pink." She glanced at the dashboard clock. "But things got really complicated afterward. I'll be at my place in about an hour, maybe less, depending on traffic."

"You're driving?"

"Yes."

"The Phantom?"

"Uh-huh."

He chuckled. "I'm impressed. I don't think Davis ever let anyone except his brother and me get behind the wheel, and we only got to drive it around the block."

"He didn't have a lot of choice tonight. Can you meet me at my apartment? I'm going to need a little help getting your boss upstairs."

"Why?" Trig's gravelly voice sharpened with concern. "What's happened?"

"A lot. I'll tell you the details when I see you." She glanced at the ruby amber artifact on the dash. "The most important thing is that we have the relic."

"That's great news."

"Trig?"

"Yeah?"

"Did you get to chapter four of my book yet? The part that talks about how important it is for two people to communicate?"

"Yes, and I agree absolutely," Trig said, very earnest now. "I underlined several paragraphs in that chapter."

"You might want to mention to your boss that he ought to read that chapter."

Trig heaved a heavy sigh. "I know he isn't always a first-rate communicator. But he's a guy. You gotta give him some leeway."

"I don't think this comes under the heading of a little leeway."

"How did he screw up this time?"

Given what she had observed about the relationship between the two men, she was fairly certain that Trig was aware of Davis's odd talent.

"It would have been useful if he had mentioned some of his small, personal quirks," she said.

"Quirks?"

"Turns out my date for the wedding is the Invisible Man."

There was a short, shocked pause.

"Green hell," Trig whispered. "He went invisible?"

"Yes." She gave him a quick rundown of the events in the alien chamber.

"How long did he stay vanished?" Trig's voice was tense and urgent.

"Not long. Maybe four or five minutes."

"Five minutes?"

"That's an estimate. I wasn't looking at a watch."

"You're sure it wasn't just a couple of minutes?"

"No, it was definitely longer than that. There were five of them, you see. And they had knives. They all pulled ghosts, of course. We were underground, so they were big ghosts."

"This is bad," Trig said grimly.

"I think Davis is okay. He told me that he was all right, and I can sense his energy waves. They feel normal again."

"He's not okay. Not if he burned silver light for more than a couple of minutes. The last time he went over that limit he ended up in a weird coma. They used all sorts of drugs on him to try to bring him out of it. He spent nearly two months in the hospital. Afterward everyone said he was lucky to be alive, let alone function normally again."

"He's okay, Trig. I'm monitoring him."

"I don't get it. How did he avoid the big sink this time?"

"I used the relic on him."

"That ruby amber thing? How did you do that?"

"It's hard to explain." She paused. "Trig?"

"Yeah?"

"I think that's what the relic does. It allows a person to manipulate someone else's psychic energy waves. It may have been some sort of alien medical device."

"Weird."

"Not so weird when you think about it. The aliens were obviously heavily into psi energy. Figures they would have needed some therapeutic technologies to deal with various kinds of psychic trauma. Look how much medical research we're doing in that field because of how rapidly psychic talents are developing in humans."

"Do you realize what you're saying? If that relic really can be used to treat human parapsych trauma, it would be a genuine medical miracle."

"The problem is," she said quietly, "I've got a nasty feeling that this is one of those good news–bad news situations."

"What do you mean?"

"The relic is pretty impressive, Trig. I think it holds out great hope for treating a whole range of psi trauma."

"I'm sensing a 'but' here."

"But I got a strong hunch that in the wrong hands it could be used as a form of mind control."

"Huh. Okay, that doesn't sound so good."

"No, it's not. Trig, Davis wants the relic to go back to Mercer Wyatt tonight."

"He's right. The sooner the relic is out of your hands and

back in the Guild vault, the safer everyone will be. Wyatt can handle Landry."

"I understand, but I've had some time to think about this, and I've come to a conclusion that Davis and Mercer Wyatt probably won't like."

Trig groaned. "Please don't tell me that you tossed that damned relic out into the desert on the theory that the device is too dangerous for mere humans to use."

"No. It is dangerous, but so is a lot of medical technology. I'm going on the theory that the possible benefit is too great to ignore. Besides, what if another one turns up someday? This one needs to be studied."

"Absolutely," Trig said quickly. "All the more reason to keep the device under lock and key in a secure place like the Guild vault."

She almost smiled. "I agree. And that's why I've decided to turn it over to a reputable medical research lab."

"Damn. You don't trust the Guild to handle the device, do you?"

"In a word, no."

There was another long pause.

"Does Davis know about this?"

"Not yet," she said. "He's still asleep. I intend to talk to him about my plan as soon as he recovers from the after-burn."

"You won't do anything without discussing it with him first, will you?" Trig sounded very worried.

"No."

"All right. I'll be waiting at your apartment when you get here. You'll need some security tonight, anyway. I doubt very much that Landry would try anything in Cadence. This is Mercer Wyatt's town, after all. But whoever searched your apartment the other night and then raised those twin ghosts is still running around."

"Any luck with that angle?"

"I've got one good possibility," Trig said. "I was waiting for Davis to get back before chasing it down, though.

Figured he'd want to handle it himself. Listen, about this plan of yours to turn the relic over to a research lab."

"Yes?"

"Think the dust bunny will go along with it?"

She looked at Araminta, who was munching on a cracker topped with pink cream cheese. "I have no idea."

Chapter 27

*Her screams woke him. He jerked upright in bed,
searching for the source of the danger. He saw Janet
in a patch of moonlight. She was on her feet, backing
away from the bed with a horrified expression. She
held out both hands as though warding off a demon.*

"What is it?" he said. "What's wrong?"

*"You." She choked on another scream. "I know you
told me what it would be like, but I never realized . . .
never expected to wake up in the middle of the night
and . . . I'm sorry, I just can't deal with it."*

*She whirled and ran from the bedroom, her night-
gown flapping wildly at her heels.*

*He looked down and saw that at some point he
had kicked off the covers during the night. The upper
half of his leg from knee to hip was missing.*

HE OPENED HIS EYES AND LET THE REMNANTS OF THE
dream fade away. Through the sliding glass door he could
see the faint green glow of the Dead City night giving way

to a cloudy dawn. For a few seconds he was disoriented. Wrong bed, wrong apartment, wrong view.

Then the memories slammed through him. He'd pulled silver light, enough to go invisible for several minutes. His heart accelerated abruptly. The fight-or-flight response kicked in, dumping adrenaline and a bunch of other bio-chemicals into his bloodstream. The last time this had happened he'd ended up in a waking coma at the Glenfield Institute.

He swung his legs over the side of the bed and surged to his feet, intent only on escape.

Max rumbled softly somewhere nearby. Davis stopped cold at the familiar sound and turned around. He saw Max at the foot of the bed, nestled into the plump quilt. Only his blue eyes were open and he was still fully fluffed: concerned, but not in battle mode.

It finally dawned on him that the room did not smell like the psych ward. Instead of the sterile, antiseptic odor he associated with that antechamber of hell, there was another scent.

He picked up the pillow and breathed deeply. Everything inside him stirred into full awareness. He knew the fragrance. He would remember it for the rest of his life. His heart rate slowed. He wasn't trapped in the Glenfield Institute; he was in Celinda's bedroom.

He recalled how she had wrapped herself around him, her body heat driving out the icy, postburn fever.

"How you doin', boss?" Trig asked from the doorway. He had a cup of coffee in one big hand.

Davis realized that the only thing he had on was his briefs. "I'm okay. A little foggy about what happened, though."

"You pulled your invisible man trick when you took on Landry's men. As near as Celinda can figure, you disappeared for about five minutes. Plus you de-rezzed a lot of ghosts."

He sat down on the edge of the bed. "What day is it? How long was I out?"

"You weren't out. Not the way you were last time. The fight with those goons Landry sent after you happened last night. You've been asleep for a few hours, that's all. Normal postburn crash this time."

"That's not possible."

Trig sipped his coffee and lowered the mug. "You're sitting there, aren't you? You look fine to me. Course, you need a shave and a shower, but aside from that—"

"What happened?"

"Celinda took care of your little coma issue last night."

Davis went very still, remembering the feel of her heat and the sense of calm that had come over him.

"How?" he asked.

"She thinks it was a combination of her talent and the relic."

"Explain."

"She told me that she was able to resonate with the relic and restore your psi-wave patterns to normal. She thinks the artifact may be some kind of alien medical device designed to treat psi-related trauma."

"Huh."

"But there's another possibility," Trig said.

"What?"

"Better brace yourself, boss. Celinda is convinced that in the wrong hands the device might be very dangerous."

A grim sense of impending trouble came over him. "Let me guess. She doesn't think Mercer Wyatt and the Guild are the right hands, does she?"

"Nope. She wants the device to go to a medical research lab where it can be studied."

"Oh, shit," he said very softly.

"Yeah." Trig sounded sympathetic.

"If the device really is that valuable or that dangerous, Wyatt is not going to agree to let go of it. Where is it now?"

"Araminta's cookie jar. Celinda told me she figures that's

the last place any of Wyatt's Guild thugs would think to look for it."

"Thugs?"

"I believe that was the term she used," Trig said.

"Swell. The most potentially significant alien artifact ever discovered is hidden in a dust bunny's cookie jar."

"Not like it's unprotected," Trig said quickly. "Got a feeling that anyone who tries to swipe it out of that cookie jar will have to deal with one really pissed-off dust bunny."

Davis contemplated his badly tangled case. "Got any other cheery news for me?"

"Couple of things. First, I called Wyatt last night and told him that Benson Landry was after the relic. I also briefed him on what happened out there in the desert at the old ruin site."

"What did he say?"

"Pretty much what you'd expect a guy in his position to say. He told me not to worry about Landry anymore. He'll take care of him."

"One less thing to worry about. Did you tell him the relic had turned up again?"

Trig exhaled heavily. "No. I thought I'd let you handle that. As far as Wyatt's concerned, the relic is still missing."

"Something to look forward to. Anything else?"

"Picked up a couple of fairly solid rumors about a guy who may have been the hunter you met up with in the lane the other night. He's a former Guild man named Brinker who turned ruin rat a few years ago. Evidently he's capable of generating a dopp ghost."

"Got anything else on him?"

"He managed to eke out a living for a while working the underside of the antiquities business. But a couple of years ago he ran into an illusion trap. The experience left him with a bad case of parapsych trauma. The Guild took care of his medical expenses, but he never fully recovered. According to my information, he's living in a flophouse in the Old Quarter."

"Got an address for him?"

"Sure do," Trig said.

"Sounds like I need to have a conversation with this Brinker."

"One thing doesn't add up, though," Trig warned.

"What's that?"

"Like I said, according to my information, Brinker is a real burnout case. Can't even hold a job. Frankly, he doesn't sound like the type who could get it together enough to engineer a complicated search for a stolen relic."

Davis thought about that. "I see what you mean."

Trig checked his watch. "It's four thirty. Want me to stick around any longer?"

"No. I can handle things now. Go home and get some sleep."

"Right." Trig started to turn away. "Call me if you need anything."

"I will. Where's Celinda?"

"Sound asleep on the sofa. Finally."

Davis frowned. "What do you mean, *finally*?"

"She had a hard time getting to sleep. Didn't stop tossing and turning until about three AM. No big surprise, given what she went through."

"She was amazing," Davis said.

"Yeah, I got that impression." Trig paused. "And to think you didn't believe any woman could handle the invisibility thing."

"I said Celinda's amazing." He made his tone go neutral. "Doesn't mean that she wants to have a long-term relationship with a Guild man who does a carnival act."

"Don't be so negative, boss. Keep in mind that she knows your big secret, and she didn't freak out."

"I repeat, it doesn't mean she wants to get involved with me."

"Looks like the two of you are already involved, if you ask me. By the way, I stopped by your place on the way over here last night and picked up some fresh clothes for you."

Trig nodded toward a small overnight case on the floor. "Wasn't sure what you had left from the wedding trip."

"Thanks."

Trig went down the hall. A moment later the front door opened and closed very quietly.

Davis got to his feet and then stopped, unable to decide what to do next. He couldn't get the image of Celinda asleep on the sofa in the other room out of his mind. The urge to go down the hall and look at her was almost overwhelming.

But now she knew he was a circus freak.

"Probably a bad idea," he said to Max.

Max yawned and stretched contentedly. Then he flipped over on his back, closed his eyes, and went back to sleep.

"How come your love life is so much simpler than mine?" Davis asked.

There was no response.

After a while it occurred to Davis that he probably needed a shower.

Chapter 28

WHEN HE EMERGED FROM THE BATHROOM A SHORT TIME later, he listened very intently for a moment. No sounds of movement came from the living room. Evidently, Celinda was still asleep. Max had disappeared from the bed. A dull, silvery gray light infused the sky.

He opened the suitcase that Trig had packed and found several items including a black crew-neck T-shirt and a pair of black trousers. He donned the T-shirt and trousers and then stopped to listen again.

There was still no sound from the living room. He considered his options. He could either stay here in the bedroom until Celinda awakened, or he could go out into the kitchen and see if Trig had left any coffee.

It was a no-brainer.

He went barefoot down the hall. The drapes were open, allowing the pale light to illuminate the living room. He told himself that he would go straight into the kitchen and not even glance at the sofa. He discovered immediately that his normally inexhaustible well of willpower had run dry.

Celinda was sound asleep amid a tangle of sheets and

blankets. Her face was turned away from him on the pillow. He came to a halt, unable to move beyond the sight of her lying there in the early morning light. The memories of their night together in Frequency flooded back, igniting his senses.

Forget it. Whatever you could have had with her is probably finished.

As though she had been awakened by his thoughts, she stirred, opened her eyes, and turned her head to look at him.

"Hi," she said in a voice softened and warmed by sleep.

"Hi," he said. He couldn't think of any other intelligent conversation. *Do you still want me?* was what he really wanted to ask.

"How are you feeling?" she said.

"Normal. Thanks to you." Again the unspoken question went through his thoughts: *Do you want to go to bed with a freak?*

She looked around the rumpled bedding. "Where are Max and Araminta? Don't tell me they took off again?"

"No." He inclined his head toward the small balcony. "They're dining alfresco at the moment."

She followed his gaze. The sliding glass door was open a few inches. Araminta and Max were perched on the railing, munching cookies while they watched the sun come up over the Dead City.

"They were both pretty cool last night, weren't they?" Celinda said proudly. "I couldn't believe how they went after those thugs."

"You were pretty cool, yourself."

"Mmm. Well, you did most of the work. All I had to do was drive us all home."

He groped for words. "Sorry I didn't have a chance to tell you about what I can do with silver light."

"Trig explained it." She contemplated him for a long moment. "It's a little disconcerting to watch someone disappear, especially when you don't know there's a rational explanation."

"It's more than disconcerting." He remembered the dream about Janet. "Even when people do know there's an explanation, they can't deal with it. It's just too damn weird."

She searched his face with sudden understanding. "That's what happened to your engagement, isn't it? Your fiancée found out that you can go invisible, and she couldn't handle it."

"I told Janet the truth. I even went invisible in front of her once to let her see what it was like. I could tell it bothered her, but she insisted she could deal with it. I don't do it very often because it's such a huge psi drain. But once in a while it comes in handy in the course of my work. As long as I don't push it for more than a couple of minutes, I'm okay." He paused. "Until a few months ago I was always in complete control."

"What happened?"

"I think all those drugs they gave me while I was in a coma had some kind of long-term side effects. Occasionally now, when I dream, I pull a little silver light without realizing it."

"Without amber?"

He nodded. "Janet and I were together one night when it happened. I woke up to the sound of her screams. Looked down and saw that a chunk of my leg was missing."

She gave him an understanding look. "An awkward moment in a relationship."

"Yes," he said. "It was definitely that."

"That was when the two of you decided you weren't a good match?"

"Things hadn't been going well for a while," he admitted. "We got engaged before I wound up in the hospital. After I got out, we both pretended that everything was back to normal. But it wasn't. We started having problems."

"What kind of problems?"

"I lost most of my clients, for one thing. No one wanted to risk hiring a known burnout case. Business was bad. The rumor went around that I would never recover from the psi trauma. Some of our friends started avoiding us."

"I see."

"At any rate, the night I accidentally pulled the silver in bed was the last straw. Janet grabbed her keys, ran out of the apartment in her nightgown, and drove to her parents' house. The next day her father phoned to say that they were all very sorry, but everyone hoped I would understand that no one wanted my genes in the family."

"Well," she said briskly, "that certainly explains why you like to sleep alone."

"Beats waking up to a screaming woman in the middle of the night."

She arched her brows. "I would just like to point out that you really can't blame the matchmaker for what happened. I'll bet you never mentioned your unusual talent when you filled out the questionnaire, did you?"

"No. I told you, it's not the kind of thing you advertise."

"How did you expect your marriage consultant to find you a good match when you didn't provide her with your full parapsych profile?"

"What the hell was I supposed to do? List 'invisibility' in the Description of Psychic Talents section? Give me a break. She'd have figured me for some kind of nutcase. And if I had proven that I could do it, she would have told me I was unmatchable. Right after she stopped screaming, that is."

"That's always the way it is." Celinda made a tut-tutting sound. "The client is less than forthcoming on the question- naires and then complains when the match isn't perfect."

Was she teasing him? He couldn't believe it.

"Damn it, Celinda."

She drew her knees up under the bedclothes and wrapped her arms around them. "I did some thinking on the way home last night while you were sleeping. It's not like there isn't a long tradition of myths and legends about people who can make themselves invisible or appear to do so. Some of the stories go back to Old Earth tales."

"I know. Trust me, I've done the research. A lot of the tales are linked to military or combat traditions."

"Ninja warriors?"

"Among others. I found a couple of legends involving invisibility when I studied records of an Old Earth group called the Arcane Society, too."

She frowned. "I remember running across a mention of the Society in a History of the Paranormal class I took in college. It was an organization devoted to psychic research, wasn't it?"

"Yes. There are also plenty of stories about Old World magicians who could pull off invisibility."

She watched him very steadily. "What do you think?"

He shrugged. "We're human. Something here on Harmony is pushing the evolution of psychic talents in the population, but that probably wouldn't happen if we didn't already carry some innate genetic ability to access the paranormal plane. I think it's possible that there may have been a few humans back on Old Earth who could do what I do."

She thought about that. "The talent is obviously rare. It's likely to stay rare, too. Judging from what I saw last night, it exacts a huge price in terms of physical and paranormal energy."

"Yes."

She searched his face. "Trig told me how you wound up in the hospital for a long period of time after you rescued a little girl who had been kidnapped. To avoid the kidnappers you had to keep yourself and the child invisible for over five minutes. He said the resulting coma lasted for weeks."

"The *real* problem," he said quietly, "was that I wasn't unconscious that whole time."

She stared at him, eyes widening with sympathetic horror. "Dear heaven. You mean you were aware of what was going on around you, but you couldn't communicate?"

"For the first three days or so after I collapsed I was

completely under. But after they got me into the hospital, they started experimenting with their damn drugs in an effort to bring me out of the coma. They succeeded, but only partway. I could walk if someone steered me. I could eat if someone fed me. But I couldn't initiate any action. I couldn't speak."

She tightened her arms around her knees, hugging herself. "I was in a similar kind of limbo after Landry shot me full of that heavy-duty tranquilizer drug. But at least I was only trapped for a few hours. I can't even imagine how bad days and weeks in that condition would have been."

"The orderlies used to take me outside to sit on the veranda." He grimaced. "They probably figured that looking at the gardens would be soothing. But I hated those gardens. Every time they sat me down on that damn veranda, all I could think about was how badly I wanted to walk away from that place."

"I understand."

"In fairness, it wasn't the fault of the doctors. They'd never seen anything like my case before. They had no protocol for treating me, so they went with the experimental approach. In their place, I'd have done the same thing."

"What happened?" she asked. "How did they finally bring you around?"

"They didn't. For the most part, all the drugs did was suppress my psi senses and tranquilize me into a stupor. Eventually they tried a drug that was not very effective. I was able to surface long enough to say a few words."

"What words?"

"'Stop the damn drugs.'"

"Good choice. How long did it take you to recover?"

"Took about three days for the drugs to wear off enough so that I could move on my own without falling down. The first thing I did was check myself out of the hospital." He smiled very thinly. "The director did not approve."

"How long would the psi coma have lasted if they hadn't given you the drugs?"

"Who knows?" He shrugged. "For obvious reasons, I don't have a lot of practical experience with the problem. Going invisible for more than a minute or two just requires too much energy. Take it from me, it's not pleasant sliding into even a short-term coma." He shoved a hand through his hair. "The dreams are not sweet."

"You dream while you're in that state?"

"Yes." He felt his jaw tighten. "After what happened last night, I should have been out for at least three or four days, maybe longer. I've never burned that much psi before. For all I know, I might not have come out of it at all. But what I experienced was just a routine hunter crash, the kind I get after working a normal level of silver. Trig said you used the relic on me?"

"It not only enhanced my own natural ability to read psi energy, it allowed me to manipulate your patterns. During the fight underground, I was able to use it to enhance the fear of two of the hunters." She gave him a very sober, serious look. "It's a very powerful tool, Davis."

He did not want to fight this battle now, he thought.

"I see," he said neutrally.

"One more thing."

"What?"

She fixed him with a determined look. "Bet you ten bucks I wouldn't have screamed. At least not because I woke up and discovered that part of you was invisible."

"Celinda." He stopped. He had no clue what to say next.

"Of course, I might have screamed for another reason," she added. Her eyes were very green now. "The same reason I screamed the other night in the hotel room in Frequency."

"I'm a freak, Celinda."

"*No*, don't you dare say that. It's not true."

She came up off the sofa bed like a small whirlwind. He had time to register the fact that she was wearing a very demure white nightgown that covered her from throat to toes before she was standing directly in front of him, eyes brilliant with outrage.

"Listen to me, Davis Oakes, you are not a freak. Benson Landry is a freak. Trust me, with my kind of talent, I know the difference. You are a good man, a fine man. You are a brave, honorable man. You are all the things that Landry is not."

"Hey," he said, taken aback by her fierceness. "I appreciate the pep talk, but I'm no hero."

She gripped his shoulders with both hands, tried to shake him a little. "Yes, you are. You're *my* hero."

She wrapped her arms around his neck and kissed him hard.

His reaction was immediate. He was suddenly hot and desperate for her. He pulled her close against his chest, aware of the gentle, ripe feel of her breasts through the thin fabric of the modest nightgown. He realized that her nipples were hard.

She did not try to retreat. As far as he could tell, she was as hungry for him as he was for her. He scooped her up in his arms and carried her back down the hall to the bedroom.

He got rid of the nightgown and dropped her lightly onto the rumpled bed. Within seconds he was out of his own clothes and falling on top of her. She was soft and damp, and the scent of her body made his head spin.

She coiled around him as she had last night, but this wasn't like last night. Last night had been all about warmth and connection, about holding on the way you hold on to a lifeline. This morning was about headlong desire, heat, and reckless thrills.

They struggled against each other for the embrace. The wrestling was no holds barred. When her hand curled around his erection, he sucked in his breath. When he looked down at her, he saw the sensual challenge in her eyes. She opened her mouth a little, giving him a shadowy glimpse of the tip of her tongue.

In retaliation, he caught her wrists and anchored them in one hand above her head. She taunted him with a sexy, seductive smile that let him know more clearly than words that as far as she was concerned, she had won the small battle.

He kissed the smile off her mouth, leaving her gasping for air and twisting to get free. He moved his hand down the length of her body, over her breasts, past her soft belly. He found the wellspring of her damp heat and explored the swollen flesh until she went wild.

He could have sworn that invisible energy flared between them. In some way he could not explain, he was resonating with her on the psychic as well as the physical plane.

Her release gave him more satisfaction than anything he had ever experienced before in his life. He had to cover her mouth with his own to stifle her little scream of pleasure so that it would not reverberate downstairs and arouse Betty Furnell's curiosity.

When the last of the tight little shivers inside her was finished, he released her wrists. She immediately rolled him onto his back and took him inside her.

"My turn to be on top," she whispered, eyes alight with sultry challenge.

She was wet and tight and welcoming. Nothing had ever felt so good.

His climax hit him in surging waves that dazzled his senses a thousand times more than any dose of alien psi energy ever could.

Perfect.

Chapter 29

AN HOUR LATER SHE WAS IN THE KITCHEN MAKING breakfast. She had showered and dressed in a pair of snug, dark brown pants and a crisp white shirt. A brown head-band restrained her freshly washed hair.

Araminta and Max watched the breakfast preparations from the top of the refrigerator. Both were munching slices of fresh, sweet amberglow melon.

Davis emerged from the bedroom hallway, dressed once more in the black T-shirt and black trousers. The masculine satisfaction in his eyes made Celinda grow warm all over again.

He watched her pull the pan off the heat. "Trig said you think the relic could be used as some sort of mind control device."

So much for cozy chitchat. She braced herself for the battle.

"I think it's possible, yes, especially when it's pumped up with alien psi underground." She divided the scrambled eggs onto two plates. "I have a hunch that it requires some-one with my type of talent or something similar to resonate with it, however. That's why it sat unnoticed in the Guild vault all these months."

"Trig also said that you want to see it turned over to a medical research lab. But if it really is a potential weapon, it's better off under lock and key in the Guild vault."

She put the pan down and looked at him. "We're in dangerous territory, and there are no guarantees. But if the device is turned over to a reputable lab with a lot of fanfare and media attention instead of being handled secretly by the Guild, it is far more likely that it will be studied with a view toward its therapeutic properties."

"How do you know that?"

"The medical world has a long history of working with medicines and machines that can kill as well as cure. The Guild will think only in terms of using it as a weapon."

Davis was silent for a while.

"You may be right," he said eventually.

"I know I'm right. This is the only way to go, Davis. You have to trust me."

"I'm going to call Wyatt as soon as we finish breakfast, but I can't promise you that he'll see things your way."

"I think he will be reasonable if you remind him of a couple of small details," she said quietly.

"What details?"

"First, if he tries to take that relic without my permission, I'm going to go straight to the media and put out the word that the Cadence Guild discovered an alien mind control device and is conducting secret research on it."

Davis wasn't impressed. "Wyatt can handle the media. Who do you think the reporters are going to believe? A disgraced matchmaker from Frequency City or the head of the local Guild?"

She winced. "That was cold, but you're right. Okay, that brings us to the second little detail."

"Which is?"

"I just told you that I don't think there are many people around who can figure out how to work that device. That's probably why Araminta wanted me to have it in the first place. She must have sensed that I could resonate with it. I wouldn't be surprised if she thought it would make a nice toy for me."

They both looked at Araminta, who was unruffled by the attention.

Celinda took a deep breath and prepared to play her high card. "You can inform Mercer Wyatt that I will cooperate in research on the relic only if that research is conducted in a respectable medical lab and if the results of that research are made public."

"Well, hell," Davis said, stone-faced. "Nothing I like better than starting off the day by blackmailing my one and only client."

Some of the tension she had been feeling receded.

"Thanks," she said quietly.

"Don't thank me. This is a long way from a done deal. And even if Wyatt agrees to make arrangements for a medical lab to study the device, you'll still have to figure out how to convince Araminta to go along with the plan."

They both looked at Araminta again.

Araminta muttered something. Max promptly scampered down onto the counter and pried the lid off the cookie jar. He removed a cookie and drifted back up to his perch. Araminta took the cookie from him and began to nibble daintily.

"We both know that dust bunnies have some psychic qualities," Celinda said quietly. "I'm hoping that if she senses that I really don't want that relic, she'll lose interest in it."

"Sure about that?"

"No," she admitted.

Davis sat down behind the counter and picked up his coffee mug. "Maybe you can distract her with a really big wedding cake. She didn't get a chance to finish the last one."

"That's a thought."

"Something else we should talk about," he said.

"What's that?"

"You can't go to work today or any other day until this situation is under control."

"Davis, my job is very important to me."

"I realize that. But keeping you safe is my first priority. I can't protect you and work on this case at the same time, not if you insist on going into your office at Promises, Inc."

"But Mrs. Takahashi won't understand."

"She will when I call her and explain that this is Guild business."

He was right. Morosely she surveyed the eggs and toast. "My worst nightmare. I've become Guild business."

He cocked a brow. "Your *worst* nightmare?"

She sighed. "Okay, not my worst nightmare. But a nightmare, nonetheless."

She sat down beside him. They ate their eggs and toast in what she thought was a surprisingly companionable silence, given that three minutes ago they had been locked in a contest of wills. Maybe it was the early-morning sex.

"Probably the early-morning sex," Davis said. "It seems to put me in a good mood."

She wrinkled her nose. "Don't tell me you can read minds. Going invisible I can deal with. Mind reading is a deal breaker."

"I can't read minds, but sometimes I'm a really good guesser. That's what makes me such a hotshot private investigator."

"No doubt."

Someone knocked on the door.

"I'll get it," Davis said.

He eased himself off the stool and went into the small front hall. Celinda listened to him greet their visitor.

"Good morning, Mrs. Furnell," he said. "You're looking very bright and cheerful today."

"Thank you." Betty sounded pleased. "Everyone always says that orange is my color."

"Everyone is right," Davis said.

"I wondered if I could borrow a little milk for my cereal. I ran out, and it's too early to go to the store."

Celinda stifled a sigh. "Come on in, Mrs. Furnell. I'll get the milk for you."

Betty appeared, beaming. "Thank you, dear." She was, indeed, very bright and cheerful looking in an orange track suit trimmed with purple racing stripes and a pair of neon orange running shoes.

"How was the wedding?" she asked.

"It was very pink and very lovely." Celinda slid off the stool and went around the counter. "My sister looked beautiful."

"You must show me the pictures."

Celinda tried and failed to resist the good manners impulse. "Would you like a cup of coffee?"

"I would love one, dear. Thank you." Betty smiled benignly at Davis. "The two of you came in quite late last night. I thought I heard a third person, too."

"My assistant," Davis said. "He had an important message for me."

"I see." She beetled her brows at him. "I must say, it was an odd time to deliver a message. He stayed for quite a while, didn't he? I'm sure I heard him leave around four."

Something clicked inside Celinda's head. She looked up from the mug that she was filling with coffee.

"You never miss a trick here, do you, Mrs. Furnell?"

Betty winked. "Not much gets by me, dear, and that's a fact. This is a very quiet place. Sound carries."

It hadn't been all that quiet recently, Celinda thought. Whoever had searched her apartment the other night must have made some noise. Furniture had been turned over and drawers had been emptied in what had appeared to be a frenzied haste.

Celinda glanced at Davis, who responded by raising his brows in silent question.

She turned back to Betty.

"Mrs. Furnell, did you by any chance hear some un-usual noises from this apartment three nights ago?"

Out of the corner of her eye, Celinda saw Davis go very still.

But it was Betty's reaction that startled Celinda. First, she went completely blank, as though utterly baffled by the question. Then she stiffened. Her fingers fluttered nervously.

"No," she said quickly. "No, I didn't hear a thing."

Celinda caught the sudden flaring of agitated psi energy. Betty was experiencing a sudden amount of stress.

"Are you certain?" Celinda pressed gently.

"Absolutely certain. I heard nothing." Betty frowned. "I don't allow any loud noises from this apartment. Told you that when you took the place. I didn't see anything, either."

Celinda exchanged glances with Davis.

"She didn't ask you if you'd seen anything, Mrs. Furnell," Davis said. "Celinda just wondered if you'd heard anything."

"Didn't see anything or hear anything." Betty was becoming more anxious by the second. She put her fingertips to her temple. "I'm getting a headache. I don't want to talk about this any longer."

Celinda took one of her hands. Betty's violently disturbed psi energy flooded her senses. Up on the refrigerator, Araminta and Max stopped whispering sweet nothings to each other and fixed Betty with alert, attentive expressions.

"It's all right, Mrs. Furnell," Celinda said quietly. "I understand that you didn't hear or see anything the other night. There's no problem. You can relax."

Betty looked at her with a dark, haunted expression. "I didn't hear or see anything," she repeated, desperate to be believed.

"I know," Celinda said.

Betty seemed to take some comfort from the reassurance, but she did not return to her previously cheerful, inquisitive state.

"I should go downstairs," she said, her voice dulled with pain. "I need something for my head."

"Mrs. Furnell, I might be able to do something about that headache if you'll allow me."

"Thank you so much, dear. I would really appreciate that. I rarely get headaches. But for the past couple of days they've been bothering me. Every time I think about—" She broke off, blinking in confusion.

"Think about what?" Celinda probed cautiously.

"I'm not sure." Betty shook her head, bewildered and frightened. "I get them when I think about *something*. But I can't recall what that something is, if you see what I mean."

"Was it something that happened the other evening?" Celinda asked.

"No, nothing happened the other night. It was just a dream." Betty's psi energy kicked up violently again. "Did you say you had some pills, dear?"

"I think I may have something more effective." Celinda smiled encouragingly. "Will you allow me to use it?"

"Yes, anything. I can't stand this feeling. It's worse than a headache. To tell you the truth, I'm afraid I might be going senile."

Celinda released her hand. She raised the plastic lid on the cookie jar, reached inside, and took out the ruby amber relic.

"What's that?" Betty asked, frowning with curiosity.

"One of Araminta's toys."

She touched Betty's hand again and rezzed a little energy through the relic.

Instantly she could clearly detect Betty's sparking, flashing psychic wave patterns. It was relatively easy to identify the most disturbed rhythms and trace them back to a distinct location on the spectrum.

Cautiously she went to work, soothing and strengthening the chaotic pulses until they resumed a normal rhythm.

Betty grew visibly calmer. Her distraught expression cleared miraculously.

"How do you feel?" Celinda asked.

"Much better." Betty blinked and then smiled. "My headache seems to be gone. That's amazing. What did you do, dear?"

"It's a form of psychic meditation that I've been studying lately," Celinda said, keeping things vague. "It's supposed to be very relaxing."

"Oh, I see. Well, I understand why it might work on you, since you're the one studying the technique, but why did it work on me?"

"I'm not sure," Celinda admitted. "The instructor said it has an effect on others around the practitioner."

"I suppose it makes sense," Betty said. "Psi energy does radiate, doesn't it? Everyone knows that some people, such as myself, who are highly intuitive, often notice when others are upset or depressed."

"Exactly," Celinda said. "Now, do you remember if you heard or saw anything unusual from this apartment three nights ago?"

"Oh, no, dear, I'm sure that nothing out of the ordinary—" Betty broke off abruptly. Her eyes widened with indignation. "Good heavens, the *burglars*. How could I have forgotten about those two dreadful men? I was going to call the police but—" She halted again, looking baffled. "But I didn't."

Davis turned slightly on the stool and rested one arm on the counter. "Why didn't you call the police, Mrs. Furnell?"

"Why, because it was all a dream." Anger flashed across her face. "No, that's not right. I didn't call the police because that dreadful man told me that it was a dream. And I *believed* him. He said that if I tried to remember the dream in detail I would get a terrible headache."

"Can you tell us exactly what happened?" Davis asked.

"I heard noises from up here. Thought the two of you had come home early and were, well, you know." Betty waved one hand. "Doing what couples do. But after a while, I realized that something was not right. I came up here with a key and opened the door. There were two men in here. I knew that they were burglars and tried to back out, but they had heard my key in the lock."

"What did they do?" Celinda asked.

"The tall, thin one grabbed me. The other one said, 'Hold her still.' Then he . . . he touched me."

Celinda was horrified. *"Intimately?"*

Betty looked startled. Then she quickly shook her head. "Oh, no, dear. He just put a hand on my arm and started telling me how everything I had heard and seen was a dream and how I would get a headache if I tried too hard to remember it."

"Where was his other hand?" Celinda asked. "Was he holding anything in it?"

Betty frowned a little. "No, I don't think so. Wait. I remember he kept his other hand in the pocket of his raincoat."

"But it wasn't raining the other night," Davis said quietly.

"No, it wasn't." Betty's lips thinned. "I remember thinking it was odd that he was wearing any sort of coat. The night was quite warm."

"Can you describe the two men you saw?" Davis asked.

"Well, I'm not sure I can give you a very useful description," Betty said uneasily. "I was a bit distracted at the time."

Celinda smiled sympathetically. "For a very good reason."

"The lights were off, of course, so I couldn't see their faces very clearly," Betty explained. "The one who held the gun on me wore a cap pulled down very low over his eyes. He was rather twitchy. I remember being terrified that he would pull the trigger by accident."

"What about the other man?" Davis asked.

Betty pursed her lips. "Tall, but not as tall as the twitchy guy. From what I could tell he was well-built. Very fit and trim. Excellent shoulders. I remember wondering if burglars worked out in fitness clubs."

"Do you recall anything at all about his features?" Celinda asked.

Betty shook her head. "I'm afraid not. As I said, it was quite dark in here."

"Anything else about him strike you as distinctive?" Davis said.

Betty hesitated. "Well, there was his voice."

"What about it?" Celinda asked.

Betty's forehead crinkled. "He didn't have a burglar's voice, although I must admit I've never spoken with a burglar before."

Celinda leaned forward across the counter a little. "What sort of voice did he have?"

"Cultured. Well-bred. Forceful." Betty thought for a few seconds. "Maybe *authoritative* is the right word. Like a doctor or a professor. He was obviously a well-educated man. He just didn't sound like a burglar, if you see what I mean."

"I understand," Celinda said.

Betty shook her head, frustrated. "I don't know why I thought the entire incident was a dream and why I never called the police. It's . . . worrisome."

Celinda dropped the relic back into the cookie jar and replaced the lid. The implications of what Betty had seen and heard made the adrenaline rush through her veins. She knew that Davis had to be thinking the same thing.

"Don't worry, Mrs. Furnell," she said. "You're not going senile. I think that burglar with the well-educated, professorial voice used a form of psychic hypnosis on you to make you think that everything you saw and heard that night was a dream."

"Hypnosis." Betty's eyes widened. "Good heavens."

"He reinforced the hypnotic suggestion by doing something to your psi senses that induced a headache every time you tried to recall what really happened."

"I suppose that would explain it," Betty said slowly. "But how could he hypnotize me so quickly in the dark?"

"Obviously, he has some sort of extremely powerful psi talent," Celinda said.

Betty looked at Davis, baffled. "I understand now why I didn't call the police. But why didn't you call them when you got home?"

Davis assumed his darkly mysterious air. "Because this is Guild business, Mrs. Furnell."

"Oh, my goodness." Betty looked thrilled. "You don't say. How exciting. You're with the Guild, then?"

"I'm working for Mercer Wyatt," Davis said.

Betty was satisfied now. "Expect the Guild can handle a couple of burglars."

"Yes, ma'am," Davis said.

"I'd better be off, in that case." Betty got to her feet. "I'm sure you've got a lot to do." She smiled at Celinda. "Thank you so much for that meditation treatment. I feel ever so much better now."

"What about your milk?" Celinda asked.

"Oh, that's all right, dear. I'll pick up some at the store this afternoon."

Davis had the phone in his hand when Celinda returned from seeing Betty out the door.

"You realize what this means?" he asked her while he rezzed the number.

"Yes," she said. "There's a second ruby amber relic, and the man with the professorial voice not only has it, he's got the talent required to activate it."

"A talent like yours."

Chapter 30

THE DOORBELL SOUNDED LESS THAN AN HOUR LATER.
Araminta and Max suddenly seemed quite excited. They
both bounced a couple of times and then quickly scampered down from the refrigerator.

"I'll get it," Davis said. He rose from the counter stool
and went into the front hall.

Araminta and Max bobbed enthusiastically at his heels.

Celinda poured herself another cup of coffee and prepared for the showdown with Mercer Wyatt. She'd heard
enough of Davis's side of the phone conversation to know
that the Guild boss was not a happy camper.

She listened to Davis greet the newcomer. To her
amazement he sounded like he was welcoming an old
friend.

"So, Wyatt sent you to do the dirty work," Davis said.
"Come on in."

Evidently it was not Wyatt who had come to lay down
Guild law. According to the press, he and his wife had a
mansion on Ruin View Drive. Maybe slumming in this part
of town was beneath a man of his exalted station.

Then she heard a woman's voice, warm and vivacious.

"Hello, Davis. Good to see you again. How are you, Max? And who's this?"

"That's Araminta," Davis said. "She lives here."

"I hear you've got a problem on your hands," a man said, sounding a little amused.

"Are you all right, Davis?" The woman was concerned.

"I'm fine," Davis assured her. "But the case has gone to green hell."

"Got that impression," the man said. "What's going on? When he called, Wyatt told me this was supposed to be a simple retrieval operation."

"Things got complicated," Davis said. "Come on into the kitchen and have some coffee. There's someone you need to meet."

Celinda waited for them behind the counter, instinctively seeking a barricade between herself and the sure-to-be-intimidating representatives of the Guild.

The dark-haired man with the specter-cat eyes and the redheaded woman who accompanied him were not at all what she had expected. The vibes of both were powerful. The man could be ruthless, she thought, but never cruel. He did not look like a typical hunter. His hair was cut short, and he wasn't dressed in khaki and leather. Instead, he wore a stylish, expensively tailored mix of trousers, jacket, and open-collared shirt. The face of his watch was amber. He could have passed for a pricey business consultant.

The woman had smart, insightful eyes. She wore a conservative, skirted suit and heels. There was something about her that made Celinda think she might have an academic background.

Most reassuring of all was the dust bunny the couple had brought with them. He sported a small yellow bow on top of his head. Max and Araminta had already taken charge of him, leading him straight to the cookie jar on the counter.

"Celinda, this is Lydia and Emmett London," Davis

said. "Emmett's an old friend of mine. Lydia and Emmett, Celinda Ingram. The bunny with the yellow bow on his head is Fuzz."

There was a polite round of greetings. Celinda poured coffee for Lydia and Emmett, and they sat down in the living room.

"All right," Emmett said, looking at Davis, "I've got Wyatt's version of events. Give me the rest of the story."

Davis told them everything in short, terse sentences. When he was finished, Emmett contemplated the cookie jar.

"You definitely picked an innovative hiding place," he said neutrally.

"My theory is that if anyone tries to take the relic out of that cookie jar, Araminta will know about it," Celinda explained. "For some reason she wants me to have it."

Lydia nodded thoughtfully. "Dust bunnies clearly have some psychic abilities. My guess is she senses that you can resonate with the relic and, therefore, it ought to belong to you. Probably thinks it's a toy of some kind."

"That's what I concluded," Celinda agreed.

Lydia raised her coffee cup and looked at Celinda over the rim. There was a wealth of understanding in her expression. "I don't blame you one bit for not wanting to turn that relic over to the Guild."

Davis and Emmett exchanged grim looks. Celinda and Lydia ignored them.

"The thing is," Celinda said, relieved now that she had a supporter, "I think the relic has enormous potential as a medical device for the treatment of psi trauma and, perhaps, other kinds of psychic and psychiatric disorders as well. The Guild isn't exactly into high-tech medical research."

"Nope, it sure isn't," Lydia agreed. "I'm with you one hundred percent on this. The relic should go to a reputable lab."

Emmett looked at Davis. "Wyatt isn't going to relinquish control of the relic. Not if it's as powerful as you think it is."

"We've been giving the problem some thought," Davis said. "Got a proposal to make to Wyatt."

"I'm listening."

"As far as we can tell, the relic is useless unless it is activated by someone who possesses a psi talent similar to Celinda's," Davis said. "Probably a very strong version of that kind of talent."

"There can't be a lot of people running around with my particular ability," Celinda added swiftly. "The lab where I was tested when I was a teen said that they had only seen one other case in a decade, and that person wasn't nearly as strong."

"Can I try the thing?" Emmett asked.

Celinda hesitated, and then she got to her feet and went into the kitchen. Araminta, back on top of the refrigerator with Max and Fuzz, watched her take the relic out of the cookie jar but did not try to stop her.

She returned to the living room and put the relic into Emmett's hand. Araminta muttered ominously, but she did not jump down from the refrigerator.

Emmett gripped the relic firmly. Celinda felt his psi energy pulse strongly. She knew that he was trying to rez the device. Nothing happened.

He shrugged and handed the artifact to Lydia. Again Celinda sensed a powerful rush of psi energy.

"I'm an illusion trap tangler," Lydia said, turning the relic over in her fingers. "I can sense that there's some energy coming from this thing, but I can't do anything with it."

"The Guild may be able to find someone else who can rez the device," Celinda said, retrieving the relic. "But I think the odds are good that it won't be easy. In the meantime, whoever wants to experiment with this thing will need my cooperation."

Emmett regarded Celinda with a speculative expression. "That situation does appear to give you some bargaining power."

"Oh, wow," Lydia said, bubbling with enthusiasm. "We're going to strong-arm Mercer Wyatt into doing the right thing. This will be fun."

"Yeah, can't wait," Davis said dourly. "Probably be the last business I get from the Guild. Meanwhile, there's one more thing Wyatt needs to know."

"What's that?" Emmett asked.

"We think a second relic has turned up, and it's in the hands of someone who knows how to use it."

"Doesn't sound good," Emmett said.

"It's not," Davis agreed. "But I've got a strong lead. I should have some answers later this morning."

"When you get them, call me," Emmett said. "I'll arrange a meeting with Wyatt."

"One more thing," Davis said. "What about Benson Landry?"

Emmett's slow grin was icy cold. "I don't think you need to worry about him. Wyatt told me this morning that he had been assured that Benson Landry will not interfere again in Cadence Guild business. Seems like Harold Taylor, the boss of the Frequency Guild, isn't quite as weak and toothless as Landry thinks."

Celinda frowned. "What, exactly, does that mean?"

Emmett shrugged. "It means that Landry won't be a problem in the future."

She turned to Davis, who had the same cold expression on his face. He drank some coffee and said nothing.

Mystified, she looked at Lydia for clarification.

"Don't ask me." Lydia waved one hand. "When Guild men go all stony and secretive like this, you can't do a thing with them."

Celinda heard the lid of the cookie jar being removed. She looked over her shoulder and saw that Araminta was helping herself to another cookie.

"She's eating again," she said to Lydia. "I haven't had much experience with dust bunnies, but lately Araminta's appetite has seemed unnaturally strong. Do you know anything about their eating habits?"

"I don't think it's her eating habits that you have to worry about," Lydia said dryly. "More likely her mating habits."

"Uh-oh," Celinda said. "I was afraid of that."

"Fuzz became a father a few months ago. His girlfriend started hanging around a while before that. She nearly ate us out of house and home."

"Then, one morning, we were presented with a couple of baby dust bunnies," Emmett said.

"I've got pictures." Lydia reached into her purse, pulled out a wallet, and flipped it open. "Aren't they the cutest little things?"

Celinda examined the photograph. It showed Fuzz, clearly identifiable by the yellow bow in his fur, and another adult dust bunny. Between them were two tiny balls of gray fluff.

"They're adorable," Celinda said. She looked up from the photo. "So, now you've got a whole family of dust bunnies?"

"Yes, but I don't think we're going to have them for long. The babies are maturing rapidly. Fuzz and his girlfriend take them down into the rain forest almost every day to teach them how to hunt. Got a hunch the kids will be sent off on their own one of these days."

"They don't show any sign of bonding with you?" Celinda asked.

Lydia shook her head. "No, and neither does their mother. They tolerate us, but they don't seem keen on hanging around us. When the little ones are on their own, I think Mom is going to take off, too. Dust bunnies are quite sociable with each other, but I get the impression that they only pair up when a female is ready to mate."

They all looked at Araminta, who was holding court with Max and Fuzz.

"Ah, the simple life," Celinda said dryly. "No need for professional marriage consultants and Covenant Weddings."

"We humans do tend to make things more complicated, that's for sure," Lydia agreed.

Chapter 31

DAVIS STUDIED THE ENTRANCE OF THE RUN-DOWN FLOP-house through the windshield of the Phantom.

"I don't like this," he said.

"We've been over it a dozen times." Celinda unfastened her seat belt. "I'm involved in this thing. That means I've got a right to go in with you. Besides, after I read his psi waves, I might be able to give you some useful information."

She had a point, he thought.

He got out of the car. Celinda opened her door and joined him on the cracked sidewalk. Trig had followed them in his own car. He eased his battered little Float into a vacant slot, climbed out, and walked across the narrow lane to meet them.

"His room is on the second floor at the back," Trig said. "I'll go around to the alley. That way if he slips out the window or down the fire escape, I'll be able to grab him."

"Right," Davis said.

He took Celinda's arm and steered her toward the apartment house entrance. The neighborhood was deep in the

Old Quarter, only a block from the massive green wall. The Colonial-era buildings loomed darkly, blocking most of the sunlight. It was midmorning, so there was no visible glow coming from the Dead City, but you could feel the psi energy seeping up from underground.

By mutual agreement they had left Max and Araminta at the apartment along with the relic. Davis was fairly certain the artifact was safe with them. No human intruder could move as fast as the bunnies. If Araminta sensed a threat, she would most likely grab the device and run off with it.

Trig disappeared into the narrow passage that separated the apartment house from the building next to it.

The lock on the front door of the building looked as though it had been broken a long time ago. He opened the door and moved into the front hall, Celinda at his heels. The smell was a mix of rotten carpeting, garbage, and mildew.

"Whew." Celinda wrinkled her nose. "Hard to believe anyone would actually pay rent to live here."

"Probably better than sleeping in an alley."

"Not by much."

They climbed a sagging, creaking staircase and emerged in a narrow, unlit hallway. Number six was at the end of the corridor.

Davis knocked a couple of times. There was no response.

He tried the knob. The door was locked.

"Brinker," he called. "Open up. We want to talk to you. This is Guild business."

"Oh, that's sure to make him come running," Celinda mumbled.

"You'd be surprised how often it works."

"Well, it doesn't seem to be doing the trick this time," Celinda observed. "I'll bet he's halfway out the window by now."

"If he is, Trig will get him."

He reached into his pocket and removed the locksmith's tool that he had brought with him. He inserted it into the lock and rezzed it gently. It hummed briefly in his hand, trying various frequencies.

There was an audible click.

"Got it," he said softly.

Celinda eyed the tool. "Is that thing legal?"

"It is if you're a licensed and bonded locksmith."

"That doesn't quite answer my question."

"I know."

He opened the door. "Brinker?"

There was no answer. None was needed. The unmistakable miasma of death wafted out into the hallway.

Celinda took a step back. She looked at him with shocked eyes.

He moved into the shabby studio apartment. The body was on a cot, sprawled amid dirty sheets. There was no sign of physical injury, just the pale gray color of death. A number of prescription medicine bottles stood on the end table together with a syringe. Two of the bottles were empty.

Davis picked up one of the bottles and looked at the label. Ice gripped his insides.

"Psi-trauma meds," he said. "They tried this stuff on me while I was in the hospital."

"Looks like he OD'd," Celinda said, following him slowly into the room. "How sad. I wonder if it was accidental or a suicide."

"There's a third possibility," he said quietly.

She gave him a sharp, searching look. "Murder?"

"If this is our man, he was with someone else the night they searched your apartment. Mrs. Furnell said the second man spoke like a professor or a doctor, remember? He seemed to be the one in charge."

Celinda shuddered. "Someone with a medical background would have known how to kill him with drugs. Is that what you're thinking?"

"Crossed my mind."

"What's the name of the doctor who provided that prescription?"

He checked the bottle again. "Looks like Brinker was being treated at a local street clinic."

"Why would someone murder him?"

"Don't know for sure, but I can think of a couple of possibilities offhand. Maybe he knew too much. He was being treated for psi trauma. Maybe he had become too unstable. Or maybe his employer didn't need him anymore." Davis touched the dead man's arm. "I'm no medical examiner, but I don't think he's been dead very long. A few hours, maybe."

He put down the bottle and crossed the small space to raise the window. Trig stood in the alley, looking up. Davis waved him upstairs.

It took only a few minutes to search the studio. By the time Trig walked through the door, Davis had checked the closet and gone through the drawers in the battered dresser.

"Damn," Trig said, looking at the body with a glum expression. "Looks like we're going to have to call Detective Martinez again. Got a feeling she's going to be a mite put out about this."

Davis closed the kitchen drawer and turned to contemplate the room. "Once she gets involved, things will get even more complicated. We need to find Brinker's employer before the Cadence PD opens up another murder investigation."

Celinda looked up from the stack of mail she was going through. She held a crisp-looking white envelope in one hand. "I don't know if this is important, but it's the only piece of mail here that isn't addressed to current resident."

Davis took the envelope from her. Another chill went through him when he saw the return address.

"What is it, boss?" Trig asked, frowning.

"A letter from the Glenfield Institute," Davis said without inflection.

"Huh." Trig made no further comment.

Celinda's brows snapped together. "Why are you both

looking as if that letter is a note from the City-State Tax Service?"

"The Glenfield Institute is where I ended up when I went into that extended coma I told you about," Davis said. "It's the private parapsych hospital where the Cadence Guild sends hunters who get burned."

"I see." Understanding lit her eyes. "Not a lot of happy memories, in that case."

"No," he said. He ripped open the envelope, pulled out the neatly folded sheet of business letterhead, and read the letter aloud.

Dear Mr. Brinker:

   It has come to my attention that you missed your last three follow-up appointments at the Institute. Please call immediately to reschedule.

The signature was that of Harold J. Phillips, DPP.

"Phillips is the head of the Glenfield Institute," Davis said. "I've had a couple of letters from him, myself, in the past few months. He didn't like the fact that I checked myself out of the institute. Thinks I need follow-up care like Brinker, here."

"Well, clearly you don't," Celinda said firmly. She glanced at the body on the bed. "But Brinker may have needed some."

Davis looked at Trig. "Call Martinez. Fill her in on what happened here. Remind her this is still Guild business."

"Sure," Trig said. "But she isn't going to like it."

"I know. Once you've made the call to her, check with the director of the street clinic that issued these meds. Tell him the patient died and that the Guild wants to talk to the doctor who was treating Brinker."

"Got it," Trig said. "What are you going to do next?"

"Looks like I no longer have a choice," Davis said. "Got to make that appointment at the Glenfield Institute."

Chapter 32

DAVIS LOOKED AS CALM AND CENTERED AS ALWAYS, BUT Celinda was intensely aware of the tightly leashed tension beneath the stony surface. His energy patterns were sharp and hotly colored just as they had been last night when he had prepared to do battle with Landry's men.

She stood with him in front of the massive iron gates that guarded the Glenfield Institute. The large stone building was designed to look like a gracious mansion. It was surrounded by at least a couple of acres of manicured gardens, ponds, and fountains.

She looked at Davis. "You okay?"

"I'm not going to have hysterics, if that's what you mean."

She smiled. "I know. You're under complete control."

He cocked a brow. "You can tell that?"

"Sure can. I call 'em as I read 'em. You're definitely in control."

"Thanks for letting me know that. I can't tell you how much better that makes me feel."

A groundskeeper approached the gate.

"Security," Davis said to Celinda. "The theory is that if they're dressed like gardeners, the patients won't notice."

"Obviously, you noticed."

"Security people always look like security people. They can't help themselves."

"What can I do for you?" the groundskeeper asked, eyes watchful.

Davis handed him a business card. "We're here to see Dr. Phillips. Guild business."

The guard frowned at the card and then spoke quickly into his phone. There was a brief pause while he listened to the response. He nodded respectfully at Davis.

"I'll escort you to Dr. Phillips's office," he said.

He rezzed them through the gate and then led the way along a white gravel path to the colonnaded entrance.

Inside the lobby, a woman in a business suit waited for them. Celinda did a quick check. The vibes were all wholesome.

The woman smiled warmly at Davis.

"It's good to see you again, Mr. Oakes. We're so glad you decided to return. Dr. Phillips has been very anxious to speak with you."

"This is Miss Ingram," Davis said coolly. "Celinda, this is Dr. West."

Celinda smiled. "Doctor."

Dr. West inclined her head. "Perhaps you would care to wait out here while Mr. Oakes consults with Dr. Phillips?"

"She's with me," Davis said, taking Celinda's arm. "And this isn't a consultation. It's Guild business. We'd like to see Phillips immediately."

Dr. West's smile faded into an expression of grave concern. "Of course," she said, sounding a little anxious now. "Come with me."

She led them into an expensively paneled and carpeted office. A receptionist smiled at them, but before she could speak, the door of the inner office opened. A small, rumpled man with a crown of thinning gray hair bounded out. He grabbed Davis's hand and pumped it energetically.

"Good to see you, Davis," he said, beaming. "How are you feeling?"

"Normal, thanks." Davis freed himself. "This is Celinda Ingram. She's a friend. Celinda, Dr. Phillips."

"Dr. Phillips," she said.

Phillips turned to her, still smiling broadly. "A pleasure, Miss Ingram. What do you say we all go outside onto the veranda? It's a lovely day."

She opened herself to the psi energy emanating from the little man. His warmth and smile were genuine.

Within minutes they were all seated on a wide, shaded veranda overlooking the lush gardens and a tranquil pool. The setting was very restful, Celinda thought. Maybe too restful for a private investigator. No doubt about it, the place would probably have driven Davis crazy, even if he hadn't been medicated.

"We've been very worried about you, as I'm sure you're aware," Phillips said earnestly, speaking to Davis. "But seeing you here today, I am vastly reassured. You appear to be in excellent health."

"I appreciate your concern." Davis's tone could have frozen hot lava. "But I didn't come here today to talk about my case. I want to ask you about one of your other patients, a man named Robert C. Brinker."

"I see." Disappointment flashed briefly across Phillips's face. "I thought perhaps you had finally decided to respond to my letters. I know that your experience here was extremely unpleasant. Please believe me when I tell you that we did the best we could under the circumstances. We had never seen a case like yours before. We thought for a time that we were going to lose you altogether or that you would be trapped in a coma for the rest of your life. We were desperate."

"About Brinker," Davis said flatly.

Phillips hesitated and then evidently decided to surrender to the inevitable. "You know I am bound by rules of confidentiality."

"This is Guild business," Davis said. "In any event, the patient is deceased."

"Dead?" Phillips was clearly shocked. "How did he die?"

"The cause is still under investigation, but there is a high probability that it was murder."

"Good Lord." Shaken, Phillips leaned back in his chair. "This is terrible."

"Brinker was a Guild man," Davis said. "His death occurred in the course of an investigation that I am pursuing on behalf of Mercer Wyatt."

Phillips pondered that closely for a few seconds and then nodded once. "Well, under those circumstances, I suppose I can talk about Mr. Brinker's case. But I'm not sure if I can supply you with any useful information."

"I'd like to see the file."

"Very well." Phillips got to his feet. "I'll be right back."

He disappeared through the glass doors of his office. When he returned, he had a blue folder in one hand. He gave the folder to Davis.

"Brinker was brought here after he sustained a very serious psi burn in the catacombs," Phillips said, sitting back down. "The trauma was bad enough, but it was made much worse by the fact that he had a long-standing drug habit that had rendered his parapsych profile extremely fragile and unstable."

Davis flipped open the folder and leafed through the notes, pausing occasionally to read more carefully. "It says here that when he regained consciousness, he was prone to both visual and auditory hallucinations. In other words, he heard voices?"

"Yes." Phillips sighed. "It was a very sad situation and complicated, as I told you, by his addiction history."

Davis went back to the file. "He was treated by several doctors. I recognize most of the names."

"No doubt."

"They're all still here at the clinic?"

Phillips looked troubled by the question. "All but one. Seton Hollings was on the staff at the time Brinker was a patient. He left us shortly before you came to us as a patient."

Davis looked up at that, very focused. He might not be sensitive to psi wave patterns, Celinda thought, but there were other ways to read people, ways a good private investigator no doubt utilized instinctively.

"Why did Hollings leave?" he asked.

Phillips hesitated. For a few seconds, Celinda was afraid he might not answer at all. She wasn't sure what Davis would do if that happened. He wanted answers.

"I'm not certain if the reasons for Hollings's dismissal come under the heading of Guild business," Phillips said quietly.

Davis fixed him with a steady expression. "If he was dismissed in connection with the Brinker case, it does."

Phillips struggled with his professional ethics a moment longer and then exhaled heavily. "Very well. It's not as though I have any interest in protecting the bastard."

The outrage in the words made Celinda straighten a little in her chair.

"You didn't like Dr. Hollings?" she asked.

"He was a disgrace to the profession." Phillips got to his feet and started to pace the veranda, hands clasped behind his back. "In the beginning we were delighted to have him on the staff. He came to us with credentials that positively glowed. But later we learned that most of his publications and references were fraudulent. What's more, he had been dismissed from his previous post."

"Don't you run background checks on your people?" Davis asked.

"Of course. But they are fairly routine in nature. We don't conduct in-depth investigations. Hollings was very clever. He had gone to great lengths to make himself look good on paper, and I'm sorry to say he succeeded."

"When did you discover that he was a problem?" Davis asked.

Phillips came to a halt, his expression grim. "When I realized that he was conducting unauthorized experiments on a small number of the most severely traumatized patients."

"Patients like Brinker?" Celinda said.

"Yes." Phillips's mouth tightened at the corners. "The nature of Brinker's parapsych illness made him extremely vulnerable."

"What sort of experiments did Hollings perform on him?" Davis asked.

"Hollings was a leading light in dream state research. As you may know, new research has confirmed that the dream state is the only state in which the barriers between the normal and paranormal planes are not clearly defined."

"No," Davis said. "Can't say I did know that."

"The study of the dream state is a new and rather esoteric field," Phillips explained. "Hollings was fascinated with the subject. He was also an expert with psi drugs. I fear he combined the two skills to conduct experiments that can only be described as mind control."

Davis watched him closely. "How did he attempt to control Brinker?"

"To be quite honest, I have no way of knowing how much damage he did to poor Brinker, because shortly after Hollings was dismissed, Brinker, himself, disappeared. In the past nine months I have sent a number of letters to the address that we had on file for him, but he never responded." Phillips rubbed his forehead in an agitated way. "Now you tell me that he is dead."

"I want to talk to Hollings. Where did he go after he left the institute?"

"Certainly not to a reputable hospital or clinic here in Cadence. I would never have given him a reference, and he knew it. In fact, I filed a complaint with the License Review Board of the Association of Para-Psychiatrists. But by the time they got around to acting on it, Hollings had vanished."

"What do you mean?" Celinda asked.

"To be frank," Phillips said, "I suspect he assumed a new identity. All I can tell you is that the last time I checked, there was no doctor in the city practicing under that name."

Davis looked thoughtful. "Brinker had an apartment here in town. That means that if Hollings is involved in this thing, he's probably still in town, too."

Phillips raised his brows. "What makes you think Hollings is connected to Brinker?"

"I know coincidences when I see them, and there are a lot of them here. The fact that both Brinker and Hollings have a connection to this place is one of them."

"I see." Phillips inclined his head with a grave air. "I wish you luck in finding him."

"Thanks." Davis closed the folder and got to his feet. "The Guild appreciates your cooperation."

"Let me be quite clear about something," Phillips said, surprisingly brusque. "I did not cooperate in order to please the Guild."

Davis looked at him, waiting.

"I offered my assistance because I trust you, and I trust your motives." Phillips's eyes narrowed. "And because I don't want Seton Hollings doing any more damage with his talent."

Davis was silent for a few seconds. Then he seemed to relax a little.

"I appreciate it," he said.

Phillips met his eyes. "I also did it because I am hoping to convince you to return to the institute so that my staff and I can learn from the mistakes we made with you. Thus far, your case still comes under the heading of one of a kind. But in the last several years, a number of new types of psychic talents have begun to emerge in the population. New forms of psi trauma are appearing along with those talents."

"Forget it," Davis said. The ice was back in his voice. "I'm not interested in becoming a research subject again."

"Being a doctor is a lot like being a policeman, Davis. As soon as we subdue one criminal ailment or condition, another pops up. We are always fighting a new war. We need allies and spies and raw intelligence. You have a great deal to teach us. I am asking you to help us in this never-ending battle."

Davis shook his head. "No more drugs."

"No drugs," Phillips promised. "You have my word on that."

Davis looked at Celinda. She gave him an encouraging smile, letting him know silently that she approved of Phillips.

"I'll think about it," Davis said.

Chapter 33

SHORTLY BEFORE MIDNIGHT, DAVIS CLOSED THE CADENCE
City directory and dropped it on the floor beside the sofa. He
leaned back, stretched out his legs, and looked at Celinda.

"Who the hell knew there were so many people running
around claiming to be experts in various forms of psi therapy?" he said.

She put down the pad of paper she had been using to
take notes. The task of sorting through the list of practi-
tioners in the directory in an attempt to pick out the mysterious Dr. Hollings had not been successful.

The balcony door was partially open. Max and Araminta were outside on the railing. They were sitting very
close together, taking in the night. A few minutes ago Max
had come inside long enough to fetch another cookie for
Araminta.

Glumly she eyed what she had written.

"From the looks of it, most of them are self-proclaimed
therapists and counselors," she said. "The number with genuine parapsych degrees of one kind or another after their
names is only a small subset."

"The problem is that the city-states don't have any laws dictating who can hang out a shingle calling himself a therapist or a counselor." He picked up her list. "We've got everything from shady gurus to full-fledged doctors of para-psychiatry here." He frowned at one of the names she had written. "What the hell is a psychic lifestyle counselor, anyway?"

"I'm not sure, but it's nice to know there are some out there in case I ever need one."

He leaned his head against the back of the sofa and closed his eyes, thinking. "None of the people on that list jumps out at me. Got a feeling our man doesn't advertise in the phone book."

She considered that. "It wouldn't be surprising, not if he's going after a high-end clientele. Promises, Inc., doesn't advertise, either. We work strictly by referral."

"Referral," Davis repeated. He raised his lashes halfway, a predatory gleam in his eyes. "I'll bet your competitors know who you are, though, don't they?"

"Definitely." She was unable to suppress a twinge of pride. "Everyone in the matchmaking business here in Cadence is well aware of Promises, Inc."

"Maybe the way to find Hollings is to talk to some of his competitors."

The psi energy of the hunter was pulsing strongly in him. He was running on adrenaline, she thought. Whether he realized it or not, he had not completely recovered from the heavy psi burn in the ruins.

"There's nothing more you can do tonight," she said. "You need sleep, Davis."

"I'm too rezzed up to sleep. I'm closing in on him; I can feel it."

"All the more reason why you should rest." She got to her feet and held out her hand. "Come on, let's get you into bed."

Instead of coming up off the sofa, he captured her wrist in his hand and tumbled her down onto his lap.

"Got a better idea," he said.

He kissed her before she could offer a protest. She did not require her psi senses to realize that he was more than just restless and edgy; he was as hard as quartz. The adrenaline and testosterone bio-cocktail that had aroused all of his hunter's senses was having some predictable side effects.

She put her arms around his neck and kissed him back. Holding her locked in the embrace, he reached out and de-rezzed the lamp on the end table beside the sofa. The living room was plunged into deep shadows.

Turning, he stretched her out on the sofa beneath him, peeling off her clothes with quick, urgent motions. Sensual psi flared hotly in the darkness. Her own senses quickened in response. She could feel the rush of sexual hunger that was heating his blood. It burned through her, as well, creating an urgent ache deep inside. A moment ago she had been intent only on getting him into bed. Now all she could think about was getting him inside her.

Invisible energy sparked and flashed between them. He got her blouse open and went to work on the waistband of her trousers. She managed to unfasten his shirt, put her arms around him, and stroke the warm, tight skin of his muscled back. He unbuckled his belt and got rid of his trousers and briefs in a couple more swift, efficient moves.

She reached down between them with one hand and curled her fingers around his rigid length. He made a sound that was part groan and part hungry growl.

The next thing she knew, he had pushed up her knees and slid halfway down the length of her body. When she felt his mouth on her, she gasped, half-shocked and wholly thrilled. She sank her fingers into his hair.

The glorious, glittering, throbbing release hit her like a blast of high-powered alien psi, rocking all of her senses. She grabbed one of the pillows and slapped it over her mouth to stifle her thin, high shriek.

Davis surged back up her body and buried himself inside

her. It was an act of possession and desperate need. He yanked the pillow away from her face and kissed her throat. His thrusts were heavy and powerful and fast.

A moment later he raised his head. Every muscle in his body was tensed as though he was some great, wild beast about to bring down prey with a killing blow.

His climax struck hard. She put her hands around his neck, pulled his face down, and kissed him, swallowing his roar of satisfaction.

When it was over, he collapsed on top of her, crushing her into the sofa cushions.

"Can't get enough of you," he whispered against her breast. "I could come just by looking at you."

She smiled into the shadows, trailing her fingertips along his damp skin. "More fun this way, though."

"Oh, yeah." He did not open his eyes.

She edged herself out from beneath his crushing weight and tugged on his arm.

"Come on, Davis. It's time to go to bed."

"I'll just sleep here," he muttered into the pillow.

"No. You need a good night's sleep. You won't get that here on the sofa. It's too small for you."

"What about you? Where will you sleep?"

Most of the languid satisfaction she had been savoring faded. *I prefer to sleep alone. Don't take it personally.*

"I'll use the sofa again tonight," she said. "It works fine for me."

Grumbling, he rolled off the cushions and allowed her to steer him down the hall to the darkened bedroom. She pulled back the covers. He fell into bed, closed his eyes, and was instantly asleep.

She pulled the sheet and quilt up over him and went back into the living room to the open balcony door. She spoke softly to Max and Araminta.

"Are you two coming in tonight?" she asked.

They hopped down off the balcony and tumbled into the apartment. She closed the door and locked it very carefully.

She checked the cookie jar one last time to make certain the relic was still safely stashed inside, and then she went to the hall closet, took out a pillow and a blanket, and arranged them on the sofa.

For a long time she lay there looking up at the ceiling, Araminta a heavy little bundle of lint beside her.

"The thing is, I do take it personally," she said to Araminta.

Araminta opened her baby-blue eyes and blinked a couple of times.

Celinda gave it ten more minutes before she pushed aside the blanket, got up from the sofa, and went down the hall to the bedroom. Davis was sleeping so soundly when she got into bed beside him that he never even stirred

HE CAME AWAKE TO THE SENSATION OF A HAND ON HIS shoulder.

"Wake up," Celinda said. "You're dreaming."

He opened his eyes and saw that a pale dawn light was replacing the green glow of night outside the window.

He looked at Celinda. "What are you doing here?"

"It's my bed, remember?"

"You slept on the sofa."

"Changed my mind. By the way, you will notice that I'm not screaming."

"What the hell?" Still dazed with sleep, he levered himself up on his elbows.

She glanced down. He followed her gaze. His forearm from elbow to wrist was invisible. The fingers of his seemingly unattached hand gripped the rumpled sheet.

She held out her own hand, palm up. "You owe me ten bucks."

Chapter 34

"SOUNDS LIKE YOU'RE TALKING ABOUT TITUS KENNINGTON." Martin Skidmore lounged deeper into his padded leather chair, folded his hands across the broad expanse of his belly, and regarded Davis with an expression that contained a mix of disgruntled competitiveness and reluctant admiration. "What can I say? The man's good. He managed to snag a couple of high-end clients right after he opened up for business. Overnight he went straight to the top. Referral only."

Skidmore's office was located in a shiny tower not far from the headquarters of the Cadence Guild. The discreet sign outside the door announced that he was a psychic lifestyle counselor. He was the third therapist on the list that Davis had put together. He had limited the names of those he wanted to interview to counselors who clearly catered to a high-end clientele on the assumption that Hollings would have gone after the same market. Anyone who could afford a lifestyle counselor had to be pretty well-heeled. If they actually stumbled into Hollings working under an assumed name, Celinda would recognize his psi energy.

"What kind of counseling does Kennington do?" Davis asked.

Skidmore's expression twisted in disdain. "I've heard he calls it dream therapy. Bunch of guru-babble, if you ask me. But there's no denying he hit an amber mine. I hear he's even got Senator Padbury's wife as a client."

"Do you know where his office is located?"

"Over on Burwell Street in the Old Quarter. Don't know why he set up shop there. It's not the most fashionable address in town, that's for sure. Maybe he likes the atmosphere."

"Maybe." Davis got to his feet. "You've been very helpful. The Guild appreciates your cooperation."

"Any time. Always happy to do a favor for the Guild."

"I'll mention that at headquarters." Davis turned to leave. He stopped briefly at the door. "What does a psychic lifestyle counselor do?"

"I can help you explore your unique para-rez potential and guide you toward a truly fulfilling and satisfying life on both the normal and paranormal planes."

"Cost a lot to get all that?"

Skidmore smiled benignly. "Of course."

Davis let himself out into the reception area of the office. Celinda was waiting for him.

"Well?" she asked, rising quickly.

Davis savored the hit of anticipation that he always got at times like this. "Nailed him. I'm going to his office now. With luck, I'll surprise him and maybe get some answers or evidence."

"I'm coming with you."

"Damn it, Celinda—"

"I'm the only one who will be able tell you for sure whether he's the man whose psi waves I read that night in the lane."

She was right. Time was short, and he needed a positive ID as fast as possible. His biggest worry at the moment was that Kennington had already gotten nervous and skipped.

"All right," he said. "One thing I think I should mention."

"What's that?"

"If you're ever short on ideas when it comes to buying me a birthday present?"

"Yes?"

"Don't get me any psychic lifestyle counseling sessions."

"Okay, I'll stick with cuff links."

They went down to the garage and got into the Phantom. He rezzed the engine and then called Trig.

"We're on our way to the office of a Dr. Titus G. Kennington," Davis said. "I think he's our man. Address in the Quarter. Burwell Street."

"Want me to meet you there?"

"Yes. Parking is mostly on the street in that part of town, but there will be an alley entrance. Keep an eye on it. If you see someone leave Kennington's building by the back door, follow him."

"Got it."

Davis ended the call and drove out of the garage. The distance between the downtown office corridor and the Old Quarter wasn't far in terms of miles, but there was a couple of hundred years' difference when it came to atmosphere.

Within a very short span of time they were back in the narrow, twisted streets and lanes of the city's oldest neighborhoods. He parked a block away from the address he had been given and got out of the Phantom. Celinda joined him on the sidewalk. She stood quietly for a moment, looking at the dark street. He did not like the uneasiness of her expression.

"What?" he asked.

"If Kennington is the man we're looking for, you need to be prepared for the fact that he's a lot like me," she said quietly.

"Bullshit. He's nothing like you."

She looked at him, her eyes as shadowed and somber as the neighborhood around them. "I told you, I sensed his psi

energy the other night. He's strong, Davis. And he appears
to possess the same kind of talent I've got."

"So?"

"So, there's something I haven't told you about my type
of parapsych profile. I don't just read other people's patterns; under certain conditions, I can . . . influence them a
little."

That stopped him. "What the hell are you talking about?"

"It requires physical contact," she said, still disturbingly
serious. "At least it does for me. I've never told anyone
about this, because by the time I realized what I could do, I
was old enough to understand that people would be afraid
to get close to me if they thought I could manipulate their
psi waves."

"Maybe we could talk about this later," he suggested.

"No, you need to know what you're up against. Listen to
me, Davis. You once asked me if Landry had raped me after he drugged me. I told you he didn't."

He touched the side of her face very gently. "It's all
right. You don't have to talk about it."

"It was the truth," she continued. "He didn't assault
me, not in that way. But he fully intended to. The reason
he didn't was because the drug only suppressed my ability to move. My psi senses were unaffected. Sexual arousal
is heavily influenced by psi patterns. When he put his
hands on me, I was able to dampen his arousal enough to
make him lose interest. It had the same effect as a cold
shower."

He searched her face. "Are you telling me that Landry
didn't rape you because he couldn't get it up?"

"Yes. He didn't realize what I was doing, of course. As
far as he was concerned, he just couldn't get aroused. He
said something about not wanting to waste time on an ugly
bitch like me, slapped me a couple of times, and then he
called room service."

"Son of a bitch," he said softly.

Her jaw tightened, and her chin came up in a way that he was coming to recognize.

"You now know why I've never found a good match for myself," she said. "There aren't many men who would want to risk falling in love with a woman if they knew she had the ability to shut them down in bed."

He smiled slowly. "Got news for you, sweetheart. Nothing you could do to my psi waves could make me lose interest in you."

She blinked. Her eyes widened. "I realize you're very strong. That's one of the reasons why I knew right from the start that we—" She broke off abruptly, frowning a little. "Doesn't it make you a little uneasy to know what I can do to a man?"

"You manipulated my psi waves once before, remember? After the fight with Landry's men."

"Yes, but I used the red gadget on you that time and for a different purpose. I'm trying to tell you that I can influence your psychic waves even without the artifact."

"I'm not worried." He gave her a quick, wicked grin, showing a lot of teeth. "But I'm warning you, if you try your little cold shower trick on me, I'll get even by going invisible in places that will make you think twice about doing it again."

She blushed and rushed on. "The thing is, if Hollings tries to control you with his own innate talent, I'm sure you're strong enough to block him if you realize what he's doing and act quickly enough. But if he uses the relic on you, it will be a different story."

"Think so?"

He didn't sound at all concerned. She wanted to shake him.

"I know so," she said evenly. "Listen to me, Davis, if he uses the relic, you will have only a two- or three-second window to protect yourself. That's the length of time it will take him to identify your psi waves and figure out which ones to manipulate. You'll have to act immediately, or you'll be overwhelmed."

"Got any suggestions?"

"I've had years to learn how to tune out other people's psi. But you've never had to do it. Throwing up a mental barricade won't be instinctive for you. I'm not sure how to prepare you."

"Describe this mental barricade thing."

Finally, she thought. He was starting to take this seriously.

"The mind can only produce so much energy, and that energy can only be focused in a limited number of ways at one time," she said. "We can all multitask to some extent, but there are limits. If you think Hollings is using the relic on you, you'll need to focus as you've never had to focus before in your life. Try concentrating all of your psi power on something linked to your survival instinct. It's the most primitive and most powerful instinct any human possesses."

"Think that strategy will work?" he asked.

"I don't know," she admitted. "I've only used the relic on one occasion, and you were in no condition to resist. I have no idea what will happen if a powerful talent like you actively tries to fight it. I'm winging it here."

He gave that a few seconds' thought and then resumed walking toward Hollings's office. "All right, now I'm going to give you some advice. Don't get between me and Hollings, no matter what happens. If anything occurs inside that office that makes you think we're in trouble, you run, you do not walk, to the nearest exit and yell for Trig. He'll be close by on the street."

She looked around. "I don't see him."

"The panhandler in the doorway over there." He did not look toward Trig. "He uses more traditional methods, but in his own way, Trig's almost as good at going invisible as I am."

Some major cash had been dropped into the renovation of the two-hundred-year-old building that housed Hollings's office. A small sign declared that visitors were expected to announce themselves by picking up the phone beside the locked front door.

Davis stopped a few feet away from the door and examined the area surrounding the phone. There was a camera mounted above the device. He was careful to keep out of range.

"You make the call," he instructed Celinda. "Tell whoever answers that you were referred by a friend and that you want to make an appointment. Use the senator's wife's name, if necessary."

"If Hollings is watching the monitor, he'll recognize me."

"Odds are a guy running an upscale operation will have a receptionist working for him. Even if he does see you, he's going to be damn curious to know why you're here."

"What about you?"

Davis shrugged. "Now you see me . . ."

"Now you don't?" She didn't look reassured. She looked worried.

"It will only take a few seconds to get through the door. I told you, I don't get into trouble unless I go invisible for several minutes."

She wasn't entirely satisfied, but she picked up the phone. She listened for a moment and then responded, smooth and glib.

"I'd like to make an appointment for a consultation . . . How did I hear about Dr. Kennington? A close friend told me about him. She said he had done wonders for her. Her name? Jennifer. Jennifer Padbury. Yes, the senator's wife." There was another pause. "Thank you."

There was a sharp *snick*. The door was unlocked. Celinda pushed it open and moved into a dimly lit lobby. Davis pulsed his own psi power through the amber in his watch, resonating with the dissonance-energy waves at the silver end of the spectrum.

Celinda had been right, he wasn't fully recovered from the long period of invisibility in the old ruins, but he had sufficient juice to manipulate silver ghost light long enough to slip past the camera and through the door into the lobby.

He went invisible and followed her.

Chapter 35

DAVIS DISAPPEARED. SHE COULD FEEL HIS STRONGLY pulsing psi energy and knew that he was right beside her, but all she could see was a faint shimmer in the air. It was disconcerting, but it wasn't terrifying. As long as her other senses assured her that he was nearby, she could handle the invisibility thing. *If I were blind, I wouldn't even know that he had vanished.*

She closed the lobby door. Davis materialized beside her. She could see signs of strain at the corners of his eyes.

"Are you sure you're okay?" she asked in a low voice.

"I'm fine. Stop worrying." The hungry anticipation of the hunter laced the words.

She surveyed the small lobby. It was richly paneled and thickly carpeted. A long, low wooden table that looked like a genuine Colonial antique stood against one wall. On top of the table was an alien antiquity, a green quartz vase that contained a bouquet of elegant emerald roses.

There were two doors; one was unmarked. The other bore a small sign inviting clients to enter.

"That will be the receptionist's office," Davis said very

quietly. "Go on inside and keep her busy for a few minutes."

"What are you going to do?"

He looked at the second door. "That's probably the private door to Hollings's office." He took the highly illegal lockpick out of his pocket. "I'm going to have a look around."

"What if he's in there?"

"So much the better."

She wanted to tell him to be careful, but she was pretty sure he wasn't listening. Davis was on the prowl.

She opened the door of the receptionist's office and walked inside. An extremely polished, professional-looking woman sat at the desk. She was dressed in a conservative business suit. The sign on top of her desk said that her name was Miss Allonby

"Please sit down." Miss Allonby's tone was as crisply refined as her appearance. "I don't believe I caught your name?"

"Susan Baker." Celinda took a seat. "As I told you a moment ago, I was referred by Senator Padbury's wife."

"Yes, of course. You do understand that Dr. Kennington is extremely busy. He rarely takes new clients these days."

"I'm hoping he'll make an exception for me."

Miss Allonby rezzed the computer on her desk and turned toward the screen. "I'm afraid the first available appointment isn't until the end of next month."

"That will be fine," Celinda said.

Chapter 36

THE LOCKPICK FOUND THE FREQUENCY. THERE WAS A soft click. Davis opened the door and walked into the room. A heavy dose of alien psi rezzed all his senses. He didn't need to survey the room to know that there was a bolt-hole into the catacombs somewhere nearby.

The distinguished-looking man seated at a large desk near the window looked up, startled.

"You've got the wrong door," he said, patrician features darkening in an irritated scowl.

"I don't think so, Dr. Hollings."

Recognition flashed across the face of the man who called himself Kennington. Alarm and something close to panic followed almost immediately. He leaped to his feet, staring at Davis as if he couldn't believe his eyes. "What are you doing here?"

"Guild business. Among other things, I've come to collect the other ruby amber relic."

"I don't know what you're talking about." Hollings had recovered some of his composure now. Very casually he started to reach toward the top drawer of the desk.

Davis took the mag-rez out of his pocket. "Hands in the air, Hollings."

Hollings's jaw clenched, but he raised his hands. Davis crossed the room, went behind the desk, and opened the drawer. A mag-rez gun gleamed dully inside. He scooped it out and ejected the cartridge.

"I assume this used to belong to Brinker?" he said.

"I don't know what you're talking about."

"You should know better than to keep one of these things this close to a bolt-hole," Davis said. "There's a lot of alien psi floating around this room. No telling what might happen if you actually pulled the trigger."

Fury leaped in Hollings's face. "Listen, you son of a bitch, I don't know what you think you're doing—"

The door of the receptionist's office opened directly behind Hollings. Davis saw a dark-haired woman in a severe suit. She stared, openmouthed, at the scene in the inner office. Celinda was directly behind her.

"What in the world is going on in here?" the receptionist gasped. "Doctor? Are you all right? Shall I call the police?"

Hollings did not reply. He launched himself at Davis, eyes wild. He seemed oblivious of the gun in Davis's hand. Somehow you just don't expect a sensible person to charge a man holding a mag-rez, Davis thought. But it only went to show how unpredictable things could get when the situation escalated into violence.

Miss Allonby screamed.

He didn't dare fire the mag-rez. If he missed or if the alien psi warped the shot, he could easily hit one of the women.

He moved, trying to sidestep Hollings, but he came up hard against the desk chair, which spun away beneath his weight.

Hollings plowed into him. He was already off balance, thanks to the encounter with the chair. The force of the impact sent him sprawling.

Hollings did not seem interested in engaging in fancy hand-to-hand combat. He ran toward a door at the back of the room, yanked it open, and vanished into the unlit space behind it.

Davis rolled to his feet and went after him. The last thing he heard before he followed Hollings into the darkness was the receptionist. She was still screaming.

Chapter 37

MISS ALLONBY FINALLY QUIT SHRIEKING. CELINDA EASED her down onto a client chair.

"Take it easy," she said soothingly. "Would you like a glass of water?"

Miss Allonby looked up at her, bewildered and fearful. "What is this all about?"

"Dr. Kennington's real name is Hollings, and I'm sorry to inform you that he is involved with stolen antiquities. The Guild hired Mr. Oakes to retrieve a relic that was taken from the Guild vault."

"Dr. Kennington?" Miss Allonby was thunderstruck. "Dealing in stolen antiquities? Why, that's impossible. His list of clients includes some of the most important people in Cadence."

"Listen, Miss Allonby, I never thought I'd hear myself say this, but this is Guild business. There's someone outside watching the front door of this office. He'll know what to do. I'll go get him."

"It's all right," Miss Allonby said. She gazed into the

middle distance and miraculously regained her composure. "I already know what to do. I have my instructions."

There was no time to decipher that odd comment. Celinda gave her one last reassuring pat on the shoulder and then went through the second door into the building lobby.

The all-too-familiar waves of twisted energy flooded her senses just as she reached to open the front door.

"If you're looking for the panhandler who was watching this place, don't waste your time," Benson Landry said behind her. "I took him out of the picture a few minutes ago."

Chapter 38

THE OLD, DIMLY LIT STEPS LED STRAIGHT DOWN TO A jagged gouge in the catacomb wall. Davis could see the slice of eerie green light waiting at the bottom. Hollings was just ahead of him, a dark figure bounding down the two-hundred-year-old staircase.

A few seconds later Hollings stood silhouetted briefly against the emerald glow. Then he vanished into the tunnels. Davis leaped the last few steps and went through the opening at a run. He had to keep Hollings in sight. He didn't have the man's amber frequency. Without it and minus one of the new locator devices, he wouldn't be able to track Hollings if he lost visual contact.

But when he got through the ragged hole in the wall, he had no trouble spotting his quarry. Hollings wasn't trying to flee deep into the catacombs. Instead he was going through another, man-sized opening in the green quartz wall.

Humid heat and the chaotic scents and sounds of the rain forest spilled out into the tunnel. Nothing else followed. The thick foliage grew right up to the opening, but not a single stray leaf or vine drifted out into the tunnel. No creatures wriggled or slithered through the gap. The invisible psi barriers the aliens had installed to keep the jungle from invading the catacombs held fast.

The wall of psi had no effect on humans. Hollings fled through the gate into the rain forest. He looked like a man who knew where he was going, a man with a plan.

Davis went after him, moving from the sterile green quartz tunnel into the verdant rain forest in a single stride. When it came to pursuits, the jungle was no better than the catacombs. In the tunnels a man could vanish by going around a corner. Here in this underground world of green, he could disappear by concealing himself behind one of the vine-choked trees.

Hollings was making no effort to hide, however. He shoved his way frantically through a forest of tall fern trees. Davis followed, opening his hunter's senses. He probed for the telltale whisper of dissonance energy that would be all the warning he got before he blundered into a ghost river or a psi storm.

Hollings showed no such hesitation. He had obviously come this way on other occasions and felt confident that the path was clear of ghost energy and other hazards.

Davis was less than ten feet away when Hollings stopped and whirled around.

"This is far enough," Hollings said. He raised one hand, aiming the ruby amber relic as though it were a gun. "You're a dead man, Oakes."

It wasn't the threat that made Davis pause; it was the slashing wave of psychic energy that slammed across his senses, deadening them.

"You fool," Hollings shouted. "You have no conception of the kind of power I can wield down here."

Another tsunami of psi crashed across his numbed senses. Everything started to darken around him.

Try concentrating all of your psi power on something linked to your survival instinct.

Celinda. He seized on the name like a talisman. It glowed like a jewel in the gathering night.

Another ferocious wave of energy slammed through him. This time everything went black except for Celinda's name.

Names have psychic power. He did not know how he knew that, but he was absolutely certain of the knowledge. Celinda's name had the power he needed to fight the on-rushing tide. He concentrated on it.

At first it was only a name, but after a couple of pounding heartbeats there was more. Emotions became attached to the name, faint at first and then gradually strengthening. Hunger, longing, a desire to keep her safe.

Safe. He had to fight back. If Hollings won this battle, Celinda would be in mortal danger.

The silent, screaming waves of energy continued to cascade against his senses, but they began to splinter and fall apart when they crashed against the name *Celinda*. Keeping her safe was more important than his own life.

The tide of energy ceased as abruptly as it had begun.

"No," Hollings screamed. "It's impossible."

Davis could breathe once more. His psi senses rebounded.

He saw that Hollings was moving again, leaning down to reach into a small cave. When he straightened, Davis saw a mag-rez gun in his hand.

"You're crazy," Davis said. "You can't use that thing down here."

Hollings was beyond reason. He aimed the mag-rez at Davis.

Davis reacted instinctively. He pulled silver, went invisible, and dove for the ground.

Hollings's eyes widened in horror. "Where are you? Where did you go? You can't hide from me."

He started firing. The first two shots went wild. The third time he rezzed the trigger, the mag-rez exploded in his hand.

By the time Davis reached him, he was dead.

Chapter 39

"I SHOULD THANK YOU, CELINDA," LANDRY SAID. HIS smile was hellish. "If it hadn't been for you, Hollings would never have contacted me for help in retrieving the second relic. I wouldn't even know the damn things existed."

"He told you his real name?"

"Sure. Hollings and I are *partners*." Landry smirked. "Temporarily, that is."

Erratic, flaring psi pulsed and surged. What little control Landry still wielded over his insanity was slipping badly.

There was no sound from the inner office. Celinda prayed that meant that Miss Allonby had gone into her own office to call for help.

"You're a hunter," Celinda said. She was shivering, but she managed to keep her tone calm and steady. She had to give Miss Allonby time. "A very powerful hunter, it's true, but you don't have the kind of psychic talent it takes to manipulate the relic."

"Not a problem. Hollings will work it for me until I locate others who can do what he can. That shouldn't be hard.

I've got the resources of the Guild behind me. Once I've re-placed Hollings, I'll get rid of him. Don't trust the slippery bastard."

"That plan sounds a little shaky, if you ask me."

"I don't want your opinion." His eyes sparked with rage. "All I want from you is the other relic."

"Why would I give it to you?"

"Because if you don't, I'm going to kill you."

"You'll kill me anyway once you have the relic."

"True." He smiled slowly. "But there are different ways to die. Fast and slow. You're lucky. You've got a choice."

"You think the local Guild won't notice that something happened to me?"

"There won't be any evidence. You'll commit suicide by walking off into the rain forest without tuned amber. If anyone does eventually find your body, there won't be any-thing left of it except bare bones. The jungle is like the Guild, you see. It takes care of its own problems."

"You're forgetting one very important factor. Davis Oakes."

"Oakes is a dead man. Hollings will take care of him with the relic."

"Don't count on it," she said tightly.

"The relic is very powerful when it's used belowground. Hollings won't have any trouble dealing with Oakes."

A figure moved in the doorway. Celinda saw Miss Al-lonby standing there, a trancelike expression on her face. She did not appear to notice the gun in Landry's hand.

"I'm afraid both of you will have to come back some other time," she said, severely polite. "I have to burn Dr. Kennington's papers now. He left strict instructions."

Landry scowled. "What the hell are you talking about?"

"Dr. Kennington was very clear," she said primly. "He told me that if anyone tried to harm him or take him away, I was to burn his papers immediately."

"Ghost-shit," Landry said, suddenly comprehending.

"His research. You can't destroy those papers, you stupid woman. I'm going to need them after I get rid of him."

Miss Allonby stopped long enough to give him a stern look. "I'm just doing my job."

"Take one more step, and I'll kill you."

Miss Allonby drew herself up proudly. "I'll have you know I am a professional. I would not dream of failing to execute my responsibilities."

"Stop, you stupid bitch," Landry bellowed.

Miss Allonby tut-tutted. "Language, sir. Language."

Landry started to aim the mag-rez gun at her. Celinda readied herself to spring at him. She would go for his gun arm, she thought. It wasn't much of a chance, but it looked like the only one she was going to get.

As if he had read her mind, Landry hesitated. Then he took two steps forward, hooked an arm around her throat, and dragged her hard against his body.

She gasped for air. He was half-strangling her, but she did have physical contact. Struggling to breathe, she opened her senses to the sick tide of psi energy that pounded at her and began to probe delicately.

Certain that he had her under control, Landry concentrated on Miss Allonby.

"Don't move," he ordered.

"You are not my employer, sir," Miss Allonby informed him. She turned her back to him and started to walk into the office.

Crushed against him, wide open to his psi patterns, Celinda was intensely aware of the slight jump in tension as Landry prepared to pull the trigger. He was taking his time, hesitating just a bit. Probably worried that someone outside in the street would hear the shot, she thought. Whatever the case, it gave her a precious few instants of time. She had one advantage. She knew Landry's energy patterns all too well. She still encountered them in her nightmares.

The roaring pulses of cold, crazy rage were shatteringly

clear on the paranormal plane. The problem was that the pattern was so frighteningly abnormal. Desperately she tried to establish a counterpoint rhythm capable of dampening the most violent psi waves.

She knew she was having a measure of success when she opened her eyes and saw that Miss Allonby had disappeared into the office. Landry had not pulled the trigger.

"What's happening?" His hand tightened around her throat. "What are you doing to me? *I can't rez the trigger.*"

She did not even try to answer. All her concentration was on disrupting his energy rhythms.

He started to shake. Still pinned against him, she could feel the tremors going through his body, just like that night when he had tried to rape her. On the psychic plane, all was chaos. She heard the gun clatter on the floor.

Landry shouted something. He sounded terrified. Abruptly he released her, spinning away from her. His breath came in great, gulping gasps.

"Don't touch me," he screamed. "Get away from me. You're doing something to me. I can feel it."

Crouching, she scooped up the mag-rez gun, gripping it in both hands.

Landry stared at her, shocked and enraged. Now that they were no longer in physical contact, he was already recovering.

He looked at the gun in her hand and uttered a derisive laugh. "What do you think you're going to do with that?"

"Shoot you," she said.

"Not a chance. You don't have the nerve. Besides, there's no way a stupid little bitch like you would know how to use a mag-rez."

She lowered the barrel of the gun, aiming at a point just in front of his boots, and rezzed the trigger.

The shot roared like thunder in the small room. Landry jumped back and then stared, stunned, at the hole in the floor where the bullet had plowed into the two-hundred-year-old wood.

Celinda raised the barrel of the gun so that it once again pointed at his midsection. "As you can see, I've been practicing. I've waited for this moment for a long time, Landry."

He must have read her intention in her eyes, because his face went oddly slack with fear.

"No, wait," he whispered. "You can't do this—"

There was a sound from the office doorway behind her.

"I think we can let the Guild deal with him now," Davis said quietly.

"I haven't noticed that it has been able to do that very well," she said. She did not take her eyes or the gun off Landry.

"It will this time," Davis said, moving up to stand beside her. He held out his hand. "You have my word on it."

She flicked a glance at him, uncertain.

"You don't want to do this," he said. "Trust me; once you've done it, you can't ever forget it. Landry's not worth the psychic burn."

"But I have to be sure. I can't let that bastard threaten my family ever again."

"He won't," Davis said. "I know you don't buy the old saying, but the Guild really does police its own."

Chapter 40

TRIG LOOKED UP AT THEM FROM THE HOSPITAL BED. THE tension that had been chewing at Davis's insides ever since he had found him in the alley, badly dazed and bleeding profusely, eased. There was a large white bandage around Trig's head and traces of pain at the corners of his eyes, but the doctor had assured everyone that the blow had done no permanent damage.

"They said you got off lightly because the cap you were wearing gave you some protection," Davis said.

Trig grimaced. "I heard the bastard coming up behind me at the last second and tried to move. Too little, too late. Sorry, boss. Guess I was worrying too much about the doctor and not enough about Landry."

"It's not your fault," Celinda said. She looked at Davis across the bed, eyes narrowing. "We had been assured that the Guild would take care of Landry."

Luckily, Alice Martinez responded before Davis had to come up with a response.

"The Cadence Guild has made some progress when it comes to cooperating with us," she said coolly. "But it has a long way to go. Someone should have picked up the phone and called me at a much earlier stage."

"Yeah?" Trig squinted up at her. "And what could you have done about a major honcho from the Frequency Guild? Especially given that there was no hard evidence against him."

"I could have let him know that he was under suspicion," Alice shot back, undaunted. "If Landry had been aware that both the cops and the local Guild were keeping an eye on him, it's a good bet he would have hit the road back to Frequency City."

"Bad bet, Martinez." Trig gingerly touched the bandage around his head. "The guy was a nutcase. Nothing would have stopped him."

Alice cleared her throat and then said very politely, "The guy *was* a nutcase? Past tense? Are you telling me that we're wasting our time looking for him?"

Trig blinked a couple of times. "Uh—"

He turned helplessly to Davis.

Davis realized that Celinda and Alice were looking at him, too.

"Evidently there was a problem shortly after the Guild picked up Landry at Hollings's office," he said. "According to my sources, Landry went crazy, broke free of his guards, and tried to escape into the rain forest. There's an open gate in the tunnels that run beneath Dr. Hollings's office."

"I see," Alice said, clearly annoyed. "I assume the Guild guards gave chase?"

"Sure." Davis shrugged. "But Landry was in a panic. He blundered into a bad ghost storm. There wasn't anything anyone could do until the storm had passed. By then it was too late. His body is scheduled to be sent back to the headquarters of the Frequency City Guild later today."

"I don't suppose it occurred to anyone at the Guild that the Cadence PD might want a medical examiner to take a look at the body before it is returned to Frequency?" Alice asked, going even colder.

"Maybe you should talk to Mercer Wyatt," Trig suggested helpfully. "He's real big on cooperating with the police."

"Yeah, we've noticed that," Alice said, glaring at him.

"Hey, don't look at me, Detective," Trig said quickly. "I'm just an innocent bystander."

"Sure." Alice switched her attention to Davis. "You know, I keep hearing that as far as the Cadence Guild is concerned, the good old days of taking care of things with the triple-S method are over. But somehow there seem to be a lot of exceptions. Next time you talk to Wyatt, tell him that he owes me a favor for letting this one go. Understood?"

"I'll relay the message, Detective," he said.

Alice nodded once, flipped her notebook shut, and strode out of the room.

Trig waited until she was gone before he whistled softly. "You think she wears that gun to bed?"

Celinda glowered at him.

"Sorry," Trig said, abjectly apologetic. "I realize that kind of crude sexual innuendo is not the hallmark of a man who is ready for a committed, fulfilling relationship. It won't happen again."

"I see you got as far as chapter eight of my book," Celinda said approvingly. She rounded on Davis. "What is this triple-S method the Guild uses to take care of problems?"

"It stands for *shoot*, *shovel*, and *shut up*," Davis explained. "Old Earth saying, I think."

"Hmm." She absorbed that. "Well, this is one time I'm not going to complain about Guild methods. I can't tell you how relieved I am to know that Landry is gone for good."

"We'll make a Guild supporter out of you yet," Trig said, grinning.

"Don't count on it," she replied. "By the way, since you're going to the trouble of actually reading my book, unlike some people I could name, I'll give you some free matchmaking advice. Remember, under normal circumstances it would cost you a small fortune."

"I realize I could never afford you," Trig said eagerly. "What's the advice?"

"You and Detective Martinez are made for each other. I suggest you give her a call as soon as you're out of here."

"Yeah?" Trig's eyes gleamed.

She held up a hand, palm out. "Regardless of what happens, I definitely do not want to hear whether or not she wears the gun to bed. Is that clear?"

"Absolutely," Trig promised.

Chapter 41

IT WAS THE FIRST TIME HE'D HAD A CHANCE TO INVITE her to his place. Luckily it was the housekeeper's regular cleaning day, so the apartment was in reasonably good shape. He picked up a bottle of champagne on the way home and dealt with dinner by ordering in. The night was warm and clear, so he served the pizza and salad on the balcony overlooking the Dead City.

They had talked about everything except themselves for the past three hours. Unwinding, Davis thought. They had both needed some time to relax after the events of the day.

Sometime after dinner he went back inside to get the bottle of Emerald Glow liqueur that he had bought along with the champagne. When he returned he saw that Celinda had risen from the lounger and was now leaning against the balcony railing. Araminta and Max were perched next to her.

For a moment he just looked at her, aware of the sensation of deep, hungry longing welling up inside. She was turned partially away from him, one arm resting on the railing as she gazed pensively at the view of the ruins cloaked

"I realize I could never afford you," Trig said eagerly. "What's the advice?"

"You and Detective Martinez are made for each other. I suggest you give her a call as soon as you're out of here."

"Yeah?" Trig's eyes gleamed.

She held up a hand, palm out. "Regardless of what happens, I definitely do not want to hear whether or not she wears the gun to bed. Is that clear?"

"Absolutely," Trig promised.

Chapter 41

IT WAS THE FIRST TIME HE'D HAD A CHANCE TO INVITE her to his place. Luckily it was the housekeeper's regular cleaning day, so the apartment was in reasonably good shape. He picked up a bottle of champagne on the way home and dealt with dinner by ordering in. The night was warm and clear, so he served the pizza and salad on the balcony overlooking the Dead City.

They had talked about everything except themselves for the past three hours. Unwinding, Davis thought. They had both needed some time to relax after the events of the day.

Sometime after dinner he went back inside to get the bottle of Emerald Glow liqueur that he had bought along with the champagne. When he returned he saw that Celinda had risen from the lounger and was now leaning against the balcony railing. Araminta and Max were perched next to her.

For a moment he just looked at her, aware of the sensation of deep, hungry longing welling up inside. She was turned partially away from him, one arm resting on the railing as she gazed pensively at the view of the ruins cloaked in the starry night. He could see the curve of her cheek and the sweet, echoing arcs of her shoulder, breast, and hip.

He took a grip on his self-control, walked to the table, and poured two small glasses of the Emerald Glow. Her fingers brushed against his when he handed one of the glasses to her.

"Thanks," she said, turning to smile at him. "I need this. I'm exhausted, but I think I'm going to have trouble sleeping tonight."

"It's the adrenaline." He swallowed some of the Emerald Glow, savoring the green heat. "It jacks you up and wears you out at the same time. Takes a while to de-rez. You've been through a lot in the past few days."

"Not my usual routine, that's for sure." She searched his face. "I don't think it's been routine for you, either. You never said what happened when you followed Hollings down into the rain forest."

He leaned both elbows on the railing, cradling the little glass in one hand, and looked out at the glowing ruins. "He used the relic on me. Felt like I was standing in front of a huge dam that had just broken. A wall of psi crashed over me, wiping out everything, my normal as well as my paranormal senses. It was chaos." He stopped for a beat. "I thought I was dying."

"*Davis.*" She put her glass down and moved closer, sliding her arm around his waist. She leaned into him, letting him absorb her warmth the way she had the night she had driven him back to Cadence after the encounter with Landry's men. She didn't say anything more.

He set his own glass aside and pulled her tightly to him, breathing in her scent.

"You were right about the strategy to combat the effects of the relic," he said into her hair. "I focused on something really important to me, something that was even more important than my own survival. I hung on to it the way a man hangs on to a life preserver when the ship is going down."

She pressed her forehead against his shoulder. "Thank heavens it worked. I wasn't sure if it would."

Very gently he eased back and used one finger to raise her chin so that she had to meet his eyes.

"It was your name I used to anchor me in the storm, Celinda."

"My name?" She sounded bewildered.

"I didn't want to die, I *couldn't* die, because that would leave you in mortal danger from Hollings. I know that according to that book of yours, it's probably way too soon to say this, but I love you."

"Oh, *Davis*." She flung herself hard against him. "I love you, too. I've loved you from the moment I walked into my office at Promises, Inc., and sensed your psi energy. I knew that day that you were Mr. Perfect."

"Let me get this straight." He laughed a little, as the euphoria hit him. "You fell in love with my psi wave patterns?"

She raised her head. "I always knew I would recognize the man of my dreams when I met him."

"Hang on a second. Doesn't that theory run counter to the advice in your book? Trig said that in chapter one it states very clearly that there is no such thing as love at first sight."

"If there is ever a second edition of the book, I'll make it a point to correct that obviously inaccurate statement."

Chapter 42

THE EXECUTIVE SUITE OF THE HIGH-RISE TOWER THAT
housed the headquarters of the Cadence Guild had a very
fine view of the Dead City. The interior décor of Mercer
Wyatt's private office was as sleek and sophisticated as that
of any other seriously successful CEO in the city. Very
mainstream, Celinda thought. If you didn't know much
about Guild history, you wouldn't even guess that you were
dealing with an organization that was steeped in secrecy,
outmoded traditions, and archaic rules.

"I've given your suggestion concerning how to handle the
relics a great deal of thought, Miss Ingram," Mercer Wyatt
said.

He was standing in front of the windows, looking even
more formidable in person than he did in news photos or
when he was being interviewed by a rez-screen reporter.
From his hawklike features, silver hair, and specter-cat
eyes to the heavy amber rings he wore on his hands, he
projected an image of power.

It was his eyes that had caught her attention when they
had been introduced a short time ago. Emmett London had

the same eyes. There were certain similarities in their psi patterns, too. She knew, without being told, that the rumors were true. Emmett was Wyatt's son.

Celinda was glad that she and Davis were not facing the Guild boss alone today. They had brought plenty of backup. Emmett and Lydia London were present. So was Max, who was perched on the back of Davis's chair, and Araminta, who was peering out from the tote at Celinda's feet.

But Wyatt had some backup of his own, namely his elegant, attractive, much younger wife, Tamara. Davis had explained that Wyatt considered her his most trusted confidante. Tamara was a hunter, one of a statistically small number of women who possessed dissonance-energy para-rez talent. There were rumors circulating to the effect that Wyatt was grooming her to take over his position as head of the Guild. No one believed for one moment that he could do the impossible and install a female as the next boss of the Cadence Guild. But Wyatt had a reputation for getting what he wanted.

It was that reputation that was worrying Celinda this morning.

"It's not a suggestion," she said, keeping her tone very polite and respectful. No sense pissing off the Guild boss any more than absolutely necessary. "I must insist that both relics be turned over to a reputable medical research lab. If you want a *suggestion*, I'll give you one. Put Dr. Phillips of the Glenfield Institute in charge of studying the therapeutic aspects of the relics."

Wyatt frowned. "I realize you are concerned about the Guild's intentions toward the relics. I understand that your unfortunate experience with a member of the Frequency City Guild has left you with a poor impression. However, I assure you that the Cadence Guild adheres to the strictest standards."

"You're right," she said. "I don't trust the Guild establishment. In my opinion, the organizations lack an appropriate system of checks and balances. However, I will acknowledge that they have a role to play in society."

Wyatt's silver brows rose. Something that might have been amusement gleamed in his dangerous eyes. "Do you, indeed? That is very open-minded of you."

"The Guilds are, however, peculiar blends of business corporations and emergency militias," she continued. "I am convinced that if any Guild, including the Cadence Guild, gets its hands on the relics, they will view them as possible weapons. While I believe that they have only a very limited potential in that regard, it irritates me to think that the possible therapeutic qualities will be ignored."

Tamara, seated on a black leather chair, crossed her knees and looked suddenly very curious. "Why do you believe that the relics have only limited potential as weapons?"

Celinda looked at her. "Several reasons. Based on my admittedly limited experience, I am convinced that only someone who possesses the type of psi talent that I have and that Dr. Hollings had can activate them. What's more, it has to be a very strong form of that talent. That means that the pool of people who can resonate with the relics is probably going to be extremely limited." She paused for emphasis. "And I'm betting that no ghost hunters will be in that pool."

"Why not?" Wyatt asked sharply.

Lydia answered with a triumphant smile. "She's right. It's a known fact that when a particularly strong talent exists in an individual, it is not generalized across the psychic spectrum. It always takes a specific form such as the ability to resonate with ephemeral or dissonance energy. There is no recorded instance of a person possessing two equally powerful forms of psi talent. That certainly implies that no strong ghost hunters will be able to rez the relic."

"You'd have to rely entirely on non-Guild talent to conduct your research," Emmett observed in a businesslike manner. "That means you wouldn't have full control."

Wyatt's mouth tightened. Celinda knew he did not like hearing that.

"Celinda and Lydia have a point," Davis said. "One way

or another, you're going to have to turn the research over to an outside lab. Why not make it a medical lab?"

There was a long beat of silence before Tamara said thoughtfully, "They're right, Mercer."

Wyatt looked at her, scowling, but he didn't argue.

"There's another factor that you should keep in mind," Celinda added quickly. "Although I'm sure that there are other people around who can rez that relic for you, the fact is, with Hollings dead, I'm the only one you know for certain who can do it."

Wyatt looked suddenly fascinated. "Are you trying to blackmail me, Miss Ingram?"

"No, of course not." She took a deep breath. "What I'm telling you is that if you want my cooperation in testing the relics, the research will have to be done on my terms."

Wyatt nodded. "Certainly sounds like blackmail to me."

Lydia cleared her throat. "There's another aspect of this thing that you might want to consider. If you do turn the relics over to a legitimate medical research lab, you stand to reap some extremely good publicity for the Guild."

Tamara inclined her head. "True. Mercer, there's not much point retaining control over the relics if we can't make use of them, but if they do turn out to be therapeutic medical devices, we can gain some excellent press. We provide security for the Glenfield Institute because that is where we send our people when they get hurt in the line of duty. We'll be able to protect the artifacts there. Also, we know Dr. Phillips, and we trust him."

Wyatt stopped prowling and came to a halt. It was obvious that he had made his decision. He was a CEO who knew how to cut his losses.

"Very well, Miss Ingram," he said. "The relics will be entrusted to Dr. Phillips and his staff for further research. Are you satisfied?"

"Yes." She looked down at Araminta, who was munching a cookie. "There's just one tiny little problem left."

Chapter 43

AN HOUR AND A HALF LATER, CELINDA AND DAVIS SAT on the veranda of the Glenfield Institute. Araminta, perched on the arm of Celinda's chair, was eating a lemon square that Dr. Phillips had given her. There were several more lemon squares arranged on a plate on a nearby table. Max had scampered off to investigate the gardens.

"You say these ruby amber relics might actually be able to counteract the effects of serious psi trauma?" Dr. Phillips studied the one he was holding in his hands.

Araminta had raised no objection when the relic that had been in Hollings's possession had been turned over to Phillips. Celinda was still uncertain how she would react when the second one was handed to him.

"To be perfectly honest, I have no idea how effective they'll be," Celinda said. "All I know is that I was able to strengthen Davis's psi waves the other night to keep him from sliding into a coma after he pulled ghost silver. I was also able to manipulate the waves of two of the men he fought underground."

"I told you what Hollings did with that thing when he and I faced off underground," Davis said.

"A double-edged sword," Phillips said quietly. "Historically that has often been the case with many of the most significant advances in medicine. Antibiotics and drugs, surgical procedures, instruments, machines, and all the rest. They must be treated with the utmost respect because they can kill or cure."

"Which is why we're giving you the relics," Celinda said. "I'll do what I can to help you research the appropriate uses of the devices, but I think in the long run you'll be better off if you can find some people in the medical profession who possess my kind of psi talent."

Phillips continued to examine the relic. "We will begin a search immediately. I can't tell you how excited I am by the possibilities. We have had so few effective treatments for psi trauma. Ultimately, as in Davis's case, it generally comes down to whether or not the patient has the psychic strength to fight his or her way back to recovery. Sadly, too many don't make it. These relics offer great hope."

"Here goes," Celinda said.

She reached into the tote and removed the relic that Araminta had insisted she purchase. Araminta went very still and alert on the arm of the chair, watching intently.

Celinda put the relic down and picked her up. She held her in both hands and looked straight into her baby-blue eyes. "I know you don't understand what I'm saying, but I'm hoping you can sense that I really want Dr. Phillips to have the relic. It's very important to me, Araminta. He's a good man, a fine doctor. He'll put this thing to good use. Okay?"

Araminta blinked a couple of times. Celinda put her back down on the arm of the chair. Then she picked up the relic and handed it slowly to Dr. Phillips.

Araminta followed the action with close attention. Then she gave what was evidently the equivalent of a dust bunny shrug and scampered up onto the table to help herself to a third lemon square.

"There you have it," Davis said. "Another great moment in medical history made possible by a dust bunny and a plate of lemon squares."

Chapter 44

Ten Days Later . . .

"ANOTHER WEEK, ANOTHER WEDDING," DAVIS GROWLED.

"What do you expect?" Celinda laughed. "It's the season. Besides, you shouldn't complain. You look terrific in a tux."

They stood together with the other guests and watched the bride and groom take the floor for their first waltz as a married couple. The new Mrs. Boone looked spectacular in an old-fashioned wedding gown and a veil that fell all the way to her heels. Her husband, Cooper Boone, looked every inch the powerful Guild boss that he was in his formal uniform adorned with the insignia of his position as head of the Aurora City Guild.

The ballroom was filled with high-ranking Guild men and Guild families from all four city-states and a lot of the small towns in between. Everything about the wedding had been old-style Guild traditional, right down to and including the quartz-green and amber-yellow floral arrangements and the towering wedding cake trimmed with amber and green roses. Green champagne flowed freely from a half-dozen fountains scattered around the brilliantly lit chamber.

Elly and Cooper Boone circled the floor, clearly lost in each other.

A perfect match, Celinda thought. She dabbed her eyes. Other couples were taking the floor now, including Lydia and Emmett and Tamara and Mercer Wyatt.

"You just met Cooper and Elly today," Davis said, amused. "You hardly know them. Why the heck are you crying?"

"I can't help it." She blinked away the tears. "I'm a matchmaker. It goes with the territory."

"Are you going to cry at our wedding?" he asked with grave interest.

She sniffed and tossed the tissue into a nearby container. "No, of course not. Brides never cry at their own weddings. They're too busy making sure everything is under control."

"Good." He caught her hand, gripping it tightly. "I wouldn't want anyone to think you were having regrets at the last minute."

"Never." Satisfaction welled up inside. "You're Mr. Perfect, the man I've been waiting for all of my life."

He laughed and drew her out onto the dance floor. "I'm a long way from perfect," he said, taking her into his arms. "But what I feel for you is absolutely perfect. I love you, Celinda."

She glowed in the sweet certainty of his love.

"I love you, Davis," she whispered.

A SMALL GROUP OF UNINVITED WEDDING GUESTS SURveyed the happy scene from the cover of a buffet table draped with amber and green. Each was dressed for the occasion. Fuzz wore an amber-yellow ribbon. The bride's special pal, Rose, glittered in a sparkling bracelet draped around her neck. Max and Araminta were adorned with gleaming paper clips that secured little tufts of fur on top of their heads in a rakish fashion.

From the perspective of a bunch of hungry dust bunnies, the glorious wedding cake loomed a mile high, and the champagne fountains flowed like rivers.

If the humans would rather dance than eat, that was their problem. Dust bunnies knew what to do with a fully loaded buffet table.

TURN THE PAGE FOR A LOOK AT

SIZZLE AND BURN
A Novel of the Arcane Society
by Jayne Ann Krentz

Available January 2008 from G. P. Putnam's Sons

. . . BURN, WITCH, BURN . . .

The voice was a dark, ghostly whisper in her head. Raine Tallentyre stopped at the top of the basement stairs. Gingerly she touched the banister with her fingertips. That was all the contact she needed. The voice, thick with bloodlust and an unholy excitement, murmured again.

. . . Only one way to kill a witch. Punish her. Make her suffer. Burn, witch, burn . . .

It was the same voice she had heard when she had brushed against the counter in the kitchen a few minutes ago. It whispered of darkness, fear, and fire. The psychic traces were very fresh. A deeply disturbed individual had come through this house in the recent past. She could only pray that the freak was the type who limited himself to twisted fantasies played out in his head. But she'd had enough experience to know that probably wasn't the case. This bastard was the real thing: a human monster.

She shuddered, snatched her hand off the banister, and wiped her palm against her raincoat. The gesture was pure instinct, a reflex. The coat, long and black, was wet because it was pouring outside, but no amount of water could wash away the memory of the foul energy she had just sensed.

She looked back at Doug Spicer and heard another voice, her aunt's this time. The warning came straight out of her teenage memories. *Never tell them about the whispers in your head, Raine. They'll say you're crazy, like me.*

"I just want to take a quick look around the basement," she said, dreading what lay ahead.

Doug peered uneasily down into the darkness at the foot of the stairs. "Do you really think that's necessary, Miss Tallentyre? There will probably be mice or maybe even rats or snakes. Don't worry, I can take the listing without a thorough examination of the basement."

Doug was the proprietor of Spicer Properties, one of three real estate companies in the small town of Shelby-ville, Washington. She had contacted him when she had arrived that morning because he was the only agent who had bothered to get in touch with her after learning of Vella Tallentyre's death. He had inquired delicately about taking the listing. She was more than happy to give it to him. It was not as if she had been besieged by enthusiastic agents. For his part, Doug was relatively new in town and struggling to establish his business. They needed each other.

Dressed in a crisply tailored dark gray suit and pale blue tie, with a handsome brown leather briefcase in one hand, Doug looked every inch the professional real estate agent. Sleek, designer glasses framed his pale eyes. His car, parked in the drive, was a Jaguar.

She guessed him to be in his late thirties. His hairline was starting to recede and he had the solid, well-fed look of a man who, while not yet overweight, had definitely started to put on extra pounds. He had warned her that the gloom-filled house, with its aging plumbing and wiring, would not be an easy sale.

"I'll be right back," she assured him.

She couldn't tell him that she really had no choice now that she had picked up the psychic whispers of a man who fantasized about killing witches. She had to know the truth before she could leave the house.

"I did a little research and called Phil Brooks after I spoke with you," Doug said. "He told me that your aunt cut off his pest control service shortly before she, uh, left town."

Shortly before I took her away, Raine thought. She curled the hand that had just touched the railing very tightly around the strap of her purse. *Shortly before I had to put her into a very private, very expensive sanitarium.*

A month ago Vella Tallentyre had died in her small room at St. Damian's Psychiatric Hospital back in Oriana on the shores of Lake Washington. The cause of death was a heart attack, according to the authorities. She had been fifty-nine years old.

It dawned on her that Doug probably didn't want to get his pristine suit and polished shoes dirty. She didn't blame him.

"You don't have to come with me," she said. "I'll just go to the foot of the stairs."

Please be a gentleman and insist on coming with me.

"Well, if you're sure," Doug said, stepping back. "I don't see a light switch up here."

"It's at the foot of the stairs."

So much for the gentlemen's code. What had she expected? This wasn't the nineteenth century. The code, if it ever had existed, no longer applied. After what she had just been through with Bradley, she should know that better than anyone.

The thought of Detective Bradley Mitchell proved bracing. The ensuing rush of feminine outrage unleashed a useful dose of adrenaline that was strong enough to propel her down the stairs.

Doug hovered at the top of the steps, filling the doorway. "If the light isn't working, I've got a flashlight in my car."

The ever helpful real estate agent.

She ignored him and descended cautiously into the darkness. Maybe she wouldn't give him the listing, after all. The problem was, neither of the other two agents in town was eager for it. It wasn't just that the house was in such a neglected state. The truth was that it was unlikely any of the locals would be interested in purchasing it.

For the past few decades this house had been the property of a woman who had been certifiably crazy; a woman who heard voices in her head. That kind of history tended to dampen the enthusiasm of prospective clients. As Doug had explained, they would have to lure an out-of-town prospect; someone interested in a real fixer-upper.

The old wooden steps creaked and groaned. She tried to avoid touching the railing on the way down and she was careful to stay close to the edge of each tread so that she would be less likely to step in *his* footsteps. She had learned the hard way that human psychic energy was most easily transmitted onto a surface by direct skin contact, but bloodlust this strong sometimes penetrated through the soles of shoes.

As careful as she tried to be, she couldn't avoid all of it. *Make her suffer. Punish her the way Mother punished me.*

The scent of damp and mildew intensified as she went down. The darkness at the foot of the steps yawned like a bottomless well.

She paused on the final step, groped for and found the switch. When she touched it, she got a jolt that had nothing to do with electricity. *Burn, witch, burn.*

Mercifully, the naked bulb in the overhead fixture still worked, illuminating the windowless, low-ceilinged space in a weak, yellow glare.

The basement was crammed with the detritus of Vella Tallentyre's unhappy life. Several pieces of discarded furniture, including a massive, mirrored armoire, a chrome dining table laminated with red plastic, and four matching red vinyl chairs were crowded together. Most of the rest of the space was filled with several large cardboard boxes and crates. They contained many of the innumerable paintings that Vella had produced over the years. The pictures had one unifying theme: they were all dark, disturbing images of masks.

Her heart sank. So much for taking a quick look around and retreating back up the staircase. She would have to leave her perch at the foot of the stairs and tour the maze of boxes and crates if she wanted to be certain that there were no terrible secrets buried down here.

She really did not need this. She had problems enough at the moment. Settling Aunt Vella's small estate had proved remarkably time-consuming, not to mention depressing. In the middle of that sad process she had been forced to face the fact that the one man she thought could accept her, voices and all, found her a complete turn-off in the bedroom. On top of everything else, she had a business to run. Late October was a busy time of year for her costume design shop, Incognito. No, she did not need any more trouble, but she knew all too well that if she ignored the whispers, she would walk the floor until dawn for days or even weeks. For some reason she could never understand, finding the truth was the only antidote for the voices.

Stomach clenching, she stepped down onto the concrete floor and put out a hand to touch the nearest object, a dusty cardboard box. There was no help for it now. She had to follow the trail of psychic whispers left by the freak.

"What are you doing?" Doug called anxiously from the top of the staircase. "I thought you said you were just going to have a quick look around down there."

"There's a lot of stuff here. Sooner or later I'm going to have to clear it out. I need to get an idea of how big a job it will be."

"Please be careful, Miss Tallentyre."

She pretended not to hear him. If he couldn't be bothered to accompany her into the darkness, she was not interested in his platitudes.

There was nothing on the cardboard box but when her fingertips skated across the laminated surface of the old table she got another vicious jolt.

The demon is stronger than the witch.

Gasping, she jerked her fingers away from the table and took a quick step back. No matter how she tried to prepare herself, she would never get used to the unnerving sensation that accompanied a brush with the really bad whispers.

She looked down at the floor, searching for footprints. If there were any, they were undetectable. In the poor light the gray dust that covered everything appeared to be the same color as the concrete. In addition, the deep shadows between the valleys of stacked boxes left much of the surface of the floor in pitch darkness.

She inched forward, touching the objects in her path in the same tentative way she would have tested the surface of a hot stove. Psychic static clinging to the dusty armoire mirror made her flinch.

She looked around and realized that she was following a narrow path that snaked through the jungle of crates and boxes. The trail led to the closed door of the old wooden storage locker. A heavy padlock secured the sturdy door.

A very shiny new padlock.

She knew before she even touched it that it would reek of the freak's spore.

She came to a halt a step away from the locker, held her breath, and put out her hand. The edge of her finger barely grazed the padlock but the shock was nerve-shattering all the same.

Burn, witch, burn.

She sucked in a deep breath. "Oh, damn."

"Miss Tallentyre?" Doug sounded genuinely alarmed now. "What's wrong? Are you all right down there?"

She heard his footsteps on the stairs. Evidently her small yelp of pained surprise had activated some latent manly impulse to ride to the rescue. Better late than never.

"I'm all right but there is something very wrong down

here." She fished her cell phone out of her purse. "I'm going to call 911."

"I don't understand." Doug halted on the last step, clutching his briefcase. He peered around and finally spotted her near the storage locker. "Why in the world do you want the police?"

"Because I think this basement is about to become a crime scene."

The 911 operator came on the line before Doug could recover from the shock.

"Fire or police?" the woman said crisply.

"Police," she responded, putting all the assurance she could muster into her voice in an effort to make certain the operator took her seriously. "I'm at fourteen Crescent Lane, the Tallentyre house. Tell whoever responds to bring a tool that can cut through a padlock. Hurry."

The woman refused to be rushed. "What's wrong, ma'am?"

"I just found a dead body."

She hung up before the operator could ask any more questions. When she closed the phone she realized that Doug was still standing at the foot of the stairs. His features were partially obscured by the shadows but she was pretty sure his mouth was hanging open. The poor man was obviously starting to realize that there were reasons why the other local real estate agents hadn't jumped on the Tallentyre listing. He must have heard the rumors about Aunt Vella. Maybe he was starting to wonder if the crazy streak ran in the family. It was a legitimate question.

Doug cleared his throat. "Are you sure you're okay, Miss Tallentyre?"

She gave him the smile she saved for situations like this, the special smile her assistant, Pandora, had labeled her *screw you* smile.

"No, but what else is new?" she said politely.

* * *

THE OFFICER'S NAME WAS BOB FULTON. HE WAS THE HARD-
faced, no-nonsense, ex-military type. He came down the
basement stairs with a large flashlight and a wicked looking bolt cutter.

"Where's the body?" he asked, in a voice that said he
had seen a number of them.

"I'm not certain there is one," Raine admitted. "But I
think you'd better check that storage locker."

He looked at her with an expression she recognized
immediately. It was the everyone-here-is-a-suspect-until-
proven-otherwise expression that Bradley got when he was
working a case.

"Who are you?" Fulton asked.

"Raine Tallentyre."

"Related to the crazy lady, uh, I mean to Vella Tallentyre?"

"Her niece."

"Mind if I ask what you're doing here today?"

"I inherited this house," she said coldly. He'd called
Aunt Vella a crazy lady out loud. That meant she no longer
had to be polite.

Clearly sensing the mounting tension in the atmosphere,
Doug stepped forward. "Doug Spicer, Officer. Spicer Properties. I don't believe we've met. I came here with Miss Tallentyre today to take a listing on the place."

Fulton nodded. "Heard Vella Tallentyre had passed on.
Sorry, ma'am."

"Thank you," Raine said stiffly. "About that storage
locker . . ."

He studied the padlocked door and then glanced suspiciously at Raine. "What makes you think there's a body in
there?"

She crossed her arms and went into full defense mode.
She had known this was going to be difficult. It was so
much simpler when Bradley handled this part, shielding
her from derision and disbelief.

"Just a feeling," she said evenly.

Fulton exhaled slowly. "Don't tell me, let me guess. You think you're psychic, just like your aunt, right?"

She flashed him her special smile.

"My aunt *was* psychic," she said.

Fulton's bushy brows shot up. "Heard she ended up in a psychiatric hospital in Oriana."

"She did, mostly because no one believed her. Please open the locker, Officer. If it's empty I will apologize for wasting your time."

"You understand that if I do find a body in that locker you're going to have to answer a lot of questions down at the station."

"Trust me, I am well aware of that."

He searched her face. For a few seconds she thought he was going to argue further but whatever he saw in her expression silenced him. Without a word he turned to the storage locker and hoisted the bolt cutter.

There was a sharp, metallic crunch when the hasp of the padlock severed. Fulton put down the tool and gripped the flashlight in his left hand. He reached for the latch with gloved fingers.

The door opened on a groan of rusty hinges. Raine stopped breathing, afraid to look and equally afraid not to. She made herself look.

A naked woman lay on the cold concrete floor. The one item of clothing in the vicinity was the heavy leather belt coiled like a snake beside her.

The woman was bound hand and foot. Duct tape sealed her mouth. She appeared to be young, no more than eighteen or nineteen, and painfully thin. Tangled dark hair partially obscured her features.

The only real surprise was that she was still alive.

Penguin Group (USA) Inc.
is proud to present

GREAT READS — GUARANTEED

**We are so confident you will love
this book that we are offering a
100% money-back guarantee!**

If you are not 100% satisfied with
this publication, Penguin Group (USA) Inc.
will refund your money!
Simply return the book before
November 1, 2007 for a full refund.